THE HAUNTING OF
BLACKWATER COTTAGE

CLAY WISE

~1~

"*I*f one more person says, 'I'm sorry,' I'm going to lose my fucking mind," I say as I take the joint from my best friend, Holly.

I look up at the door to the little bathroom as I'm taking a hit, sucking the smoke deep into my lungs and holding it there.

"They don't know what else to say," she replies while leaning back and looking up at the ceiling.

I'm sitting in the stall, with my legs sticking straight out, and Holly is on the counter, her eyes half-closed. I hand the cigarette back to her, and she takes a long draw.

"If you don't know what else to say, then don't say anything." I close my eyes and lean my head back against the hard, tile wall.

"We should probably go back out there," Holly says,

after letting the smoke drift slowly out of her mouth. "They're going to wonder where we are."

"If my mom knew we were doing this, she'd be *so* pissed," I say, chuckling quietly.

Suddenly, the handle of the door rattles, and I look at Holly, both of our eyes wide as saucers.

"Ally?" my mom asks.

I cover my mouth with my hand and start giggling, and Holly does the same before she suddenly tumbles off the counter onto the floor, causing both of us to start laughing. My mother knocks on the door.

"Are you in there?" she asks, her tone a little more annoyed.

"Yeah," I reply, and Holly looks at me and puts her finger to her lips.

"Are you okay?"

I just nod before realizing that I should probably say something since she can't actually see me through the door.

"Umm…yeah. I'll be out in a minute."

"Okay," she replies, and I listen as she walks away.

Holly starts laughing again, which starts me laughing. She hands me the joint, and I take one last pull before tossing it into the toilet and flushing. I blow the smoke toward the ceiling and stand up, wobbling slightly on my heels. I hold the sides of the stall for a moment until I feel a bit steadier. Holly opens her clutch and hands me a little mouth spray. I give myself two shots, rolling the minty flavored mist around on my tongue for a few seconds.

She does the same and then slips the little vial back where she found it. "You ready?" she asks.

I nod and then pause for a minute. "Steven would have hated this whole day," I say.

She nods and puts her hand on my shoulder, squeezing gently. "Oh yeah. He would have wanted us to be singing, dancing, and drinking," she replies with a sad smile.

"Don't worry. I plan on the drinking when I get home."

I reach for the door handle, but my fingers slip off the bright-silver knob a couple of times before I get it.

"You sure you're okay?" Holly asks, grinning at me.

"I'm fine."

I finally get the door open, and I step outside into the little hallway. Luckily, no one is watching us as we both walk down the corridor, running our hands along the walls to help keep our balance. Eventually, we reach the end of the hall and emerge into a larger space that leads to several visitation rooms. I look left and then right, not exactly sure which room we were in until I spot Steven's picture on an easel outside of the one just around the corner.

There are a few people standing outside in the hall, milling about in small groups, engrossed in conversations of their own. Holly and I move past them, moving as quickly as we dare. As soon as we step into the room, my mother looks at us, and I can tell she's not happy with me. I feel Holly take my hand and squeeze it gently. Somehow, her touch and the knowledge that she's there give me the strength I need.

I take my seat again, a few feet from the casket where Steven is lying. Holly takes the chair next to mine, setting her hand on my leg. I avoid looking at Steven, as I have the entire time we've been here. My mother steps over after speaking with a few people who I think were probably neighbors of ours, or maybe they were co-workers of Steven's, or maybe one of them was our mailperson. Honestly, I don't know, and I don't really care.

"Everything okay?" she asks quietly, leaning a little closer to me.

"As good as it can be."

She frowns slightly and then looks at Holly. "Were you seriously smoking weed in the bathroom?" she asks.

I glance at Holly, and she shrugs. "Not that it's any of your business, but yes," I reply.

"Oh, Ally." She shakes her head and gives me that disapproving look. "What would Steven say?"

"He'd probably say, 'Can I have a toke?'"

She shakes her head, and I glance at Holly. She grins and gives me a little wink.

"Can you at least try to behave? It's your husband's funeral, for God's sake."

"Really? Is it?" I ask, the volume of my voice rising slightly. "I hadn't realized. In that case, I should probably go smoke another joint."

A few people glance over at us, but they quickly look away, returning to their own conversations, although I'm sure I'm the subject of most of them. Holly squeezes my leg softly, and I pause for a moment and take a breath, holding it for a second before releasing it slowly.

"Sorry," I say. "I'm just trying to cope."

My mother nods, and her expression softens. "I know, honey. I'm sorry, too," she replies, gently touching the side of my face. "Do what you need to do."

She gives me a warm smile before turning and walking over to stand next to the coffin, greeting the line of people that had begun to pile up. I look around the room, wondering why most funeral homes are designed to look like, well…homes. I suppose it's to make you feel more comfortable, but this isn't supposed to be comfortable. We stand in this "house" and whisper among ourselves about how terrible it is and what a loss it is, and then later, we talk about how "nice" the whole affair was.

Fuck that. It's all awful, every last goddamn minute of it.

Suddenly, I look up into the face of a young couple standing directly in front of me. They both look appropriately sad and mournful, and the man extends his hand.

"We just wanted to say how sorry we are for your loss," the man says, and I shake his hand.

Holly pats my leg in an attempt to keep me from going off the deep end.

"Thank you," I say, putting on a smile that feels painful the entire time I'm talking with them.

"He was such a wonderful person," she says.

I just nod in response. They give me one final sad and consoling look before moving on. I take a deep breath and let it out slowly, with a quiet sigh.

"You're doing so good," Holly whispers to me.

"How much longer is this?" I ask, looking down at my watch.

"Maybe half-an-hour."

"I can do that."

"There's a little get-together after," she says.

"Oh, fuck me."

5

* * *

IT'S NEARLY three o'clock before the last of visitors walk out of the doors of the restaurant where we held the luncheon. Steven's parents left earlier than most of the rest of the attendants. We never really got along, and I'm sure they're glad not to have to talk to me again. A few minutes later, the only ones left are Holly, my mom, and me.

"You doing okay, honey?" Mom asks me as we're all sitting at one of the tables, nibbling on cheese slices and celery sticks.

"I'm fine, Mom."

"I thought everything was very nice."

And there it is, I think.

"Sure," I reply without much enthusiasm.

Holly catches my eye and gives me a little nod.

"Did you want me to come home with you tonight?" Mom asks me.

"No. That's okay."

"Are you sure?" she asks again, leaning in a bit closer and placing her hand gently on top of mine.

"I'm fine, Mom. I really am."

She looks at me, a loving expression on her face, but I can also tell she doesn't believe me. Honestly, I'm not sure if I believe it myself.

"All right, honey," she says, standing slowly. "If you say so."

Holly and I also get to our feet, and she embraces both of us, one at a time.

"Call me if you need anything," she says.

"I will," I reply. "Love you, Mom."

"I love you, too. Nice to see you again, Holly."

"You too, Mrs. Hawkins."

She turns and starts to head toward the door, but she stops just before reaching the exit and looks back at us. "Take care of my little girl," she says to Holly.

"I will. Don't worry."

She nods and smiles warmly before turning the corner and disappearing. I close my eyes and sigh, sitting down again, leaning back in the chair, and looking up toward the ceiling.

"Now, tell me how you're really doing," Holly says, taking her seat next to me again.

"I'm really okay." I open my eyes and look at her, smiling softly.

"You would tell me if you weren't, right?"

"I would."

"No, you wouldn't," she replies, shaking her head.

"Yeah. You're probably right."

We sit for a few minutes, listening to the sounds of the rest of the restaurant as people chat and eat in the main dining room. Eventually, a couple of employees walk in to start cleaning up, but they stop short and look at us.

"I'm sorry. We can come back," a young lady says quietly.

"It's okay. We're leaving. Thank you," I say, standing and picking up my purse off the side of the chair.

Holly and I walk out, moving quickly through the restaurant and exiting into the bright sunshine of the mid-June day. I have to shield my eyes from the glare for a few seconds before I'm able to retrieve my sunglasses from my purse. I slip them on and instantly feel the relief. Holly touches my arm as we're walking to her car.

"You sure you don't want me coming home with you?" she asks.

I shake my head. "I'm really okay, Holly," I reply, gently patting her hand.

"Can I at least give you a lift?"

I look around for a few seconds before answering. "I think I want to walk," I say. "It's only a few blocks."

Holly looks at me, and I can tell she doesn't like the idea, but I also know she won't fight me on it.

"Okay," she finally says after a long pause. "Make sure you call me if you need anything."

"I will," I reply, and we embrace, holding each other tightly.

I close my eyes and relish in the feel of being held, breathing slowly and deeply until we finally step apart. She unlocks her car, tosses her purse onto the passenger seat, and turns back to me.

"You'll get through this," she says.

"I know."

She nods and then climbs into her car, watching me the entire time she's backing out of her space, nearly colliding with a pickup truck behind her. As soon as she pulls out of the parking lot, I sigh deeply and then start walking down the sidewalk that leads to my house. It's hot out, but it's not unbearable, and there's a pleasant breeze that helps to make things more comfortable.

As I walk, my thoughts are all over the place, moving from basic concerns about things I need to do tomorrow to what to do for dinner tonight, but they always seem to come back to one main theme—what am I going to do now? As I pass a small red brick house on my right, I watch a young father playing with his two children in their yard, tossing a brightly colored ball back and forth and laughing together. The front door opens, and a woman appears in the opening and calls out to them, but I'm so caught up in my own thoughts that I don't even know what she said.

Suddenly, I have an overwhelming need to get home. I begin walking faster, and within a few minutes, I'm at my doorstep, even though I don't remember how I got here. I fumble for the key in my purse, finally locating it after what seems like minutes of searching. I manage to get it inserted into the lock, although my hands are shaking so badly, I can barely turn the knob. After getting the door open, I stumble inside, dropping my belongings onto the floor and collapsing with my back pressed against the hard, cold wood of the door.

I sit for a moment, and then I let out a scream that is so full of pain and loss and sorrow that it feels like it's going to tear me apart…and then the dam bursts.

2

~2~

"Are you sure about this?" Holly asks as we're sitting on the back porch, sipping coffee and devouring a box of cinnamon rolls.

I look across the yard and sigh quietly. There are tiny yellow finches darting in and out of the bushes and butterflies of all sorts flitting throughout the flowerbed, and then I catch a glimpse of the bright, white gazebo Steven had built for us two years ago.

"I'm sure," I reply. "I love this house, but everything reminds me of him."

"Is that a bad thing?"

I look over at her and smile. "It's not a bad thing, exactly," I reply, pausing for a moment. "I don't know how to explain it."

She smiles back at me as she wipes her fingers on a

napkin. "You don't have to explain it, Ally. I understand what you mean. You'll never forget him, but you don't need to be reminded of him every moment of every day."

"Exactly."

"What did your mom say?"

"She wasn't happy. She asked if maybe I just needed more time."

"And what did you say?"

"It's been ten months. I'm going to feel the same in ten years. We talked for a while, but eventually, she seemed to accept it. She doesn't like it, but she understands it."

"So, the same as me."

I look at her and cock my head to the side.

"I'm kidding," she says. "Sort of."

"You know I need to do this, right?"

She nods and smiles at me. "I know you do, and it's only Massachusetts. It's not the other side of the world."

"Yeah. You can come to visit any time you want."

"Oh, I will be, especially when Derek starts driving me crazy. Maybe we'll have a girl's weekend."

"That sounds perfect."

I take another bite of one of the rolls, and Holly does the same, and for a period, we fall silent, just enjoying the company of the other.

"How did you even find this place?"

"You remember Jenny?"

"Jenny, who sold you this house?"

"Yeah. I just called her and told her what I was looking for. She reached out, and about a week later, she sent me the pictures."

"What's it called again? Black…?"

"Blackwater Cottage," I reply, picking up my iPad and pulling up the images.

The first six are of the exterior of a smallish, dark-gray house, with a central door and four flanking windows on the front, with a small dormer directly above the entrance on the steeply sloped roof. There are several other windows, on both the first and second floors, along with two chimneys on either end of the structure. Two of the photos feature the property, which consists of a long, narrow, grassy piece of land that slopes upward as it approaches a cliff's edge that overlooks the ocean beyond.

The remaining pictures are of the interior, many of which feature rooms that are in severe need of updating. It looks livable but without many of the creature comforts most people are used to. My favorite room is located at the back of the house. It's a small but bright space with windows on three sides. It should make a perfect studio.

"It needs some work," Holly says.

"Yeah."

"Have you actually been there?"

"No. Just in pictures."

Holly sits back in her chair and looks at me. "So, you bought a house on the internet without visiting it?"

"Yep," I reply with a sly grin. "I know it's nuts, but I sort of feel that I need to do something nuts."

She chuckles and nods. "I get that."

"I had a home inspector check it out, just to be safe. He said it needs some work, which I sort of expected, but he also said it's pretty solid, considering. The place is more than two hundred years old, and it's been empty for a lot of that time. I have a contractor lined up to help me with the tough parts of the renovation."

"Well, at least you did some of it right."

"There was something odd, though."

"What?"

"I couldn't find anyone in Duxbridge—that's the closest town—who was willing to help me work on the house."

"There are no contractors there?"

"Oh, there are several, but when I mentioned the name of the place, they all said they were too busy."

Holly looks at me and frowns. "That is odd. Do you think they were actually busy?"

"I don't know, but the town doesn't seem like the sort of place that they would be swamped with jobs, you know what I mean?"

"Oh yeah."

I sigh and take another sip of coffee before setting the cup down on the little glass table. "You don't think I'm crazy for doing this, do you?" I ask.

Holly sits for a few seconds without answering and then smiles at me. "Not at all. I think you need a change. I think you need a place to clear your head and to decide what you want to do next. How are you affording all this, by the way?"

"Well," I say with a sigh, "he had life insurance, of course, and then his company had one on him as well, and when I asked Jenny about selling this place, she put it up 'off market' for a few days, and we had fifteen offers within the first twenty-four hours, and they hadn't even seen the place in person."

"Sounds like you," she says, grinning at me.

"Ha ha. Anyway, I ended up accepting an offer that was $70,000 over asking."

"Holy crap!" Holly says. "Maybe we should sell our house."

We both laugh, and I start flipping through some of the pictures again, and I look over at Holly. "The place reminds me of something out of *Wuthering Heights*," I say. "Or *Sleepy Hollow*."

My phone rings suddenly, and for some reason, I jump. Holly shakes her head and grins at me before plucking another roll out of the quickly emptying box. I check the screen and touch the accept button, and the image of a good-looking, middle-aged man with short, dark hair and a short, neatly trimmed beard appears.

"Hello?" I say.

"Mrs. Hawkins?"

"This is she."

"Hi. This is Jerry."

"Oh. Hi, Jerry. What's going on?"

"Um…I've just been up to the house again," he says before pausing for an awkwardly long time.

"Okay."

"Are you planning on coming up here anytime soon?"

"Do you need me to?" I ask, glancing over at Holly, who raises her eyebrow.

"It would probably be a good idea."

"That doesn't sound good, Jerry. Is there some sort of problem?"

He sighs and clears his throat before continuing. "Not exactly, but there are a few things we should talk about."

"Can you just send me pictures?"

"Um...I could, but...I just think you should come up and see some of this, and we can talk about a few other issues."

"You're making me feel a little...nervous."

He sighs quietly. "It's not that bad, Mrs. Hawkins."

"Call me Ally, please."

"Ally. It's not as bad as I'm probably making it seem. I just think you should come up here and see the house you bought sight unseen before we start working on it."

I nod. "That's probably not a bad idea," I reply with a little chuckle.

"Yeah. So, maybe this coming Tuesday, around one o'clock?"

"That should work."

"Okay. I'll see you then. Bye for now," he says with a warm smile.

"Bye."

I end the call and look over at Holly. "I guess I'm going on a road trip."

~3~

The trees slide by me on both sides of the road as I follow the route through the heavily wooded terrain. Traffic is light on the small two-lane highway that winds and weaves its way through the forest. I've only seen three other cars over the last two hours, and they were heading in the opposite direction. I glance down at my gas gauge and frown. The light isn't on yet, but the needle is barely hovering above the *E*.

"Shit," I mutter to myself.

The road begins a slow, sweeping turn to the right, and as it begins to straighten out again, I pass a sign for some sort of local gas station.

"Hey, Siri."

Bing.

"How much farther?"

"Your destination is forty point three miles away. You should arrive in approximately thirty-nine minutes."

I spot the taller road sign for the station in the distance, and I begin to slow down. I put on the blinker, even though I'm the only vehicle on the road for miles. I pull off the highway into the little parking lot. The station looks like something out of the *Andy Griffith Show* or maybe *Wrong Turn*; I can't quite decide. I stop next to the two ancient gas pumps and put the car in park. I wait for an attendant to emerge from the tiny office, but after a minute or two, I climb out and open the fuel door on my car and insert the nozzle after removing the cap.

I flip the little bar up on the side of the pump and squeeze the handle. The old-style, analog display counts up my purchase, the black and white numbers flipping past at a fairly fast clip. Even while I'm filling the tank, no one comes out of the building to check on me. When I finish, I hang the nozzle back on the side of the pump and walk over to the office. When I push open the door, a little bell suspended on a coiled length of copper rings loudly.

The interior of the station is as much a throwback to the last fifty years as the exterior. There are two rows of shelves filled with all manner of candy, chips, beef jerky, and even a variety of canned goods. There are a series of glass jars lined up along the front counter filled with penny candy, although the sign says "10 Cents" on each one.

An elderly gentleman in a pair of blue and white overalls with a stitched-on nametag reading "Vernon" looks up from the newspaper he's reading and smiles at me. "Afternoon," he says with a genial expression.

"Hi."

"You got gas?"

I nod and smile at him. "It was thirty-five seventy-two," I say.

"You can just give me the thirty-five. Sorry about not coming out to pump it for you, but my legs don't work quite as well as they used to."

"Don't worry about it," I reply, waving off his concerns.

I hand him two twenties, and he rings the transaction on the ancient cash register and hands me a five in return.

"You just passing through?" he asks.

"I didn't actually see anything to pass through," I reply, and he chuckles.

"That's true enough. The town, or what's left of it, is down the next left off the highway."

"Okay. You been here a long time?"

"Fifty-five years."

"That's impressive."

"It's not that difficult to just stay in one place for a long time," he says, smiling warmly at me.

"I've heard that."

"So, what brings you up this way?"

"Going to look at a house."

"Hmm. Had enough time in the big city?"

"How did you know that?"

"You sort of get a feel for it," he replies.

"I just felt like I'd stayed in one place for too long," I say, grinning at him.

"Good for you. So, where is this house?"

"Duxbridge."

"Nice place. I'm sure you'll like it."

"That's good to hear. Well, it's been nice talking with you. I should probably head out."

"Well, if you're back this way, stop in. I'll be here."

"I will. Goodbye."

"Goodbye and good luck."

I walk back out to my car, listening to the bell ringing a few times as I cross the parking lot. After climbing back in, I pull out and back onto the highway. After about another thirty minutes or so, I find my attention wavering and eyes threatening to shut as I'm driving, the combination of the infinite number of trees and the endless yellow line lulling me toward sleep. I shake my head and pull over onto the shoulder for a moment. Reaching into the little cooler on the floor of the passenger side, I pull out an Alani and pop the top. I take a swig out of the bright-purple can and then pick up my phone and load the Audible app. I search through my library and select *No Country for Old Men*. As soon as the audio starts, I pull back onto the road.

Another ten minutes later and I finally pass a road sign for Duxbridge, stating that the town is five miles farther on. I sit up a little straighter in my seat and start paying more attention to the landscape as it zips past the windows. The trees have begun to withdraw, replaced by low meadows and fields dotted with large rocks, shrubs, and the occasional scraggly tree. When the exit for the town appears, I slow down and make the turn, rolling onto a smaller side road that looks like it's barely wide enough for two vehicles to pass each other without an issue, although it's well maintained.

I glance at my phone.

12:21.

A few minutes later, I begin encountering the first buildings I've seen for some time, save the gas station I stopped at earlier. The houses are small, but they look like they're loved and cared for. There are no mini-mansions, and none of the homes appear newer than the late 1800s. I pass a couple of small farms, complete with bright-red barns and white houses. Groupings of sheep, goats, and even a few cows wander in the fields, some of them looking up at me as I pass before returning to their grazing.

Not long after, the road begins to descend slightly, and after following a long, lazy turn to the right, the town of Duxbridge comes into view, nestled in a tiny valley between low hills on one side and tightly packed trees on the other. The sign for the town proudly states that the village was founded in 1791 and currently boasts a population of 721. That number seems exceedingly optimistic, but it could include some of the surrounding farms and other scattered houses.

As I descend the hill, I finally pass the first vehicle I've seen in more than an hour. The driver, an older gentleman with a shock of white hair, gives me a friendly nod as we briefly catch a glimpse of each other. Just as I reach the boundaries of the little downtown, I spot a tiny cottage situated on a rocky outcropping on the opposite side of the hamlet. It has to be my house, but it's so far away that I can't make out any details; however, I can see that there's a little winding road that leads up to it.

Officially, it's part of Duxbridge, but it seems as if it exists on its own, isolated and private. I tear my eyes away from the house and study the tiny downtown district of Duxbridge as I roll slowly along the beautifully maintained street. There are a surprising number of businesses, including several restaurants, a hair salon, a barbershop, a tiny little hardware store, among several others, and the avenue is crowded with vehicles on both sides. I pull into one of the few empty spots, parking diagonally along the sidewalk, and I climb out, stretching my legs and back for a moment before stepping up onto the curb and moving toward the entrance for a small café with the amusing name of Egg-Me-On.

I pull open the door, disturbing the coil and bell, just like back at the gas station, and step inside. Several patrons look up from their midday meals as I walk in, but after a few nods and friendly smiles, they return to their food. A long counter, fronted by a row of stools, is set against the left-hand wall, while small tables and chairs fill the rest of the space. A young lady with brown hair pulled back into a ponytail and a quick smile catches my eye from behind the counter where she's refilling coffee cups from an orange-handled pot. Her nametag says "Emily" in bold, capital letters.

"Sit wherever you want, honey," she calls out to me.

"Actually, I was just hoping to get two coffees to go and maybe a couple of sandwiches."

"Sure," she says, setting the pot back on the warmer

and pulling out the little pad and pen from the pocket on her bright yellow apron. "Cream and sugar?"

"Yeah."

"And the sandwiches?"

"Umm…maybe ham and cheese and the other roast beef, if you have it."

"Of course. You want mayo on those?"

"Do you have any of those little packets?"

"Sure."

"Can you toss a couple of them in?"

"No problem. Give me a couple of minutes," she says with a friendly and engaging smile.

"Thank you," I say before she turns and slips the ticket through the small silver window into the kitchen.

An old man sitting near me at the counter eyes me up and down and then nods his head toward me in a friendly gesture. "Passing through?" he asks, his voice deep and gravelly.

"Does anyone pass through?" I ask, smiling at him.

"Not really," he responds with a little chuckle.

"I think I'm going to be moving here."

His expression changes, slightly darkening, looking at me the way you see country-folk look at city-folk when they come into their town. "Are you?"

"Yes, I just bought a house."

"Which house?" he asks, still friendly.

"Old Blackwater Cottage."

He stares at me for a moment, and I fully expect everyone in the diner to stop eating and talking and take up an interest in our conversation, as you see in quite a few movies, but that doesn't happen. Instead, he leans a little closer to me, and I do the same to him.

"You should be careful up there," he whispers.

"Should I?"

"Things are not natural up there."

"What does that mean?"

He starts to say something else when Emily returns, two brown paper sacks in her hands.

"Frank. Leave her alone, and stop with your ridiculous stories," she says, shaking her head and smiling at me. "Here you go. Watch the coffees. They're really hot."

"Thanks, Emily," I say, using her name for the first time.

"My pleasure. You have a great day and stop in again."

"I will, bye."

I pick up my bags and head to the door. As I turn around to push it open with my back, Frank catches my eye again, and he mouths the words "be careful" again. I return to my car, setting the bags on the passenger seat before slowly backing out of the space.

I follow the main road through town, passing the last of the buildings after only two blocks. The landscape soon transitions to a small neighborhood of little houses, many with picture-perfect white picket fences, side porches, and lovingly maintained yards. There are tiny side roads that lead off to areas unseen, although I feel as if you would discover more little cottages if you chose to drive down them.

After a few minutes, I leave the houses behind, and the terrain changes again. Meadows covered with short, scruffy grasses and dotted with stubborn evergreens and patches of brightly colored flowers line both sides of the narrow, winding road. Eventually, I reach an intersection where two stone pillars flank a small driveway on the right side of the road. A metal plaque engraved with the word "Blackwater" is mounted to the left-hand post. Dark-green moss, dotted with bright-yellow flowers, covers some of the stones. Tire tracks from a vehicle that recently passed between the pillars are clearly evident.

I make the turn and start up the winding gravel and sand driveway. I can't even see the house from my location, and I have to concentrate on driving to avoid veering off into the rough, grassy fields. Finally, as the road turns slightly to the right and levels out, the little cottage from the pictures comes into view. I immediately think back to Holly's comment from a couple of days ago.

Sleepy Hollow.

~4~

*a*s I pull up to the little house, Jerry waves at me from the tailgate of his old light-blue Ford F150. I shut off the engine and grab the two little paper sacks before climbing out.

"I brought lunch," I say, lifting the bags.

"That's the kind of boss I like," he replies, smiling warmly at me.

He's much better looking in person than he is on video, but that isn't to say he isn't a handsome man on the phone as well. He's dressed exactly how you would expect a construction contractor to dress—a red, white, and black plaid shirt, blue jeans, and brown work boots. He actually has a pencil tucked behind his right ear, which is something I thought you only saw in the movies or TV shows.

He hops off his seat and walks over, politely taking the bags from me and then guiding me back to his truck. He sets the food down and then gestures toward the house. "Welcome to Blackwater Cottage," he says with a wave of his hand.

I give the place a quick once over, and I shake my head.

"I can't believe I bought this place," I say, sitting down on the edge of the tailgate.

"Well, I guess you did. Now you have to start dealing with it."

"That doesn't sound good," I say, frowning at him.

He shakes his head and chuckles quietly. "It'll be all right. So, what's for lunch?"

I open the first bag and remove the two coffees, setting them down carefully between us.

"Cream and sugar?" I ask.

"Absolutely."

"Good," I say, a smile on my face. I open the second bag and retrieve the two sandwiches, holding one of the wax-paper wrapped squares in each hand. "Ham and cheese or roast beef and cheese?"

"Roast beef," he says, and I hand him his selection. "Thank you, much."

I unwrap my sandwich and grin as I look down at it. I hadn't realized how hungry I was until just this moment, and the thick slices of obviously homemade bread, combined with actual carvings from a ham instead of from a deli, make my mouth drool. Jerry looks just as satisfied with his option as he takes a big bite and chews as he gazes at the old house.

"Well, you said you had some stuff for me to see," I say, biting into my lunch. It's as delicious as it looks, maybe even more.

"Let's eat first, then we can talk. If you don't mind," he says before taking a sip of his coffee.

"That works for me."

He takes another bite and then looks out across the impressive, if not slightly intimidating, landscape before turning his attention back to me. "What made you choose this place?" he asks.

"Honestly, I don't know," I reply, looking over at the old house. "I just needed a change."

"Well, you certainly got that," he says with a grin.

"Yeah. Maybe too much of one."

"It'll be all right," he says again, his words quite reassuring.

"You say that, but you had me drive all the way up here. Is it as bad as you made it out?"

He shrugs slightly before taking another bite of his sandwich. "Probably not, but there are some things that I prefer the client to see in person as opposed to video or emails," he says.

"Like what?"

"Well," he says, wiping his mouth and tossing the napkin and the crumpled-up wax paper into one of the bags. "You ready?"

I finish off the rest of my sandwich and use the other bag as a trash receptacle. I pick up my coffee and take a sip. "Let's do this."

He nods, grabs one of those metal clipboards with a cover out of the bed of the truck, and we head over to the house, crossing the short span of scraggly grass and white pebble stones that create a sort of pathway from the gravel driveway to the front door of the cottage.

"So," he begins, "all in all, the place is in remarkable shape, considering how old it is and how long it's been since someone has lived here."

"Speaking of that. How long has it been?"

We stop at the door, and he opens the clipboard and flips through the first couple of papers.

"Well, it was originally built in 1815, and the last people who lived here moved out in 1952."

"So, it's been vacant for more than sixty-five years?"

"Yeah, and you know about the history of the place, right?" He starts to open the door, and I put my hand on his arm.

"What history?" I ask.

He looks at me, his brow furrowing slightly. "It's haunted, or at least that's what the locals say."

"Seriously?"

"Your agent didn't tell you about that?"

"No. Was she supposed to?"

He shrugs again and shakes his head. "Honestly, I don't have any idea if you're supposed to say something."

"Well, it does explain what the old guy at the café was talking about."

He cocks his head to the side. "What old guy?"

"Just some local sitting at the counter when I was picking up our food. He said I should be careful and that 'things are not natural' up here."

"Well, I don't know anything about all that. It's an old

house with a story, like most of the buildings around here."

"You don't believe in ghosts?" I ask, grinning at him.

"Not really. You?"

"I suppose not."

"I guess you don't have anything to worry about then. Anyway, let's go over everything," he says before pointing to the large stones under the edge of the house with his pen. "So, I don't see anything wrong with the foundation. They used to build these old places with granite block, and you can't get any more reliable than that."

"That's good."

We walk around the house, and Jerry points out a few things, none of which seem very serious. The place actually seems bigger in person than it was in the pictures. The roof needs to be replaced, which I sort of expected, and the gutters as well. The siding is in wonderful condition, and only a handful of the cedar shakes need replacing, although the whole house could do with a fresh coat of paint. As we're coming around the corner on the eastern side of the cottage that faces the cliffside, I suddenly stumble, tripping and nearly falling flat on my face. Jerry grabs my arm to keep me from hitting the ground.

"Whoa there," he says, smiling at me. "New at this walking stuff?"

"Been doing it all my life," I reply before looking down to see what I tripped on, but there's nothing that seems as if it could have caused it. I frown and shake my head.

"Anyway. Let's try to be a little more careful," he says, leading us to the front door.

"The outside doesn't seem too bad."

"Well, it's not the outside that's the issue."

He turns the knob and opens the door for me, and I step past him, and the moment I do, I know exactly what he's talking about.

"Oh God," I say, looking around. "I feel like I'm in a time warp or something."

Jerry laughs and closes the door behind him. "Yeah, like you're stuck in a 1950's version of the 1800s."

"You can say that again."

It's obvious where the previous owners made an attempt to upgrade the interior so that they had the creature comforts of the decade they were in. Unfortunately for me, that decade is nearly seventy years out of date. A lot of the original details of the cottage are still in place, such as the window trim, the exposed hand-hewn beams, and the massive stone fireplace in the living room. Jerry bends down, rolls back the faded blue rug, and gestures toward the wide planks that make up the floor underneath.

"King's boards," he says, smiling as he looks at them.

"Pardon?"

"The extra wide floorboards. Back in the day, any plank that was wider than twenty inches was supposed to be saved for the king and shipped back to England. Of course, by the time this place was built, that was a thing of the past, but these floors are very rare."

"Well, that's good. They look like they're in good shape."

"Amazing shape, actually."

The living room is small but cozy, dominated by a

huge fireplace that takes up most of the western wall, but the dingy-red wall-to-wall carpet and garish wallpaper featuring butterflies and flowers make me wish I was colorblind.

"How's the fireplace?" I ask, trying to ignore the floor and walls.

"It's all good. I think it was restored back in the fifties, and it's still holding up well."

"What about the other one?" I ask, thinking about the twin chimneys.

"Oh. That one is closed up. It used to be in the kitchen, but they sealed it up after they got electricity."

"All right. So far, so good," I say, and Jerry grins at me.

"Yeah…well, we haven't seen the kitchen yet…or the bathroom."

"Lead the way," I say, trying not to freak out before I've seen it.

We step through the opening into the kitchen, and I freeze in place, staring at a room that does not fit within an 1800's cottage. The lime-green backsplash, combined with the black countertops and the ancient 1950's appliances that are well beyond their use-by dates, seem completely out of place and a crime against taste and fashion.

"Oh boy," I mutter.

"Yeah. This is going to take some work," Jerry says.

"We're gutting the whole place, right?"

"That's my plan," he replies. "I'm going to assume that we're going to have to replace all the plumbing and the electrical as well."

"How much is that going to be?"

"Probably six-grand."

I shrug slightly. "I guess that's not too bad."

"It would be if the house were bigger, but luckily it's nice and small."

"What's your estimate on the kitchen itself?"

"I'm figuring about twelve thousand."

"Hmm."

"Bathroom?" Jerry asks.

"I guess," I say, shaking my head and following him down a narrow hallway.

I glance into the two bedrooms, which aren't too bad, and could be quite livable after a good cleaning, removal of hideous wallpaper, a coat of paint, and the eviction of several families of spiders. Jerry stops at one of the doors and gestures me forward. I step around the corner, peer inside, and shake my head.

"Why did people think that this looked good?" I ask, gazing at the bright-pink tile walls, tub, toilet, and sink, as well as a black tile floor.

"You got me," Jerry says, chuckling to himself.

"Gut job."

"Yeah."

"Cost?"

"Six grand."

I nod, adding the numbers up in my head and storing the total away.

"One more room," he says, opening the door at the end of the hall.

I steel myself for another horrible space, but this is the studio that I loved from the pictures, but it's even better in person. The three walls of windows let in a seemingly endless amount of sunlight, but the room is strangely cool despite the bright sunshine. In fact, it's so cold that I actually brush my hands up and down my arms.

"Just some paint?" I ask.

"That's what I was thinking," Jerry replies.

I walk over to one of the windows and look out across the narrow field toward the rocky outcropping far in the distance. As I'm starting to turn back to Jerry, my eyes change their focus from the exterior to the interior, and I catch sight of a young woman with long, dark hair, bright-red lips, and piercing blue eyes in the glass. The image is so clear and vivid that I spin around, certain that she must be standing directly behind me, but nothing's there.

Jerry looks at me and frowns. "You okay?" he asks, a confused expression on his face.

"Yeah…yeah. I'm fine. I just thought I saw something on the wall."

"Something? Like what?"

"I think it was a spider," I say, lying and hoping he believes my deception.

"Well, you do have plenty of those," he says, looking up at the ceiling and along the top of the windows.

"So…um…how long do you think it will take to get all this done?" I ask, trying to change the subject as we start walking back through the house to the front door.

"I'm going to say about four weeks, that is if I can find the help I need."

"What do you mean?"

"No one in town is willing to work on the house," he says.

"That's the same problem I had with finding a contractor. What do you think that's all about?"

He shakes his head. "I don't know. When I came into town last month when I first came to look at the place, I stopped in at one of the diners and was asking around about electricians, plumbers, and so on."

"And?" I ask.

"And I got some names, and I talked to a couple of them, but when I told them I was working on the cottage, they all suddenly came up with scheduling conflicts or other excuses."

I frown at him. "Same thing happened to me. What the hell is it with this place?"

"I don't know. Local superstitions, I guess."

"Well, if they don't want the work, can you find some people from the surrounding area?"

"I've already reached out. Problem is, it's going to cost more since they're going to have to travel to the site every day."

"I guess we don't have a choice."

He shakes his head as he steps past me to open the front door. "I don't think we do. Send me some ideas about paint colors, tiles, backsplash, countertops, light fixtures, and anything else you can think of."

"Will do. So, four weeks?"

"Four weeks."

"Okay. I'll send you the ideas, and I'm trusting you with the rest."

"I won't let you down," he says as he walks me to my car.

"I know you won't, and thanks for all your hard work in advance."

"It's my pleasure, and thanks for coming up to meet with me. Have a great trip back."

"Thanks, Jerry," I say, smiling as I climb in behind the wheel and slowly get the car turned around on the uneven terrain.

I wave as I start down the driveway, and he returns the gesture. Within a few minutes, he passes out of view as I descend the steeply sloped hill.

"*A*m I doing the right thing?" I ask out loud, even though no one else is here.

Holly and Mom popped out to get us something for lunch, and I'm sitting in the middle of a huge pile of boxes, some of them sealed shut and others yet to be closed. For a moment, I get a sense of claustrophobia as the walls created by the cardboard building blocks seem to close in on me, but the feeling passes as quickly as it came.

I stand up slowly and look around. The house, which Steven and I had made into a home, has been transformed back into a house—just a place to sleep, eat, and keep the rain off your head. The walls are bare, most of the furniture is already loaded on the two trucks outside, and even the window treatments are missing, which is at least allowing a flood of light to flow into the room. I sigh and walk over to the French doors that lead out to the little sitting area. As I peer through the glass, I catch sight of the gazebo, and I suddenly feel sorrow bubbling up inside me, and my knees feel weak.

I lean against the doors, setting my head on the glass, concentrating on the feeling of the cool panel on my much warmer skin. I close my eyes and suppress the tears threatening to break through my thin sheen of calm and control.

"Hey," Holly says quietly from behind me. "You okay?"

"Am I crazy?" I ask without turning around.

"I think we've been over this," she replies.

"I know," I say with a sigh before wiping away a few stray tears while keeping that hidden from Holly. I turn slowly and smile at her. She's standing a few feet away, a couple of bags from Chick-fil-A in her hands. "Where's Mom?"

"She's talking to the movers," she says, pausing for a moment before taking a step closer and placing her hand on my arm. "You're doing the right thing. Like I said, I don't like it, but that doesn't mean it's not the right thing for you."

"But I feel like I'm throwing away everything Steven and I built here."

"Will you remember it?"

"Of course," I reply.

She shrugs and grins at me. "Then you're not throwing away anything. You and Steven built a life here, and now it's time to pass what you built along to someone else so they can build something here."

I nod and smile back at her while sighing quietly. A moment later, my mother walks through the front door and strides over to us, a warm smile on her face.

"They're going to start on the boxes in a few minutes. They have most of the furniture loaded up," she says. "Are you sure you want to donate that entire truck full of stuff?"

"I'm sure. I don't have room for it anyway, and I'm sure someone could use it."

Holly shakes the paper sacks. "Hey. We should eat before everything gets cold," she says.

"I'll get some drinks," I say, heading toward the kitchen while Mom and Holly arrange a place for us to dine.

As soon as I step into the kitchen, I pause, struck again at how empty and bare everything is...how impersonal and cold it feels when only ten months ago it was so full of life, laughter, and love. I take in a breath and open the fridge, grabbing two beers and one can of Coke and heading back into the living room. Holly and Mom look up at me from their makeshift picnic and smile. I hand Holly one of the beers and the other to my mother before sitting down, cross-legged with them. They open their bottles and toss the caps into the corner with a laugh while I pop the top on the Coke. We clink them together over our little buffet of chicken nuggets, waffle fries, and macaroni and cheese.

I'm just about to toss a nugget into my mouth when one of the movers walks into the room, stopping when he sees us.

"Oh, sorry," he says, putting his hands up and looking embarrassed.

"It's okay," I say, looking over at him and smiling. "You guys should take a break. There are some beers in the fridge."

"You sure?"

"Absolutely."

He nods and smiles back at me. "Thank you, Mrs. Hawkins."

"Ally. You can just call me Ally."

He nods again before heading back outside through the front door. We return our attention back to the food, and the three of us sit and eat. We don't talk; we just enjoy each other's company and the food, letting our concerns and worries wait until later.

When we finish, we clean up the bags, bottles, napkins, and the empty can of pop, and I carry them out to the trash bin. The three of us walk outside, standing in the front yard for a few minutes as a couple of the movers begin schlepping out the boxes, while two more carefully arrange them in the trucks, sorting them between the smaller and larger of the moving vans.

"You sure you don't want me to come up and help you get everything moved in?" Mom asks.

"I'm all set, Mom. The guys are going to help me out, and I'm not really taking that much with me. I'll have you up as soon as I get settled."

"Don't feel bad, Ruth," Holly says. "She's not letting me come up to help her, either."

I shake my head and grin at them. "I just feel like I need to do this myself," I say gently.

"We get it," Holly says, looking over at my mom, who doesn't look quite as understanding. "At least I get it."

"Stop that," Mom says, softly chiding her and swatting at her with her hand. She looks at me and smiles, her expression full of love and sorrow. "I get it, too."

* * *

"V ERNON," I say with a polite nod as I walk into the tiny gas station.

"Ms. Hawkins," he replies with a grin as he looks up from his newspaper over the top of his small, round-lensed, wire-rimmed glasses.

"I told you, you can call me Ally," I reply as I walk back to the first of the two glass coolers at the rear of the store.

"That wouldn't be right," he says. "I'm too old school."

I nod and smile to myself before opening the door and grabbing a little bottle of chocolate milk. As I'm walking back to the counter, I pick up a small can of Pringles and a bag of cashews off one of the shelves. When I return to the counter, Vernon sets aside his paper, rings up my purchases, along with the gasoline, and gives me a friendly smile.

"So. This is it, then, huh?" he asks.

"What do you mean?" I ask, frowning slightly.

"Moving day."

"Oh yeah," I reply, grinning at him. "Today's the day. The truck is somewhere behind me. I guess I'm a resident of Duxbridge now."

He nods and smiles at me. "They're lucky to have you," he says and then looks around the store as if there's anyone else here or someone might be listening. "You be careful up in that cottage, and don't be pissing any of them off."

"Pissing who off?" I ask, picking up my items after he bags them.

"The ghosts," he whispers.

I stare at him for a moment, and then he starts chuckling. "Vernon!" I say, gently scolding him. "Don't do stuff like that."

"Sorry, Ms. Hawkins. I couldn't help it. I know there are some folks up there who think the place is haunted but don't pay no attention to that. Never went in for all that ghost rigamarole. Once you're dead...you're dead. End of story."

"Glad someone else feels that way," I say.

"I guess I won't be seeing you too much now."

"Why's that?"

"Well, you won't be making the trip from the city up here."

I shrug and smile at him. "I still need my junk food fix, and you're still the only gas station within thirty minutes."

"Good. I'm happy to hear that," he says, giving me a warm smile.

"All right, Vernon. I'll see you soon," I say as I head to the exit.

"You have a good day, Ally," he says, saying my name as if he's trying it on to see how it feels.

I stop in the doorway and smile at him. "See? I told you, you could say it."

"Still don't feel right," he replies with a wry grin.

I shake my head and step outside, heading to my car. Just as I reach the pumps, the moving van passes the station. The passenger waves at me, and I return the gesture before opening my door and setting the items on the seat. It's hot today, but I can feel a cool breeze coming from the direction of Duxbridge that carries a slight scent of the ocean. I climb in behind the wheel and pull out onto the road again, but before I do, I open the milk and the Pringles, setting them within easy reach in the cup holders. I can see the truck in the distance before it disappears behind the trees as the road begins a slow, arcing turn to the right.

I take a swig of the milk and bite down on two of the chips, relishing in the salty, sweet taste that fills my mouth. A few minutes later, I catch sight of it again, but I slow down, driving at a leisurely pace, knowing I'm here to stay rather than just coming for a visit.

I pass the sign for Duxbridge, and when I glance back at the rearview mirror, a scream catches in my throat when I glimpse a man, with a dark beard, a black pea coat with the collar turned up, and piercing blue-green eyes, the same color as the ocean, staring back at me. I slam on the brakes, and the car skids for a few feet before coming to a stop. I spin around, half-expecting to see him sitting in the back seat, but of course, no one's there. After putting the car in park, I sit for a minute, my heart racing and my breath coming in panicked bursts.

Luckily the road is as empty as it normally is as I sit and collect myself. I shake my head and sigh.

"It's got to be because of Vernon and his ghosts," I say to myself before putting the car back into gear and heading down the highway again, not entirely convinced by my muttered words.

A few minutes later, I make the turn onto the small side road that leads to town. As I'm driving, I hope no one else is coming this way while my moving van is heading the other way, as I don't think both vehicles could pass each other without some trouble. When I reach the top of the hill and begin descending toward town, I catch sight of the van in the distance as it drives through downtown on its way to the cottage.

I roll through town without stopping, passing the little diner and giving Emily a wave as she's filling out the chalkboard sign with the dinner specials. When I reach the entrance for the cottage, the truck is stopped between the two columns of stone. Two of the movers are standing outside, trying to guide the van through the perilously narrow opening. The driver is yelling something while his helpers are shouting back at him and waving their hands. I pull to a stop a few feet away and put the car in park before climbing out.

I walk across the uneven, grassy ground toward them. When they see me, one of them raises his hands in a gesture of defeat.

"I don't know if it's going to fit," he says as I approach.

"Are you serious?"

"It's really tight," he replies as we walk over to the truck.

The cab is through, but the rest of the box truck is significantly wider, and it looks like an incredibly tight squeeze.

"I think it might fit," I say, walking from one side to the other, trying to gauge the chances that it will make it through the opening.

"I don't want to damage the columns," he says with a frown.

"Don't worry about it. They're just stacked stone. I can fix them if something happens. I'm more worried about scratching your truck."

He scoffs and starts laughing. "This ol' hunk-a-junk? Don't worry about that. It's a moving van. It's supposed to be all scratched and dented."

"All right then," I reply with a chuckle. "Just give it a shot. I don't think any of us want to drag everything all the way from here up to the house." I point up to the top of the little rise where the ground levels out and where you can finally get a glimpse of the cottage.

"No, we do not," he says before walking back to the front of the van and beginning to signal his companions.

I stand off to the side, watching as they slowly move the truck through the gap, with multiple pauses to adjust the steering or to try to push the edge of a protruding stone out of the way. After about ten minutes of stopping and starting, we manage to get the van past the columns and up the long, winding driveway to the cottage.

"How long do you think to unload?" I ask the foreman as we're walking to the front door.

He looks at the house and then back at the truck as one of the other workers swings the side door open on the cargo area. "Can't imagine more than a couple of hours," he says. "You really didn't bring that much."

"You see how small the house is?"

"Hey, I'm not complaining. Less stuff for you, less work for us."

~6~

"*I* thought this was all going to be done," I say to Jerry as we stand in the obliterated kitchen.

All the appliances are gone, the old countertops are lying in a small dumpster just outside the front door, along with most of the cabinets. The walls are stripped down to bare plaster, or mortar and stone, in some places.

"Delivery issues," he says, frowning slightly. He doesn't seem as carefree and jovial as he had been the first time we met and the times that we spoke on the phone.

"Is it just that?"

He sighs and shakes his head. "I'm having issues trying to find people to work here."

"Are you serious? Is this about the 'ghosts?'" I ask, shaking my head in disbelief.

"Some of them. I think the others are just friends with the idiots and don't want to piss them off."

"Okay. So, how is everything else going? Please tell me that it's further along than this."

"Well, the exterior is all done—roof, siding, paint, gutters, and the landscaping. Most of the painting is done in the other rooms."

"Bathroom?"

"It's demoed, and the rebuild is about three-quarters of the way done. It's unfinished, but it's usable."

I shake my head. "I thought we had a timeline of four weeks," I say, looking around the kitchen again.

"We did."

"I actually gave you five."

"You did."

"And here we are."

"Here we are," he says, his voice both tired and frustrated.

I look over at him, and I suddenly feel bad. I can tell he's been working hard, the things that are done look wonderful, and the fact that the "help" is afraid to come to work at this terrifying little cottage, is hardly his fault. I smile and put my hand on his shoulder.

"It's okay, Jerry. I'm just giving you a hard time."

He seems to relax a little, his shoulders lower as if some of the tension had drained off. "You have no idea how worried I was for you to see this," he says, smiling for the first time today.

"It'll get done," I say. "I guess I can eat in town for the next couple of weeks. I've been doing it all this time anyway."

"I promise I'll get it done," he says.

"I know you will."

We stand there for a few awkward, quiet moments just looking at the wreck of a kitchen, and then we both speak at the same time.

"Well…" I say, stopping when Jerry starts talking.

"I was…"

"You go ahead," I say, grinning at him.

"Thanks. I was just going to ask if you might want to… maybe…get a bite to eat," he says, looking much less confident with himself than he normally does.

"Oh," I say, starting to mumble myself. "I…um…well, here's the thing…"

"That's okay," he says, a blush running across his face. "You don't have—"

"Jerry, I do have to explain. I just lost my husband, and I'm just not…ready yet."

"Oh…oh my God. I didn't know. I'm so sorry," he says, taking a small step away from me.

"Jerry. Stop," I say gently, and he pauses and reluctantly makes eye contact with me. "There's no way you could have known, okay? And you don't have to be sorry. It's just too soon for me…I think." I smile at him, and slowly, a smile begins to build on his face.

"So…maybe later?" he asks, a glimmer of hope in his eyes and in his grin.

"Maybe," I reply, with a sly grin of my own.

He nods and then looks back at his clipboard, flipping a few of the pages, and then closes the top down. "So, let's say two weeks," he says.

I frown, my brow furrowing slightly as I look at him.

"Two weeks?"

"For it to be done," he says, pointing to the kitchen with his pen that he then tucks behind his ear.

"Let's take a look at the rest of the house. See what needs to be finished and make a 'punch list,'" I say, hoping I used the term correctly that I had heard on some show on HGTV.

"Oh…punch list, is it?" he says, grinning at me as he opens his clipboard again and retrieves the pen from behind his ear. "Yes, ma'am."

I smile and shake my head, the awkwardness of a few minutes ago fading away in our memories.

We walk through the house, moving from room to room and taking notes—finish off the trim here, paint around the window there, and adjust the door into the bathroom. The last room we check is the sunroom, as I've begun calling it, the small window-filled studio at the back of the house. Once again, when we walk in, I get a chill, even though it's blazing hot outside. I look over at Jerry as he checks out the space, but he doesn't seem to notice the unnatural coolness of the room, or maybe he's just keeping it to himself.

"All right," he says, looking over his to-do list. "I think that does it."

"Still thinking two weeks?" I ask.

He nods. "Yeah. Nothing on here is too daunting, except the kitchen."

"And honestly, I can take care of a bunch of these little things, like painting, grouting, and stuff."

"You trying to take my job?" he asks, grinning at me.

"Hardly. I'm not touching the electricity or the plumbing. That's all you."

He smiles and chuckles warmly. "I'll get it all taken care of," he says. "See you tomorrow?"

"I'll be here."

He smiles again, and I follow him to the door. When we step outside, Jerry stops and turns back to face me. "Hey. I wanted to say I'm sorry for earlier," he says, looking awkward and shy.

"Jerry, don't worry about it, seriously," I reply with a smile and a chuckle. "It's all good."

"Okay. Good. Thanks. Anyway, see you on Monday, and we'll get this place all buttoned up."

"All right. You have a good weekend."

"You too," he says before walking over to his truck and climbing in behind the wheel.

He backs away from the house and then starts down the driveway after waving at me. I stand for a moment and watch the truck until it's out of sight. Turning, I look toward the cliffs and the clouds floating far out above the ocean, just watching them for a moment before heading back inside.

I walk back in and head to the kitchen, bypassing the stacks of boxes in the living room and entryway. I glance down the hall that leads to the studio and freeze in place, rooted to the spot as a young woman, dressed in a flowing black dress, with long, dark hair, both of which flow gently off to one side, as if propelled by an unfelt wind or unseen water, stands in the doorway. She stares back at me with bright blue eyes that glow like gemstones.

"Hello," I finally manage to utter.

Her head tilts to the side slightly as if she heard me.

I blink…and she's gone.

I stand for a moment, my heart racing, and then I slowly make my way down the narrow hallway toward the studio. I pause just outside the door.

"Hello?" I ask again into the nether, but there's no response.

The second I step across the threshold, the air chills my skin, and for a brief moment, my breath turns to mist and drifts away.

"Okay then," I mutter quietly to myself.

I SLICE a piece of the chocolate pie off with the side of my fork and then scoop it up, depositing it in my mouth. Looking down the counter, I glance at the only other customer for a moment before returning my attention to the pie.

"Well? How is it?" Emily asks as she walks over, wiping her hands on a bright red towel.

"It's amazing," I reply, giving her a friendly smile.

"Marcy will be thrilled to hear that. More coffee?"

I look at my half-empty cup and shake my head. "Better not," I say. "Can I get a glass of milk?"

"Of course," she says, turning and walking about halfway down the counter and using the machine to fill a small tumbler.

She strides back, sets it down in front of me, and then leans on the counter. "So, no food up at the new house?" she asks.

"No kitchen."

"Are you serious?" she asks, grinning at me.

"Totally." I take another bite of pie and wash it down with a mouthful of the wonderfully cold milk.

"What's the holdup?"

"Can't find anyone to do the work. Jerry's been trying, but no one wants to take the job."

"Ghosts?" she asks.

"That's what we think."

"Idiots."

I sigh and nod slowly. "Can I ask you something?"

"Sure. Anything."

I look down the counter toward the old man sitting five stools away, hunched over a bowl of soup and some sort of sandwich.

"Don't worry about him. He can't hear a thing," she says before standing up and looking over at him. "Hey, George. You want me to flash you?"

The old man looks up and waves his hand in her direction. "It's all fine," he grumbles before returning to his meal.

"See?"

"That's risky," I say, smiling at her.

She shrugs. "So, what did you want to ask?"

"What do you know about the cottage?"

"Just the stuff you hear when you're growing up around here."

"And what's that, exactly?"

"That the place is haunted."

"Haunted by who...or what?"

"By Lilly Blackwater."

"Is that it?"

She cocks her head to the side. "And by sailors who died on the rocks below the cliff."

"Why would they haunt the cottage?"

"Because Lilly lured them to their deaths."

"What? What does that mean?"

She shakes her head, and all the lights dim down suddenly and then return to normal a few seconds later. We both look up at the ceiling and giggle.

"That was weird," I say.

"It happens, especially in the summer when people are using their air conditioning."

"Anyway. You were saying. She lured them to their deaths."

"I don't remember all the details, but they say she used to stand out on the cliff, holding a lantern, which the ships would mistake for a small lighthouse, and they would end up crashing and sinking on the rocks."

"Why would she do that?" I ask, horrified at the thought and at the terrible ending that the sailors must have endured.

"Grief."

"Grief? Over what?"

"The loss of her husband. He was a ship's captain and never came back from a trip one day. She was trying to guide him home."

"Oh my God."

She pauses for a moment and leans in a little closer, although I'm not sure why other than to ratchet up the tension. "I heard there was more to it, but I don't know many of the details."

"Who would know?"

"I would probably start at the town library, and then you could go see Linda at the historical society."

"Thanks for that."

She pauses again as George gets off his stool and shuffles past us toward the exit.

"See you tomorrow, Emily," he says with a little, shaky wave.

"I'll be here, George." Just before he reaches the door, he stops and turns, looking at me. "Welcome to Duxbridge," he says to me.

"Oh…um…well, thank you," I reply, giving him a little smile.

He nods in response before pushing open the door, stepping outside, and disappearing around the corner a few seconds later.

"He does know that I've been eating here at least twice a day, almost every day for more than a month, right?"

"George doesn't really pay attention to much anymore, plus he probably already forgot that he saw you here today."

Emily grabs a fork from beneath the counter, stabs the crust end of the pie, and brings the piece to her mouth. I smile at her before taking a bite myself.

"Now it's my turn. Can I ask you something?" she asks.

"Sure."

"Why do you want to know all this? I thought you didn't believe in ghosts."

"I don't, but that doesn't mean they don't exist."

~7~

The first light of the morning sun creeps its way through the curtains, and I roll over, pulling the blanket even tighter around me. Even though it's mid-July in Massachusetts and I don't have air conditioning, my bedroom is remarkably cool. The windows that face the ocean are open, and a lovely breeze is flowing freely through them. I glance at the little clock on the nightstand.

8:02.

I groan and roll onto my back, lying for some time with my eyes closed, my brain already going through the list of things I need to get done. Sighing quietly, I sit up, letting the blankets fall off me, and I look around the room, my eyes automatically settling on my slippers, which are sitting by the door and not by my bed, where I always take them off.

I try to recall last night in my mind; I came home from the diner, did a little reading, checked my emails, and worked in the studio for a while, getting things unpacked and arranged like I prefer. I hate seeing all the cardboard boxes scattered around the cottage, so I emptied quite a number of them last night and tossed them into the dumpster out front, but my thoughts keep coming back to the slippers.

I climb out of bed and walk over, sliding my feet into them and then stepping into the hallway. I look toward the unfinished kitchen and sigh before looking down the hall in the other direction. Sunshine is overflowing into the corridor, and for some reason, I begin walking toward the studio. The closer I get to the room, the more a sense of dread begins to descend upon me, but I feel compelled to keep moving forward. When I step into the room, I look to the right at the large sketch pad standing on the easel. A thin sheet is draped over the tablet; only the bottom, right-hand corner is visible. I stand for a moment just staring at it, trying to remember when I set it up, but I can't.

Goose bumps break out along both of my arms, and the hair on the back of my neck stands erect. A chill runs down my spine and then back up again. I know I didn't put the pad on the easel, and I know I didn't put the sheet on top of either. I take a tentative step, and then I feel something under my foot. Looking down, I gaze at the short black piece of a charcoal pencil peeking out from beneath my slipper.

My gaze rises slowly to the tablet again, and I reach out for the sheet, my hand trembling slightly, although I'm not sure it's from the cold or from the fear that is slowly increasing its grip on me. Finally, I snatch the linen away, and my breath catches in my throat as I stare at the image on the paper—a sketch of a young woman, wearing a long, flowing dress, her hair draped over her shoulders. Her face is hidden by shadows, but I know it's the same girl I've seen twice now since coming here.

For the first time since entering the room, I look down at my fingers. They're black with charcoal stains.

"What the fuck?" I mutter to myself, and then I yelp as someone bangs loudly on the front door.

I stand for a few seconds, just staring at the picture before the banging resumes, and then the old doorbell rings a couple of times. I quickly grab the tablet off the easel and set it on the floor behind a small stack of boxes. I walk out of the studio, glancing back a few times before marching down the hall and up to the front door. I pull it open with a yank, prepared to light into whoever's there, but I pull up short when Jerry smiles at me, two cups of coffee in his hands.

"Oh shit," he says, as I stand in the doorway, and before I have a chance to utter a word, he asks, "Were you sleeping?"

"No. No," I say, feeling the pall from a few minutes ago slowly lifting. "I was just—"

"Oh, God. Were you taking a crap?"

"What?" I ask, not sure if I heard him right, and then he starts laughing, and I shake my head before joining him. "What the hell is wrong with you? I wasn't taking a crap, as you so delicately put it. I was unpacking some boxes."

"Oh, well, that's good," he says with a warm smile. "I'd rather interrupt that than the latter."

"What are you doing here? I thought you weren't coming back until Monday."

He looks at me for a moment, a confused expression on his face. "What do you mean? It is Monday."

I stare at him, my mind racing as I try to recall the happenings of the weekend, but everything is blank, and then slowly, a smile begins to break out on his face, and I shake my head.

"You are an asshole," I say, smiling outwardly, but a tiny bit of annoyance is only just beneath the surface, but I keep it in check.

"Sorry, I couldn't help it," he replies, and I can tell immediately that he feels bad about tricking me.

"So, what are you doing here?" I ask. "And just answer the question."

"I just figured I'd bring you some coffee since your kitchen is a mess, and we could get started on it…if you're up for it."

"You didn't have to do that," I say, accepting one of the offered cups and taking a cautious sip, just in case it's still burning hot.

"I know, but I feel bad about the delays. I'd donate my time today, so we could just work on it as…"

"Friends?" I suggest.

He nods and smiles. "Friends."

"Sure. That sounds great. Give me a minute to change,

and I'll be right out," I say, walking down the hall with him just behind.

He stops in the old kitchen while I head down the corridor to the bedroom, closing the door behind me. As soon as I'm inside the room, I look down at my fingers again, trying to rub the charcoal dust off them, but no matter how hard I try, nothing changes. I shake my head and then quickly strip out of my pajamas and pull on a pair of jeans, a T-shirt, and sneakers. I run a brush through my hair a few times and use my phone to make sure it looks good before stepping across the hall to the little bathroom.

I apply a quick swipe of deodorant and check my teeth before heading back down the hall to the kitchen, where Jerry and my coffee are waiting. He turns and smiles at me as I walk into the room, and I feel a tiny, faint tickle deep down in my belly.

"You ready to get started?" he asks.

"Let me get a little coffee in me first," I reply.

"Fair enough."

He walks over to the drywall panels leaning against the wall near the old fireplace and begins measuring one, both width and length, before returning to a section of the kitchen and using the bright-red tape measure on the wall. I can tell he's doing some calculations in his head as he steps back over to the sheets of white board. Using just the tape and a small knife, he cuts the panel to size in just a few seconds, without any pencil marks or other refer- ences. As I watch him, I'm sure there is no way that it will fit correctly, considering how fast he's moving, but a minute later, he has the panel secured to the studs using a handful of black drywall nails.

"You sure you need my help?" I ask from my position by the hallway.

He looks at me and grins. "Just because I'm good at my job doesn't mean I wouldn't welcome another hand."

"Fine, fine," I say, chuckling quietly.

For the next six hours, we work without stopping, except for brief pauses for water, snacks, or bathroom breaks. Jerry teaches me how to cut, hang, and mud drywall. Although he's much faster, more accurate, and cleaner than I am, he reassures me that I'm doing great the entire time. By four-thirty, we have ninety percent of the kitchen drywalled and ready for cabinets. It's an amazing transformation in such a short amount of time, and I have to admit that I have an incredible feeling of satisfaction as I stand in the corner, admiring our hard work.

"Well done," he says, grinning at me before taking a long pull on a water bottle.

"Thanks. I had a good teacher."

He nods and smiles, a faint blush running across his face. "You have a feel for it," he says. "It's more the student than the teacher."

And now, it's my turn to blush.

"Well, I guess that should do it for the day," Jerry says, slipping the hammer back into his tool belt hanging around his hips.

"I really appreciate this," I say, wiping my hands on a light-blue rag.

"It's my pleasure." He smiles at me, and I return the gesture with even more enthusiasm.

"All right," he says. "I guess I should head out."

"Oh…okay…um…I…," I say, stumbling over my words as I try to formulate a coherent sentence, and then before I know what I'm doing, I say, "I'm starving. Do you want to go grab a bite?"

There's a pause before he answers, and I swear it lasts for nearly fifteen minutes, although I'm sure it's barely five seconds.

"Sure. That would be great," he says, grinning widely.

"It's not a date," I find myself adding without any thought.

"Of course not. It's just a meal…between friends."

"Yeah, between friends."

* * *

THE LITTLE BELL rings above our head as Jerry holds the door for me. I step past him into the diner, and several patrons look up briefly from their meals before returning to their own conversations and companions. I catch Emily's eye as she refills coffee cups at the counter, and I spot her look Jerry up and down, and then she gives me a thumbs-up with her quickly rising and falling eyebrows.

"You want a table or the counter?" I ask him.

"Probably the counter. It's less datey and more friendy," he says with a grin.

"You don't have to keep doing that."

"Sorry," he replies with a chuckle.

Part of me wants to take a table to avoid Emily and her

approving and sly little looks, but something tells me she would wait on us even if we weren't at the counter.

"Let's sit here," I say, moving to the two seats closest to the door, where the counter turns to the left.

We sit and lean forward slightly, but neither of us says anything as we wait awkwardly for Emily to take our order. Considering how talkative we had been at the cottage and the drive down here in his truck, it's odd how we can't come up with anything to say, so we just sit in uncomfortable silence, glancing at one another and exchanging pleasant smiles or nods.

"Hey," Emily says cheerfully as she walks up, smiling at me.

"Hi, Emily," I reply.

"Who's your friend?"

"Jerry," he says, extending his hand, which she shakes before releasing and giving me a little wink.

I mouth the words "stop it," and she just smiles at me before looking back at Jerry.

"So, Jerry. What brings you two here?" she asks. "Date night?"

"Just friends," he says.

"Everything starts somewhere," she says quietly.

"What's that?" Jerry asks.

"Do you know what you want to order?"

I lower my head slightly and sigh before looking back up at her and shaking it. She just smiles and turns back to Jerry.

"How are your burger and fries?"

"Greasy and salty," she replies.

"That sounds good."

"What about you, Ally?"

"I'll take the same."

"You both want the works?"

I look at Jerry, and he nods. "That'll be good."

"Milkshakes or pop?"

"I'm going to say, milkshake," Jerry answers. "Chocolate."

"Make it two."

"All right. I'll be right back," Emily says, winking at me and dropping off her ticket at the window.

As soon as she moves away, I turn to Jerry.

"Thanks again for what you did today," I say.

He smiles at me and shakes his head. "You don't have to say thank you, and you already did, by the way. I told you, it was my pleasure."

"Well, I just…I just don't want you to think I'm not appreciative of everything you've done for me."

Again, he shakes his head and smiles, chuckling quietly this time. "You're welcome."

For a few moments, we return to a comfortable silence as we wait for our food.

"It's been a long time since I've been out on a date," I say, unable to come up with anything else to say and then immediately regretting my use of the word date.

He turns his head slowly and looks at me, a twinkle in his eye. "I thought this wasn't a date."

"It's not…I…um…"

He smiles and chuckles quietly. "I'm just having some fun. It's just a meal."

"Between friends."

"Exactly."

I smile warmly at him, and he does the same to me. We both fall silent again, and I detect the tiniest change in his demeanor as thoughts race through both our minds.

"Life is hard. Isn't it?" he suddenly asks out of nowhere, his attitude darker and quieter than just a few seconds before.

"Yeah. It can be...sometimes."

I can tell by his tone and the way his shoulders slump that the words carry the weight of truth. My mouth opens to say something, to reach out to him a little more than I have so far when Emily reappears with our food and shakes.

"Here you go," she says cheerfully, her brightness and enthusiasm banishing the shadow that had descended upon us.

The intoxicating scent of hot grease, melted cheese, and chocolate fills the air all around us, and I smile automatically.

"This smells awesome," Jerry says, taking the words out of my mouth.

"I put a little extra chocolate syrup in the shakes," she says, grinning at us.

"Thanks, Emily," I say.

"No problem. Enjoy."

"Damn, this looks good," Jerry says as he picks up his burger.

"Sure does."

For the next few minutes, the only sounds coming from either of us are murmurs of enjoyment, the sucking of straws, and the crunching of crispy French fries. About halfway through my burger, I set it down on the plate and sigh.

"Full?" Jerry asks.

"Hardly. Just taking a break."

He nods and takes another bite and a mouthful of shake. I glance down the counter, and Emily flashes me a thumbs-up and a Cheshire cat-type grin. I just smile and try to ignore her. Not long after, we both finish up, push our plates away, and lean back a little on our stools, satisfied expressions on our faces.

"That was really good," Jerry says.

"It was."

A moment later, Emily comes strolling over. "How was everything?" she asks.

"Wonderful," Jerry replies.

"That's good. Glad you liked it."

She pulls a little paper out of her pocket and sets it on the counter, directly between the two of us. Before I can even react, Jerry snatches it up, and I look at him.

"I can pay," I say.

"It's already paid," he replies, handing Emily the ticket and the cash.

"That's not fair. I didn't even get a chance."

"You snooze, you lose," he says, and Emily giggles. He looks up at her. "You can keep the change."

"Thanks. Have a good night, guys," she says, shooting me a secret little smile and a wink.

"Goodnight, Emily," I say, shaking my head almost imperceptibly.

We rise from our seats and head out. Jerry holds the door for me again, and we walk over to his truck. He darts in front of me and opens that door as well, waiting until I'm seated before he closes it firmly but not slamming it. He climbs in behind the wheel, backs out of the parking space, and heads through town, back to the cottage. The sun is just about to dip below the horizon far to the west, but the sky is still fairly bright as we pass between the two columns and then up the winding gravel driveway. I can see dark clouds beginning to gather out over the ocean, and a breeze is kicking up, the wind heavy with the scent of salt.

Jerry pulls up in front of the cottage and puts the truck in park.

"Thanks for dinner," I say, smiling warmly at him.

"It was my pleasure."

"It's not fair that you didn't let me pay, or at least split it."

"Maybe next time," he says, and we both just look at one another.

"Next time? Is there going to be a next time?"

"I don't know…maybe?"

I open my door and start to step out before pausing and looking back at him. "Maybe," I say with a wide grin.

~8~

*L*ightning flashes outside, filling the room with a brilliant illumination for a split second before a clap of thunder follows almost immediately after. I roll over in bed and look toward the window. Another flash and rumble roll through the house, just before the sound of rain and wind slashing the outside of the cottage begins. Glancing at the clock, I read off the digits:

11:15.

I lie on my back and look up at the ceiling, watching as the glow from the lightning flash across the rough-hewn beams and the clean, white plaster. Lightning ripples across the sky again, and as the light floods the room, the shadow of a woman appears briefly on the wall opposite the window facing the ocean. I sit straight up, staring at the spot on the wall where the silhouette had appeared, but now it's nothing but an empty space. I slowly climb out of bed, forgoing my slippers. Lightning bursts into the room again, the image returns for a split second, and I rush to the window.

Rain is lashing the windowpanes, but I gaze in the direction of the ocean, my eyes moving up the gradually sloping grass and the rock-covered hill that seems to reach toward the sea. I can't see anything but rain and darkness, but a second later, a bolt of lightning, shaped like a monstrous hand reaching down from the heavens, inundates the entire area with light, and I spot the shape of a woman walking toward the edge of the cliff, slowly climbing the hill, a lantern swinging from her right hand.

I continue to stare at her, blinking a few times, fully expecting her to vanish, but she doesn't. The wind and the rain slash and crash into the windows, and suddenly, I feel compelled to follow this young lady. Before I know what I'm doing, I'm stepping out into the storm via the front door, barefoot and dressed only in my pajamas. The rain stings my skin, and the wind threatens to push me over with every gust. Holding a hand in front of my face, I begin moving toward the side of the cottage as lighting flashes high in the sky, followed by deafening thunder-claps, which seem to deafen me temporarily.

As I come around the side of the house, the storm seems to grow in strength. I can taste salt on my lips, and my eyes burn as my face is pummeled by the rain. I squint into the darkness, and I spot the woman standing at the edge of the cliff, some fifty yards ahead.

I know this is stupid.

I know it makes no sense.

I know it's crazy to be out in this storm, but I feel somehow... bound to this strange apparition or ghost or spirit, or whatever the hell it is.

I march through the rain, stumbling every now and then as I trip on a hidden stone or clump of stubborn grass. I can see the figure holding the lamp with her right hand, high in the air as the storm rages around her. When I'm within a few dozen feet, I stop momentarily.

"Hello!" I shout.

She doesn't react, but I have no idea if that's because she can't hear me over the sound of the rain and the wind or if she's not really even there. I trudge forward, the gusts threatening to pick me up and toss me off the cliff, smashing my body onto the rocks below.

"Hello!" I shout again when I'm only a few feet from her.

I notice she's standing on a flat stone, or likely a spot that has been scoured clean by years and years of wind and rain and time. The light from the lantern is far too bright for a normal lamp, and I can see the beam cutting through the rain far out over the water below. One more step and she suddenly turns and stares at me, her face hidden by a combination of her long, flowing hair, the rain, and the darkness, but I can see her eyes—bright-blue orbs that glow with a deep ferociousness.

I feel riveted in place as she glares at me, unable to move, unable to speak as the storm rages all around me. Suddenly, she reaches out, grabs my arm in a vice-like grip, her fingers so cold that they feel like ice, and she pulls me over the edge of the cliff.

I scream and sit bolt upright in bed, sweat pouring off me, my heart racing, and my breath ragged and rapid.

"Just a nightmare," I say aloud, trying to calm myself.

I close my eyes and concentrate on my breathing, taking in a lungful of air through my nose and then expelling it through my mouth. Slowly, my heart rate begins to decrease, and my pulse returns to normal. I look over at the window. It's dark outside, but there's no sign of a storm. The bright, red numbers on my bedside clock read 11:17.

"That can't be right," I mutter before picking up my phone and verifying the time.

I sit for a few seconds before swinging my legs off the bed and stepping onto a soaking-wet rug. I yelp and pull back, staring down at the floor for a moment before I spot the trail of wet footprints. My eyes move from one to the next, the line leading into the room.

"What the fuck?" I ask, gazing around the room, half-expecting the woman to suddenly appear.

I pad over to the window and peer outside. The moon is high in the sky above the ocean, and stars are visible all around as if I'm in the middle of a massive snow globe. I take a deep breath and hold it for a moment as I close my eyes.

"Am I still dreaming?" I ask out loud, but when I open my eyes again, nothing has changed.

"Sleepwalking?" I think, trying to run every possibility through my head.

I've never done it before, but it's the only thing that makes any sense. I must have wandered outside in the rain and had some sort of waking dream...a lucid dream, I think they call it. As I'm standing there, I suddenly feel tired, and I move back to the bed and climb in under the sheets, pulling them tightly around me, and within a few minutes, I drift off.

The blaring of my alarm jolts me awake, and I roll over and slap the top of the clock, immediately silencing the annoying sound.

8:30.

I groan and think about rolling over and going back to sleep, but I have a lot to do. The events from the previous night are blurry, at best, but the second my feet touch the still-wet rug, everything comes back to me. I sit for a few seconds and then shake my head.

"Ghosts aren't real," I say quietly.

I stand and walk across the hall to the little bathroom, but not before glancing down the corridor toward the studio.

"Ghosts aren't real," I say, a little louder this time.

I breathe a sigh of relief when no one is standing in the open doorway. I turn on the water in the shower and look at myself in the mirror as the steam begins to fill the room. I strip down, pull the curtain aside, and step into the beautiful, claw-foot bathtub.

As I wash, I look up at the ceiling with its cracked plaster and faded paint. Some tiling still needs to be done in here, but as I stand under the hot water, I'm just grateful that it's finished enough that I can use it, unlike the kitchen. I let the water flow over me for several minutes, eternally grateful that I sprung for one of the more expensive tankless hot water systems. Finally, when the room is full of steam, and I can barely see the curtain,

I shut off the water, pull the towel down off the bar, wrap it around myself, and step out onto the little bathroom rug.

I freeze immediately as I stare at the mirror, where the words "HELP US" are scrawled on the steam-covered glass. Tiny rivulets of water are dripping slowly down from the letters, making it look like they're bleeding. My breath feels trapped in my throat. I take a step forward, my feet crushing the soft pile of the rug. Water rolls down my forehead and into my eye, and I blink. When I open them again, the message on the mirror is gone, nothing but condensation on the glass.

I sigh, wipe the water away, and scream when the visage of the man I saw in the backseat of my car is staring back at me. He opens his mouth to speak, but only water dribbles out. I spin around, but when I do, he's gone and I'm standing in the bathroom all by myself. I stand for a few seconds, chills running up and down my arms before settling deep in my spine. I look at the mirror again. There's no sign of the writing, but the condensation from the steam is completely undisturbed as if I never wiped it. I take a deep breath and let it out slowly, trying to clear my mind before padding across the hall to my bedroom while muttering to myself.

"Ghosts aren't real."

* * *

THE EARLY MORNING sun shines down on me as I sit outside the cottage at a little table, my laptop open. The bright, cheerful day seems to have banished most of the odd happenings of the night and the morning. Most, but not all. Peering at my screen, I type in a few searches on Google:

Blackwater Cottage

Lilly Blackwater

Lilly Blackwater ghost

Ghosts and dreams

Most of them generate little to no useful information. There's nothing online that adds to what I already know. In fact, Emily was a lot more helpful than more than a dozen different websites. I shake my head and close the lid of my computer just as the sound of a small motor-cycle comes drifting up to the house. I stand up and watch as a woman on a red and black bike rides up and over the rise, stopping a few feet away. She's dressed in a black leather jacket, black and red helmet, and black boots tucked under her jeans.

She pulls off her helmet, and a mass of dark-brown curls tumble free, cascading over her shoulders. She turns and starts unbuckling the top of one of the twin saddle-bags mounted to the rear of the bike.

"Emily," I call out as I walk across the gravel toward her, my eyes locked on the bike. "Is that a Vincent Black Shadow?"

She looks at me and smiles. "You know your rides," she says with a nod of quiet respect.

"My dad loved them. What is it, 1949?"

"Damn. You are good."

I crouch by the side of the bike and allow my eyes to slowly take in the beauty of the machine—the sensual curves of the exhaust, the glimmer of the sun off the wire wheels, and the lovely custom red and black paint scheme. Finally, I manage to pull myself away from admiring the cycle, and I look up at her.

"What are you doing here?" I ask.

"Lunch," she says, holding up two paper sacks in one hand and two beers in the other.

"You didn't have to do that," I say, smiling at her.

"Hey, I figured you might be tired of coming to the diner. Just thought I'd bring the diner to you." She gives me a smile, and then she looks around before turning her attention back to me.

"Is this really about lunch?" I ask, cocking my head to one side and grinning at her.

"Of course, it is…I figured you might be 'tired' from last night." She flicks her eyebrows up and down and looks at me with a goofy expression on her face.

"You are such a perv."

"So, is he gone?" she asks, looking around.

"Yes, he's gone."

"Aww…did I just miss him?"

I shake my head and sigh. "He left last night after dropping me off."

She looks disappointed as we walk back to the little table and chairs. "You mean, after you had a little…you know…waka-waka?"

"There was no, waka-waka," I say, shaking my head.

"No hanky-panky?"

"No," I reply, sitting down in my chair and opening the beer.

"Hmmm. Did he need a blue pill or something? He didn't look like he did, but you never know…I mean—"

73

"Stop. For God's sake, stop," I say, laughing as I try to swallow a mouthful of beer.

She starts laughing and unscrews the top on her bottle, and we clink them together.

"I'm kinda glad he left when he did. I wouldn't have wanted him driving home in the storm we had last night," I say.

She looks at me with a confused expression. "What storm?"

"The rainstorm last night, all the lightning, wind, and stuff."

"It didn't rain last night, Ally. It hasn't rained for a week or so. Are you okay?"

I'm just about to argue with her, but I change my mind. "I'm fine. Must have been a dream," I say instead.

"Yeah," she says while looking at me suspiciously.

"Anyway…nothing happened between us last night," I say, trying to redirect the conversation.

"That's a shame. Maybe next time," she says. "Or maybe I'll see what I can get out of him."

"What? Don't—" I start to say before stopping suddenly.

She smiles and wags a finger at me. "So, there is something there, isn't there?"

I sigh and shake my head. "Fine. Maybe," I say, admitting it to myself at the same moment that I admit it to her.

"That's more like it."

I lean back in my chair for a moment and look at her. "Do we really know each other well enough to be talking about this?" I ask.

"I think so," Emily replies with a wicked little grin.

"If you say so. What did you bring for lunch?"

"Grilled cheese."

"Just grilled cheese?"

"Just grilled cheese?" she asks, feigning offense. "It's grilled cheese with three different kinds of cheese, home-made sourdough bread, and grape jelly on the side."

"Grape jelly?"

"Oh yeah," she says as she unpacks the bags, giving each of us a sandwich, a small bag of chips, and a little plastic takeout cup of jelly. "You have to try it."

With that, she removes the top from the little container, picks up her sandwich, removes the tinfoil wrap, and then dips the corner into the jelly. I can see the steam still rising off the cheese as she takes a bite, rolling her eyes back and moaning in pleasure.

"*So* good," she says, smiling at me.

I frown at her for a few seconds before performing the same actions. After dipping the sandwich, I pause for a moment, just looking at the glob of bright-purple gel slowly melting on the corner of the bread before taking a bite. The second the sweet of the grape jelly and the salty of the cheese and the buttered bread hits my tongue, I groan the same way that Emily did.

"See. I told you. Such a shame that you had to waste that noise on a sandwich," she says, and I start laughing again.

"You are *so* bad," I say before taking another bite.

We finish off our sandwiches and beers, and then I give her a tour of the cottage. When we walk into the studio, I spot her rubbing her arms.

"You feel it, too?" I ask.

"Yeah. It's freezing in here."

"I know. I have no idea why."

"That's weird," she says as we're heading back toward the front door.

We step back outside, and Emily walks back over to her bike and retrieves two more beers.

"You always drive around with a bunch of beer in your saddlebags?"

She shrugs and sits down in her chair again, leaning back slightly. "You never know when you need a cold one."

"Well said," I say, and we both take a draw from our bottles.

She looks at the house and then around at the rocky and grassy landscape. "It's nicer up here than I thought. I can see why you picked this place," she says.

"You've never been up here?"

She shakes her head and takes another drink. "None of us ever came up here," she says. "Back in school, we would dare each other, but no one ever tried it."

"I thought you didn't believe in all this ghost stuff."

"I never said that."

"You said it was ridiculous."

"Yeah. It is, but that doesn't mean I don't believe in it."

"That makes no sense," I say, grinning at her.

"Neither do ghosts."

"Touché."

We fall silent for a few moments, just nursing our beers for the next couple of minutes, and then Emily looks at me, a much more serious expression on her face.

"How are you doing, otherwise?"

"I'm okay," I reply.

She stares at me, tilting her head to the side. "Really?"

I sigh quietly. "I'm doing better than I thought I would be at this point."

"And you feel…guilty about it?"

I sigh again and look down at my hands as I rub them together slowly. "It's only been a little over a year," I say quietly.

"And?"

I look up at her. "And…I still miss him. I still think about him every day."

"I know you do," she says, reaching across the table and taking my hands, perhaps to keep me from fidgeting with them, "but that doesn't mean you can't move on, that you can't be happy."

"I feel like I'm betraying him…somehow."

"Would Steven want you to be happy?"

"Of course, he would."

"Would you have wanted him to find happiness if you were the one who had died?"

"Yes," I reply quietly.

"Then I think you answered your own question."

I look at her and smile softly, squeezing her fingers with my own. "Thanks," I say.

"Any time, you know that, and when you do hook-up with Jerry, you need to tell me all about it."

"You really are a perv."

"I've been called worse," she says, and we both laugh before finishing off our beers.

"Now. Can we talk about something else?"

"Like what?"

"Ghosts."

She looks at me for a few seconds without reacting before suddenly standing and marching over to her motorcycle. "I think we're going to need a few more beers."

~9~

Sometime after two, Emily left, and I spent the rest of the day unpacking some of the boxes still sitting around the house and thinking about our conversations concerning the rather sad and somewhat frightening history of the cottage. She only knew so much, and she suggested again that I visit the local historical society and the town library, but both are closed on Sundays, so there's not much I can do until tomorrow.

Meanwhile, I take the time to fill my bookcases with the novels, art books, and knick-knacks that I decided I couldn't part with. Every now and then, I stop what I'm doing and walk into the hallway leading to the studio and check to see that no one's there. There never is. By late afternoon, I've lost interest in unpacking, and I take a beer out of the fridge, which is standing alone in the kitchen in front of bare walls and yet-to-be-completed electrical outlets.

Walking back outside, I step onto the little porch and look right toward the ocean and the long, sloping hill that leads up to the top of the cliff in the distance. The ground is dry, and the scrubby little grasses are slightly brown along the edges, reinforcing Emily's statement that it hadn't actually rained last night. I begin walking up the hill, and within a few moments, I notice that there's a faint trail leading to the final drop-off. It's not recent, by any means, but it's definitely there as if the ground has been compacted by the passing of feet over and over again for a very long period of time.

I follow the ghostly path through the grasses and rocks until I reach the bare, flat stone at the precipice of the hill, where the soil has been long washed away and time has worn the rock smooth. It looks exactly as it did during my…dream, or whatever it was from the previous night.

The sound and scent of the ocean far below are almost hypnotic. The waves come in one after the other, crashing against the cliffs as they constantly try to wear away their nemesis. The stone and rock are temporary when in comparison to the power and infinite existence of the ocean. One day this rockface will collapse and fall into the sea, finally submitting to the inevitability of time.

I sit down cross-legged and look out across the water, just watching the waves rolling in and then slowly receding, only to come back once again. I take a swig from the bottle and set it down next to me, and slowly, memories of Steven begin to flood into my mind:

~The time we went sledding, and he got a bloody nose

when I punched him in the face by accident after I slipped on the ice.

~When he decided he would be clever and throw me a surprise birthday party. Unbeknownst to him, I had just gotten fired that morning during a mass layoff at work. It was an awkward party, to be sure.

~His proposal at the Barnes and Noble bookstore where we first met, which then led to a much more successful party.

~The last day I ever saw him. We argued that morning about something stupid and petty. It was so unimportant that I don't even remember what it was. He called me to say he was sorry, and I told him I was, too, and then the phone went dead...and he was gone.

Tears are rolling slowly down my cheeks, and my heart feels like it's being gradually strangled by grief. I look out over the ocean again, and I gradually get to my feet. I move, inch by inch closer to the edge, tiny bits of stone dislodged by my shoes, go tumbling off into the waves far, far below. For a moment, I look down at the water and wonder how much I would feel if I just let myself fall and if it would hurt....

My phone suddenly rings, and I jerk slightly and take a small step back, jolted out of my dark thoughts. I pull it out of my pocket and read the screen: Holly.

I hit the accept button, and the video takes a moment to come on, and then I look into the face of my best friend. "Holly!"

"Ally!"

"How are you?" I ask, moving farther back from the cliffside.

"I'm doing good. How are you?"

"I'm doing okay," I say, trying to banish the last of the dark thoughts from my mind.

There's a pause before Holly responds, "You sure about that?" she asks.

"I'm sure," I reply with a little smile on my face.

"Uh-huh. So, when are you up for a visit?" she asks.

"Any time you want," I reply, a happier tone returning to my voice.

"How's sometime in the next few weeks? I'll have to check my schedule, but I really want to see you."

"That would be great! Just let me know."

"All right then, perfect. How's everything else going?"

"Not bad," I say as I begin walking back toward the cottage. "Still waiting for the kitchen to be finished up."

"Still?" she asked. "What's the delay?"

"Jerry can't find people to work on it."

"Jerry?"

"Oh...yeah, he's the contractor."

"Mmm. When is he expecting it to be finished?"

"Probably in about two weeks."

When I reach the little table just outside the front door, I pull out one of the chairs and sit down.

"Oh. Should I wait to come to visit?"

"No. No. Most of the place is done. It's just the kitchen."

"Do I need to bring my own food?" she asks with a quiet laugh.

"There are places to eat up here," I say. "I don't live in the sticks."

"Pretty close."

I shake my head and sigh. "You're terrible."

"I know it, and you love it."

I hear Derek calling her name in the background, and she turns away from the phone for a moment. "I'm coming! I'm just talking with Ally."

I hear Derek say something else, but I can't make out what it is.

"Derek says hi," she says.

"Hi, Derek."

"I hate to go, but we've got to head out," Holly says. "I'll see you on Saturday."

"Perfect," I reply. "I'll see you then."

"Bye, buddy. Love you."

"Bye, buddy," I respond the same way we always have for the last ten years. "Love you, too."

She gives me a little wave, her video disconnects, and I set the phone on the table and let out a small, quiet sigh, a smile on my face.

* * *

"You don't have pizza, do you?" I ask Emily, already knowing the answer as I stand at the end of the counter by the door.

She looks at me and laughs as she refills another patron's coffee cup. "If we did. You probably wouldn't want it," she replies.

"Yeah. You're right. Is there a place in town?"

"Sure. Go down the block. There's a little shop called Pizza 3.14," she says.

"That's clever. Is the pizza good?"

"It's pretty damn good."

"Are there any other places?"

She shakes her head. "Nope."

"Well, I guess it is what it is then."

"Trust me. I wouldn't steer you wrong."

"I know," I reply with a warm smile. "By the way. Thanks for lunch."

"My pleasure. We should do it again sometime…if you're not busy with Jerry."

I shake my head and grin at her. "You are the worst."

"I'm the best at being the worst," she says before the bell rings in the window, and she looks back toward the kitchen. "I gotta go."

"Me too," I say before exiting the diner with a wave.

It only takes me a total of twenty minutes to find the little pizzeria, order a small pie, pay for it, and be back in my car on the way home. When I get there, I set the box on the little table, walk inside, grab a beer and some paper towels, and then return to my chair. It's still very warm outside, but a cool breeze is blowing in off the water.

I lift the first piece to my mouth and take a bite. The little bit of grease cupped in the slightly curled-up piece of pepperoni, mingles with the hot, melted cheese and a spicy piece of Italian sausage, combine together into the perfect symphony of flavor in my mouth. It's probably the best pizza I've had in quite a while. All I had to do, was move to a tiny hamlet in Massachusetts to find it.

"Damn," I mutter to myself as I chew.

I take my time, purposely slowing down and enjoying every bite, every nuance of salt and spice. When I finish, I sit back in my chair and take a deep draw from the bottle.

It's mid-summer, and the light is still strong, even as the sun is beginning to set far off to the west. Now that evening is coming on, I look over at the cottage, and a tiny bit of fear begins to trickle into my mind. Every night has brought visions or apparitions, or whatever they are...but something tells me that they don't mean me any harm. The message on the bathroom mirror seems to confirm that theory.

I pick up the box, gather the towels and empty beer bottles, carry them over to the dumpster, and toss them inside. After opening the front door, I stand for a few seconds and look out at the slowly darkening sky above the ocean and marvel at the beautiful array of colors in the low-hanging clouds. I step into the entry and then proceed directly to the kitchen, stopping and studying the old bricked-up fireplace. I know it's not as useful as it probably was when the cottage was built since I now have a stove and oven to make all my meals...or I will have them at some point in the future if the kitchen ever gets finished.

Without thinking, I lean down and grab a small, one-handed sledgehammer off the toolbox sitting by the corner of the wall and march directly over to the fire-place. I smash the hammer into the brick, sending a small cloud of shattered stone and mortar into the air while pieces tumble to the floor. Seeing the destruction that I just caused makes me smile and energizes me even more. I slam the hammer into the bricks again and again and again until two of them come loose and fall into the hidden firebox behind the wall.

I crouch down and peer through the opening,

knocking loose pieces of old mortar and brick out of my way. It's too dark to see much, but it's obvious the fireplace is still intact. Now that a couple of the bricks have been dislodged, I begin making swift progress, and within about fifteen minutes, I have the majority of the wall completely demolished. There are dust, bits of mortar, and chunks of bricks scattered all through the unfinished kitchen. I retrieve a broom and a dustpan and begin cleaning up as best I can, toting heavy loads of old bricks out to the dumpster.

Finally, I sit down on the floor in front of the fireplace with a beer in hand and gaze at my handiwork. I lean back, grab the side of the toolbox, and drag it over beside me. After opening the lid, I locate an old chisel amongst the rest of the items, along with a regular hammer. I also put on a slightly scratched pair of safety goggles.

"Probably should have had these on before," I say to myself before I start chipping away the broken remnants on the old bricks.

Every minute that I work slowly transforms the fireplace and brings me an incredible sense of accomplishment. Eventually, I put the tools down and pick up the beer, draining the rest of the beautiful amber liquid inside. An ancient fireplace grate and the original arm and hook are still there, both of them covered with dust and cobwebs. I sweep the rest of the demolition debris, old dust, and ashes out of the firebox, dumping them all into the kitchen trashcan. I crawl partially into the fireplace itself and peer up into the chimney. I expect to be able to see up through the shaft and out to the sky above, but everything is black.

It takes me a few minutes of groping around inside the chimney shaft to locate the controls for the old damper. I try to move it, but it's stubbornly stuck in place. I grab the hammer and then wedge the chisel against what looks like the seam where the damper should open and carefully tap it into place. Using the chisel as a lever, I push hard against it, and slowly, the rusty old metal cover begins moving, but still, there's no light. I slide my fingers into the gap, searching for any additional blockage, and immediately, I feel something solid wrapped in what feels like burlap or canvas.

I grab my phone out of my pocket, turn on the flashlight, and shine it up the chimney. I can see there's some sort of bag or bundle that must be sitting on top of the damper, preventing it from opening. I take a few minutes to figure out how to get the thing out of there without damaging it or the fireplace itself. I scoot back out and grab the toolbox, searching through the two little drawers for a small screwdriver and a pair of pliers. I crawl back into the firebox and peer up into the dark shaft.

The little bit of light coming through the partially opened damper is enough to work in. Using the screwdriver and hammer, I gently tap the rusty joints, trying to loosen them without damaging them. I take my time, being as careful as I can while trying to ensure I'm making some progress. After a few minutes of work, I use the chisel and pliers to gently force the two leaves of the damper open. When I have it open as far I can, I reach up inside the opening and gently pull the cloth-wrapped package downward, wiggling it back and forth at one point when it becomes temporarily wedged in place.

A small avalanche of ash, sand, and a tiny bit of dried grass fall onto me as I finish pulling out the bundle. I scramble out of the fireplace and stand up, brushing the debris off my clothes while holding the little bundle firmly in my left hand, as if it might suddenly disappear. I walk into the living room and set the package on the little coffee table. After sitting down on the floor, I examine my find more closely for the first time.

Whatever it is, it's carefully wrapped in some sort of fabric, probably canvas, although it's very thick. It almost feels like I would expect a sail to feel. There's a thin leather strap that runs both left to right and up and down that holds the fabric tightly around the object inside. It's tied in a rather complicated-looking knot, and it takes me some time to figure out how to undo it. I move slowly and deliberately; all of my actions are made with a purpose designed to ensure the package and its contents are not damaged and that I show the item the proper respect. It's obvious that whatever is hidden beneath the thick, off-white textile was extremely important to someone, having been so carefully hidden.

After undoing the knot, I carefully remove the strap from the bundle, laying it gently off to the side. There's a ghostly imprint of the dark leather on the much lighter canvas. I suddenly feel a chill, and goose bumps break out along my arms. I look toward the hallway for a brief moment before returning my attention to the package. I slowly begin unwrapping the bundle, carefully unfolding the portions of the material and laying them down flat on the tabletop. Underneath this first layer is a second, much darker one. I touch it, brushing my fingers across its surface, and quickly realize that it's a portion of dark leather, partially due to the easily recognizable scent wafting up from the table.

I begin removing the thin, dark wrapping from the object, laying it out in the same way as the canvas layer. A few seconds later, I'm looking down at a book, or more likely, a journal of some sort. I lift it carefully free of the cloth and leather that has protected it for close to two hundred years and lay it on the table next to the wrappings. The book is bound in red leather and engraved with an intricate image of a three-masted sailing vessel from the 1800s. The book is held closed by two short strips of leather and a small lock on the fore-edge.

The lock itself looks to be made of silver with gold or copper inlay. There's a small keyhole and two switches that need to be compressed at the same time to open it. As I turn the book over and over in my hands, the chill seems to return. I look around the room, but there's no one here but me. There's some writing on the cover, embossed into the leather, but it looks like it's in French. Even though I can't understand anything but English, I can read the name Lilly Blackwater in graceful, flowing letters. I slowly look over my shoulder, fully expecting the ghostly form of the woman to be staring back at me...but she isn't.

I press the two releases and try the lock, but it won't budge. Looking at it, it doesn't look that strong, but the keyhole is far too small for a screwdriver head, so I leave the book on the table and walk over to the pile of boxes marked for the kitchen and dig through them until I find a small paring knife. I figure the tip of the blade should fit easily into the opening. I return to the book and sit down on the floor again. I insert the tip of the knife into the keyhole and start to turn it but immediately meet with resistance.

I pause for a moment, then I twist the knife, and the tip suddenly breaks off, and the blade slips and slices into the finger.

"Ow!" I say, dropping the knife and the book at the same time.

I hold my injured hand in the other and examine the cut. It's not deep, but it is bleeding. Getting to my feet again, I walk to the bathroom, grab the little box of Band-Aids out of the medicine cabinet, and secure one over the cut after rinsing it off under some cool water. I walk back into the living room, pick up the broken knife, and try to slice the strap attached to the lock, but the blade doesn't even mark the leather. I shake my head and sigh.

"What are you hiding from me, Lilly?" I ask out loud.

~10~

J wake with a start, my eyes jolting open. It takes them a minute to adjust to the dark and for me to recognize my little bedroom in the lonely cottage. Glancing over at the clock on the nightstand, I read off the numbers—3:44. I shift my feet, and I feel something on top of the sheets at the foot of the bed. I sit up and then scoot back against the headboard when I spot the journal resting on top of my blanket. My eyes dart around the room, searching for any intruders, corporeal or otherwise, but there's no one there.

I stare at the book for a few minutes, unable to or unwilling to move toward it. The lock is still closed. I finally let out a breath that I didn't realize I had been holding in, and I lean my head back against the wall behind the bed and close my eyes for a moment. When I open them again, the figure of the sailor is standing at the foot of the bed just staring at me, his gaze riveting me in place. My heart is racing, and I can feel sweat breaking out on my forehead and my armpits.

After a few seconds, I finally manage to open my mouth. "What...what do you want?" I ask, my voice shaky and unsure.

For some reason, the figure of the girl, who I assume is Lilly Blackwater, does not fill me with the same feeling of dread that this spirit of the sailor does. My throat is bone dry, and I feel like my heart is about to burst out of my chest when the ghostly visage lifts his arm slowly and points out of the room.

"What? Do you want me to leave?" I ask.

Every ghost in every movie I've ever seen is always trying to get the intruders in their domain to leave their house. He doesn't move. He just continues to point out of the room, and then I glance down at the book.

"Is this something to do with the book?" I ask.

He raises his head slightly, his brilliant blue-green eyes gazing at me, and then his mouth opens slowly.

"Help us," he says slowly, his voice sounding as if it's the echo of a sound carried on the wind. The words are drawn out much longer than necessary, and the effect is chilling.

"How can I help you?"

He looks in the direction he's pointing and then turns his gaze back to me. I look down at the book again, and when I look back up, he's gone. I jump off the mattress, rush around to the end of the bed, and immediately step on a wet spot where the figure had been standing. There is a trail of wet boot-prints coming in from the hallway. I creep slowly to the door and peer outside. The hall is empty, the only light coming in through the windows from the half-moon hanging high in the sky.

My eyes follow the line of wet prints down the hall and into the demolished kitchen. I pad quietly down the corridor, my gaze darting from side to side, constantly searching for any sign of the ghost, but I appear to be alone. The trail continues into the living room and ends directly in front of the fireplace. I stand for a few minutes, studying the hearth, the mantle, and the front of the fire-box, but I can't see anything the ghost might have wanted me to find. A few seconds later, I feel a deep sense of weariness, and I make my way back to my bedroom. I pick up the book, set it on the top of my dresser, and climb back in beneath the sheets.

I wake again, this time to the blaring of my alarm. I slap the top of the clock, immediately silencing the incredibly annoying sound. I know Jerry's going to be here this morning to hopefully install the cabinets and try to get a handle on the rest of the projects around the cottage. I climb out of bed and step over to the dresser to get a pair of underwear and socks. After glancing at the book, I turn away and head to the bathroom.

The entire time I'm showering, I keep opening the curtain and looking at the mirror, just to be sure no one is leaving me any messages in the mist. I step out of the tub and look nervously around the room, but again, I'm alone

—no writing, no ghostly faces staring back at me. I dart across the hall to the bedroom and dress, checking to make sure the book is still where I left it. It is. I walk out to the kitchen, and the first thought that I have is—coffee. My Keurig is still sitting in a box somewhere in the stack of boxes carefully arranged along one wall of the living room.

A few seconds later, the doorbell rings, and I find my heart speeding up and a little tickle forming in my belly. I know it's Jerry, and I take a moment to calm myself before I head to the door. The minute I open it, the tickle returns when I look at his smiling face and the wonderful sparkle in his eye.

"Morning, Ally," he says warmly before holding up two large cups of coffee, one in each hand.

"You are a godsend," I reply, smiling broadly as he hands me one of the cups.

I glance over his shoulder and spot two men climbing out of their truck and gathering their tools. "Looks like you found some help," I say.

He looks back at them for a moment and then nods. "Yeah. I had to go all the way to Millson to find them."

"Millson? Isn't that like thirty miles away?"

"Little more than that," he replies with a shrug. "But we gotta do what we gotta do."

"Yep," I say, stepping aside and gesturing him into the house.

He looks around as he's walking toward the kitchen. "I see you got a few boxes unpacked," he says, and then he stops suddenly when he spots the fireplace in the kitchen. "You've been busy." He turns and looks at me, smiling and shaking his head. "Are you just trying to make more work for me?" he asks.

"I just had an idea."

"You had an idea to demolish the kitchen even more?" He sets down his coffee, walks over, and looks at the newly opened orifice.

"Did I do too much damage?" I ask nervously.

"Not that I can see. You did a pretty good job. I'll have to find a mason who can come up and inspect the firebox and then clean up some of the edges on bricks on the ends here," he says, running his hand along the jagged remains of some of the bricks I couldn't get cleaned up.

"What about the chimney itself?" I ask. "Do you think it's useable?"

He gets down on all fours and peers up into the shaft. After a few minutes, he clambers back out and wipes his hands on his jeans, leaving a couple of dark stains.

"It looks like it. We'll have to try to find a chimney sweep to come to clean it out before you use it."

"Of course."

The front door opens, and Jerry's two co-workers walk inside.

"Ally. This is Tom and Aaron," Jerry says, introducing them.

"Tom?" I ask, and the one on the right with dark hair and a short beard smiles at me.

"That's me," he says, offering his hand. We shake, and he looks around at my little house. "I love this place."

"Thanks," I reply. "That's nice of you to say."

He gives me a nod, and I turn to Aaron.

"I can't believe you can't find people to work on it for you," he says. "I love these old houses."

"Well, I'm glad Jerry found you. I appreciate you being here."

"No problem at all," he replies.

I turn back to Jerry while Aaron and Tom head to the kitchen with their tools and other supplies.

"I'm going to head out for a little bit," I say, and I swear I catch a glint of disappointment in his eyes. "There's some water and beer in the fridge if anyone gets thirsty."

"Will you be long gone?" he asks.

"Not for too long. I just have a few errands to run."

"Oh...okay," he says, sounding even more disappointed and stumbling for words.

"I'll be back a little after lunch," I add, trying to make him feel a bit better.

"Oh. Okay, great," he says, smiling again.

I grab my purse, keys, laptop, and phone and head to the door. Just before walking outside, I stop, turn back, and look at him. "I'll see you later, Jerry," I call out to him with a smile.

"See you soon," he responds with a smile of his own and a renewed sparkle in his expression.

* * *

As I DRIVE out between the two columns at the end of the gravel lane leading to the cottage, I glance in the rearview mirror, hoping to see Jerry standing at the top of the hill, waving goodbye, but he's not there. I feel a tiny pang of disappointment, and I shake my head.

"Snap out of it, girl," I say to myself before pulling out onto the road and heading toward town.

It only takes me a few minutes to reach the business district and just a few more before I come upon the Duxbridge Library. It's a small, three-level stone building with a little parking lot out front. Cheerful flowers are planted in the beds lining the sidewalk, brightening the otherwise dreary, gray exterior. There are only two other cars in the lot when I pull in. I park a few spaces from the front door and climb out, grabbing my laptop and purse off the passenger seat.

I pull the heavy wooden door open and step over the threshold. The air is thick with the smell of old books, dust, and wood. I inhale deeply and smile as I look around the cramped but bright room.

There's a small checkout counter just to the right of the entrance. Shelves and bookcases take up every square inch of space and line every wall in sight. There are also a few small tables and chairs spaced around the main room. It's obvious the building used to be a house, even with all the modifications.

"Good morning," someone says, and I turn to face the counter. An older lady with short, gray hair is sitting on a stool behind the desk, multiple stacks of books partially blocking my view of her.

"Morning," I reply with a smile.

"Can I help you?"

"I was hoping to do be able to do some research today," I say.

"About what, dear?"

"Blackwater Cottage."

She stares at me for a moment, and I feel her eyes studying me before she speaks again. "Are you the young lady who bought the old place?"

"I am."

She seems to study me again for a few moments before continuing, "Well, it's good to meet you," she says, her mood suddenly lightening. "My name is Olivia. I'm the head librarian...well, I'm the only librarian." She chuckles and offers her hand.

"It's nice to meet you, too," I reply, shaking her hand. "I'm Ally."

"It's always good to have someone new come into our little town. It helps keep it going."

"Thanks. I love it here."

"That's good," she says and then pauses for a moment before continuing. "Have you run into anything...odd up there?"

"You could say that," I reply, and she grins at me.

"The place is legendary. I just hope it doesn't make you change your mind about staying here."

"So far, so good."

"Good for you, dear. Anyway, what can I help you with today?"

"I was actually hoping to do some research on the house. Emily said you might have some information."

"Well, we certainly do," she replies. "You'll find some of the books in the reference section under *D* for Duxbridge."

"And where is the reference section?"

"Oh, just down that way," she says, pointing behind

me. "Turn the corner and go down to the end of the shelves."

"Thank you so much."

"You're quite welcome, Ally."

I give her a polite nod and then follow her directions. When I reach the area I'm looking for, I walk over and set my laptop down on the lone table in the corner under a small window. I return to the shelves and begin searching for the volumes I might need. I run my fingertips along the spines of the books, starting in the *D* section. It only takes me a few seconds to locate the small collection of books I need. I carry them to the table and then pull out the chair and take a seat. The top edges of the pages are coated in a thin layer of dust, which isn't very surprising.

I boot up my laptop, load MS Word, and begin taking notes:

The house was built in 1815 by Captain Oliver Blackwater, originally from England, for his wife, Lilly Blackwater, a French ballet dancer. He was the captain of a trading merchant vessel, The Dominator, which sailed out of Boston on a regular transit to England. They lived in the house for four years, although he was at sea for most of that time. By all accounts, when he was home, he lavished love, affection, and attention on Lilly, who adored him.

IN MARCH OF 1820, Oliver set sail for England with a load of tobacco and other trading goods. They were expected to return to port in October. However, when the time came, the ship did not appear, which wasn't all that surprising considering weather and other factors. However, by the time December came on in 1820 and the ship had not returned, people seemed to lose faith that it would ever reappear. A few weeks later, word came from England that a ship crossing the Atlantic encountered an empty lifeboat adrift in the open ocean. It had the name The Dominator *emblazoned on the bow.*

This seemed to drive Emily mad, and not long after, she was seen standing on the edge of the cliff every night, holding a lantern in all sorts of weather. Many people thought she was trying to signal her husband's lost ship, but after a few other ships came to a bad end on the rocky shore at the foot of the cliff, due to her "false lighthouse signal," the townspeople of Duxbridge marched to the cottage and chased her to the cliff, where she stumbled and fell off the edge onto the rocks far below.

THE PROPERTY WAS THEN PURCHASED, not long after, by William Duxbridge, one of the founders of the town, but he died mysteriously a few months later, after having moved into the cottage.

I SEARCH through the rest of the books on the area, but I don't really find any additional information that I don't already know. I close up the dusty tomes and replace them on the shelves in the exact order I found them. As I'm sliding the last one into place, I feel a chill on the back of my neck, and I spin around and come face to face with the sailor. I'm only inches away from him, and I catch the faint scent of saltwater in my nostrils. He simply stands in front of me, staring straight ahead. It's hard to tell if he's looking at me...or through me, but either way, it's very disconcerting, to say the least.

My throat feels dry, and I try to speak, but nothing comes out. I feel riveted to the spot. He slowly raises his hand, just as he did in the house, and points to one of the books.

"Duxbridge," he says, extending the end of the word, his voice ragged, accompanied by a slight gurgling sound.

"The town?" I ask, and just at that moment, the librarian comes around the corner pushing a book cart. I glance at her, but by the time I look back at him, he's gone, but the chill remains.

I see her shiver and run her hands up and down her arms a few times.

"It's kind of chilly in here," she says to me as she's shelving some books. "I'll go turn down the air conditioning."

She moves along past my aisle, and I pull the one book that I skimmed through that mentioned the town, and I retake my seat at the table. The bright sunshine streaming through the little window quickly banishes the chill as I read through the old book. One hour later, except for a picture of William Duxbridge that I stored on my phone, I don't have any new information that might help.

I replace the book again and head toward the front desk. The librarian is sitting behind the counter again.

"Did you find what you were looking for?" she asks.

"Some, but I was trying to find some more detailed information about the town and its residents."

"Oh. Well, for that, you should probably go see Linda at the historical society."

"Where's that?"

"If you head back through town and then go past your place, it's on the left-hand side. You can't miss it."

"Thanks. Thanks a lot."

"You're quite welcome. Be sure to visit us again."

"I will," I reply with a smile before slipping out the front door.

~11~

*a*fter passing the entrance to my driveway, I continue down the highway, where the landscape changes again back to mostly rural farmland, dotted here and there with old, stone houses. A sign appears on the left side of the road for the Duxbridge Historical Society, and I slow down as the building comes into view. Tall trees surround the impressive stone house, creating a moody sort of atmosphere, which clashes with the otherwise idyllic countryside. I pull off the road and into the parking lot, and as soon as I do, I feel a dark cloud descend upon me, even with the clear, bright, blue sky above me.

I can't see any other cars, and the place looks closed, but I park and step out, grabbing my bag and heading toward the front door. As soon as I make the little turn on the sidewalk, I pass a small sign that says that the museum is only open Tuesday to Thursday between 9 am and 4 pm. I stand outside for a few minutes, just looking at the building, but I begin to get a serious urge to get away from the place as soon as I can.

I return to my car, climb inside, and back out of the parking space as quickly as I can. As soon as I'm back on the highway, I glance at the clock on the dash—11:49. I smile to myself and drive past my house again and back into town. After slipping into one of the spots opposite the pizza joint, I jog across the street and hop up onto the sidewalk. Just before reaching the door, an elderly woman suddenly grabs my arm and shoves a piece of paper into my hand. I'm so stunned that I don't even react for the first few seconds.

Looking down at my hand, I study the paper for a few seconds. It's folded over on itself, and it feels rough and primitive, as if it's a piece torn from some old parchment. When I look up again, the woman is nowhere in sight. I frown and open the paper, gazing at the words "cave spiritus" written in a bold but graceful script. After slipping the paper into my pocket, I pull the door to the pizza shop open and slip inside.

About twenty minutes later, I'm back in my car, three pizza boxes stacked beside me on the passenger seat, along with three two liters of Coke. When I reach the entrance to the cottage, I pull in between the two columns and drive up the winding path to the house. Jerry's truck is parked next to the one driven by his two helpers.

"At least they didn't run away," I say to myself as I'm parking.

I climb out and walk around to the other side of the car to get the pizzas when Jerry emerges from the cottage and smiles at me.

"Did you bring food again?"

"I'm just trying to keep everyone happy," I say as I walk toward the little table and chairs. "Can you grab the pop?"

"Sure." He darts over to the car and retrieves the three bottles, returning to the table a few seconds later.

"I think I have some glasses in one of the boxes just inside the living room," I say.

"Got it," he replies with a smile and dashes off, back into the house.

I look at the front door after he's inside and smile. The simple act of asking him to do something as mundane as getting something out of the car or out of the house gives me a warm feeling deep down inside my soul. A few minutes later, he emerges with Tom and Aaron in tow. When they spot the pizza, huge smiles break out on their faces.

"You didn't have to do this," Aaron says.

"I know. I wanted to. You guys are working hard," I reply, and then I stop and cock my head to one side. "You are working hard, right?"

"Of course, we are," Tom says, grinning at me.

"That's what I thought. Dig in."

"We really appreciate this," Aaron says as he picks up a slice from the box with the pepperoni and sausage pie.

"I appreciate you coming all this way to work on my home."

He waves off my compliment with a smile. "No need

for thanks." He takes a bite and groans quietly. "This is thanks enough."

"It's really pretty here," Tom adds, looking over toward the cliff and the ocean beyond.

"Isn't it?"

"I can see why you bought it."

"How could I not?"

I take a slice of the green pepper and mushroom pie and make quick work of it while we all stand around, eating and conversing. Jerry looks over at me and smiles, and I get that little tickle deep down in my belly again.

"So, how's the kitchen coming?" I ask with a hint of hope in my voice.

"Do you want to see?" Jerry asks.

"Can I?"

"Of course. It's your house."

"I just thought you might want to do a big reveal or something," I say, chuckling.

Jerry laughs along with me, and we head inside, each of us still carrying a slice of pizza. Aaron and Tom stay behind, talking amongst themselves. As soon as we're through the door, I spot a corner of the kitchen, and my mouth drops open.

"Oh my God," I mutter quietly as my eyes move from one thing to the next.

The cabinets are all installed, and the white granite countertops are in, along with the black farmhouse sink. Most of the white subway tile backsplash is up, and the entire room is painted with the exception of a few small spots.

"How did you even get the counters in? They weren't even here."

"I had the guy scheduled this morning. He showed up about ten minutes after you left," he replies with a satisfied grin.

I walk around the room while he stands by the wall, leaning against it with his arms crossed. I check the brand-new faucet in the sink, try a couple of the soft-close cabinets and drawers, and turn on one of the burners on my new stove.

"Oh my God, the lights," I say, looking up at the beautiful, brushed nickel pendants that look like lanterns hanging from the shiplap and exposed beam ceiling. "They look amazing."

"Another good design choice."

I stand in the middle of the room, just taking everything in, not even caring about the little bit of work that still needs to be done to finish things up.

"I can't believe you got all this done in four hours."

"Well, cabinets actually go up pretty fast when you've got everything prepped and ready."

"It's so up to date, but still looks...old...you know what I mean?"

He nods and smiles at me. "Yeah. The cabinet style was the right choice, and the farmhouse sink really helps bring it all together."

I look at him and smile. "You sound like an HGTV commercial," I say.

"Maybe I should get my own show."

"I'd watch it," I reply, grinning at him.

He blushes, and I look down at the floor momentarily, purposely not mentioning it.

"Give me a minute. I'm going to go change," I say, heading toward the hallway.

"I'll be here."

I slip into the bedroom and close the door, turning the lock just so no one accidentally walks in on me. I strip out of my pants and blouse and switch into jeans and a paint-smeared T-shirt that fits me really well. I glance in the mirror and quickly run a brush through my hair. When I turn around, I look toward the dresser and pause for a moment when I don't see the old journal resting on the top.

"What the hell?" I mutter quietly to myself.

I look around the room, searching for the book, but it's nowhere in sight. I open the top drawer on the dresser and look inside, just in case I put it in there and don't remember…even though I know I didn't. I return to the kitchen where Aaron is working on the backsplash and Tom is applying the final touches to the paint around the cabinets and under the windowsill.

Jerry is attaching handles to one of the last drawers. I step over next to him.

"Hey. Did you guys work on my bedroom?"

He stops and looks over at me. "No. We've been in here all morning," he replies with a frown. "Why?"

"I was looking for something I left on the dresser."

"What is it?" He glances at the other guys, and I can tell he's starting to get upset with the thought that they might have intruded on my private space or stolen something from me.

"It's an old book, like a journal, leather-bound."

"You mean that?" he asks, pointing to the living room mantle.

The diary is sitting up on the corner of the wooden beam, leaning back against the wall.

"What?" I mutter quietly to myself.

"Is that it?"

"Yeah…yeah. That's it," I reply, feeling like a fool in front of him, but I know I left the book in the bedroom. "Sorry about that."

"Don't worry about it," he says with a smile and then looks me up and down. "Based on how you're dressed, I'm going to guess you want to help out."

"If you have something for me to do," I reply, immediately pushing thoughts of the book into the back of my mind.

"Painting."

"All right then. Put me to work, boss."

He just shakes his head and sighs.

* * *

"You guys got a lot done today," I say as Jerry and I are sitting outside at the little table, a couple of beers in our hands and a couple of empties in front of us.

"I aim to please."

"Is this still going to be two weeks?"

"I'm thinking a little less now."

"Like how long?"

He takes a drink from the bottle and leans back in his chair. "Should be finished by the day after tomorrow."

I sit up a little straighter. "Are you serious?"

He nods and smiles at me. "Yep."

I eye him suspiciously, a grin slowly sneaking out. "Something tells me that you told me two weeks so you could impress me by getting it done in two days."

"Three days, actually. And how else can I keep my reputation as a miracle worker?"

"You sound like Scotty," I say, and then I pause, suddenly realizing that I just outed myself as a huge geek.

He stares at me for a moment and then smiles. "Aye, Captain," he replies with a terrible Scottish accent.

"That was bad."

"I know. I knew it the second I started doing it," he says with a laugh.

"As long as you know." I laugh quietly and then take a long draw on the bottle while looking out at the ocean just over Jerry's shoulder.

"Did you find what you were looking for?" he asks, jolting me out of my daydream.

"What? What do you mean?"

"The library. Did you find what you were looking for?" he asks, looking at me with a curious expression.

"Sort of," I reply. "I found a little information, but I need to dig a bit deeper. The librarian suggested I check at the historical society."

"Did you?"

"They're only open Tuesdays through Thursdays."

He nods, takes another drink, and then sets the bottle on his knee. The sun is starting to set in the distance, and he picks up his phone and looks at it. "Well, I guess I should be heading out so you can have some time to yourself before we're back here tomorrow morning," he says, starting to get up from his chair.

"Did you want to have dinner?" I suddenly blurt out.

He stares at me for a few seconds without saying a word, and for a moment, I'm fearful that he's going to say no, but then he smiles, and I respond in kind. "I would really like that," he says.

"What do you want to get? I don't really have anything to cook in my brand-new kitchen."

"Let me handle that," he says, getting up and heading to his truck.

"You sure?"

He nods and smiles at me. "You got lunch. It's only right that I take care of dinner," he says as he's closing the door on his truck.

"Okay. Be careful. See you soon."

He nods and waves to me before heading down the driveway. I wait for a few seconds and then head inside, moving directly to the bedroom, where I change out of my work clothes, put on fresh deodorant after smelling my pits, and then brush my hair and pull it back into a ponytail. I pick up the pants I wore in the morning, and the little paper the old lady gave me, drops onto the floor. I bend down and pick it up and unfold it again.

Cave Spiritus

I pull my phone and open Google, doing a search for Cave Spiritus, but I don't get much in return that looks useful. I study the second word for a few seconds and then search for a Latin to English translation. After it loads, I type in the words and hit translate.

Beware the spirits

I get a chill that rolls slowly down my spine. I'd never seen the lady before today, so why would she give me this?

I shake my head, stuff the paper back into my pocket, and check myself in the mirror again before I step back into the hallway. I pause for a moment, glancing down toward the studio.

There's no sign of the girl, but that doesn't mean she's not here. I turn and walk into the living room, stopping a few feet from the fireplace, my eyes lock on the journal. I run the events of last night and this morning through my mind again, and I know I left the book on my dresser, but then I suddenly feel a chill pass over my skin. I turn quickly and come face to face with the sailor again. He's standing in the doorway between the hall and the living room.

"You moved the book?" I ask, not expecting an answer.

He raises his right arm and points to the mantle again. "Find *it*," he says in the same strange, gurgling whisper.

I watch as water drips off the sleeves of his coat. His hair hangs limp and wet around his face.

"Find what?" I ask, just as the message alert on my phone goes off. I snatch it out of my pocket, glance at the screen, and when I look back, the sailor is gone. "Dammit."

I swipe the screen. It's Emily.

"Your boyfriend is just leaving."

"He's not my boyfriend."

"Maybe you ought to tell him."

"Were you nice to him?"

There's a bit of a pause before she responds.

"Not as nice as you're probably going to be...lol."

"OMG. U R terrible."

I slip the phone back into my pocket just as the sound of Jerry's truck rumbling up the driveway drifts into the house. I look over at the wet footprints where my visitor had been standing.

"Shit."

I rush over, grab some paper towels, and dart back to the spots to wipe the water off the floor just as Jerry walks in. He stops in the doorway, a large white sack in his hands.

"Something leaking?" he asks.

"No," I reply, shaking my head. "I just spilled some water."

"Oh, okay. Just want to make sure it's not shoddy workmanship."

"No, no." I shake my head and laugh. "It's all good." My eyes move to the bag. "So, what's for dinner?" I ask.

"If you give me a minute to set everything up, you can find out," he replies, stepping into the kitchen and grabbing a pair of beers out of the fridge before heading outside again. "No peeking."

"Okay...okay."

I shake my head and stand in the living room, my thoughts bouncing back and forth between Jerry and my daily phantom visitors. A few seconds later, he opens the door, holding it with one hand, and grins at me.

"Dinner is served, my lady," he says, with an odd bow and flourish of his other hand.

"Don't do that again," I say, shaking my head.

"Yeah, sorry...it sorta felt weird."

I smile and shake my head before moving past him and out the door. The little table is all prepared with two plates, regular silverware, actual salt and pepper shakers, as opposed to the little paper packets, and two cold beers with tiny rivulets of water rolling down their sides. Each of the plates is filled with a steaming T-bone steak, baked potato, with a little scoop of white butter slowing melting onto it, and green beans. Sitting just to the right of the plates are two slices of pie, one lemon meringue and one that looks like it might be French silk.

"Where did you get the plates and silverware?"

"Emily let me borrow them."

I nod, and he moves around to my other side and pulls out my chair. I look at him and smile before taking my seat. "Thank you," I say, and he nods and then sits down opposite me.

"You're very welcome."

I look over everything again and shake my head. "You didn't have to do all this."

"It's my pleasure."

"So, you got all this at the diner?"

"It's the only place I know in town," he replies with a grin.

"And my girl helped you out?"

He half-nods and half-shakes his head.

"What does that mean?" I ask, smiling at him.

"She did, but she kept giving me these weird looks mixed with smiles and, I swear, a couple of giggles."

"Yeah…that might have been my fault."

He looks at me and frowns slightly. "How's that?"

"She was texting me while you were there."

"Seriously?" He chuckles and shakes his head. "Are you two in high school?"

"Sometimes I think she is."

"Anyway," he says. "Let's eat before it gets cold."

I nod in agreement, and we both dig in.

~12~

"Chocolate or lemon?" Jerry asks.

I look at them both and then back at him. "Which do you prefer?"

"I like them both."

I study his face for a few moments, wondering if he's just saying that or if he really means it.

"Why don't we split them both, then we can each have some?"

"That sounds perfect." He picks up one of the knives. Then he quickly divides both slices down the middle and sets one of each on my plate.

"They look delicious," I say.

"I'm sure they taste better."

"You know, they do say you taste with your eyes first."

"Really, because I've always found taste works better

with your mouth," he replies before cutting and scooping a portion of the lemon pie into his mouth.

I do the same and smile at him as the wonderful tartness of the pastry explodes on my tongue. "I think you're probably right."

We both chuckle, and within a few minutes, both of the desserts are gone, and our bellies are filled.

"Thank you for dinner," I say after a couple of moments of silence.

"Anytime," he replies with a warm smile.

We sit for a while, both of us looking out toward the ocean, watching the clouds twist and climb around each other in the distance.

"Can I ask you something?" Jerry says quietly.

"Sure."

"You don't have to answer it if you don't want to. I know I'm just your contractor, but—"

"You're more than that...just so you know," I say.

He nods and smiles at me. "Thanks."

"You're welcome. So, what's your question?"

"Why did you buy this place? Why move to this little cottage?"

I look at him for a few seconds without answering. I simply study his face and his body language, and then he starts talking again before I have a chance to respond.

"I'm sorry. I shouldn't be asking you something like—"

"I lost my husband," I blurt out, and he seems to freeze in place, saying nothing. "I felt like I needed a change."

He nods silently, and then I see a sadness in his eyes that I glimpsed a few days ago. "I lost my wife," he responds with a quiet sigh.

"I'm sorry," I reply, saying the one thing that I hate for people to say to me.

"Me too…for you."

"How long has it been?"

He leans back in his chair and looks past me. "Two years, three months, and nine days," he replies.

I nod and shake my head. "Isn't amazing how specific we can be when thinking about this? Eleven months and two days."

"I think pain focuses the mind," he says with a grim smile.

"Yeah, it sure does."

"Cancer," he says, and I frown.

"Sorry?"

"She had cancer."

I nod and sigh. "Car accident."

"I almost feel like that's worse," he says. "At least I had time to say goodbye."

I look down at the table for a moment before looking back at him. "What's her name?" I ask.

"Elizabeth…or Lizzy."

"Steven."

We both fall silent again, just sitting in the warm evening air.

"That's why I didn't want to call our first meal…a date," I say.

"You're not sure you're ready."

"Yeah…exactly."

"I get that, but you don't need to explain."

"I feel like I do. You deserve the truth."

"I feel like I need to apologize. Maybe I'm coming on too strong."

I shake my head and smile. "You're not," I say with a chuckle. "It's on me."

He sighs and shakes his head this time. "Well, that put a real damper on the evening," he says, grinning grimly at me.

I shake my head and manage a small but genuine smile. "Hardly. There's no use in trying to run away from the past, it's always there, and you can never get any further from it, no matter how much you try."

He nods and smiles at me. "So…what do you do for a living?" he asks, obviously trying to change the subject.

"I'm a graphic designer."

"An artist, huh? I guess that explains the studio."

"Yeah. It's been a while since I've worked, but I like to stay in practice."

"Well, you're really good."

I look at him and lean back a bit in my seat. "What do you mean?"

"The picture of the woman in black."

"The charcoal drawing? Where did you see it?" I ask, frowning slightly.

"It's on the easel," he replies, and then he seems to read my face, and his expression changes dramatically. "Oh my God. I wasn't snooping, I promise. I just walked in to do some final paint touchups, and it was right there."

"It was on the easel?"

"Yeah. I didn't mean to invade your privacy."

"You didn't. Don't worry," I say, trying to reassure him. "I just don't…I don't remember putting it there."

"Who else would have put it there?" he asks.

"The ghosts," I reply without even a pause.

* * *

"I'M SORRY. THE WHAT?" Jerry asks, leaning forward in his chair.

"The ghosts."

"Um…you're telling me there are ghosts in the house?"

"Yeah."

"You've seen them?"

"I have."

He pauses for a few seconds, just looking at me from across the table. "How many?"

"Just two…so far."

"Wow. Aren't you scared?"

Now it's my turn to pause. "Honestly. No."

"How could you not be scared…they're ghosts?"

I shake my head. "They never seem threatening, at least to me, even the one who appeared in my car."

"Wait, wait, wait," he says. "You've seen them in your car?"

"Yeah," I reply, beginning to doubt whether it was a good idea to go down this road…but it's too late now. "One time."

"One time is one too many as far as I'm concerned. Are you serious that you're not scared?"

I nod slowly. "They seem to need something from me."

"How do you know that?"

"Well, when they talked—"

"Hold on again. They talked to you?" He looks at me with an expression of incredulity on his face.

"The one did. To be honest, it's not like we're talking directly to each other. It's more like…he's saying things and I'm just hearing them. I've asked them questions, but they never answer. I'm not sure if it's because they can't hear me, they don't want to answer, or they can't answer."

"What have they said?"

"I saw one in the library, and he said Duxbridge."

Jerry frowns. "Are they talking about the town?"

"I don't know."

"What else have they said?"

"Help us."

He sits back in his chair and stares at me. "What do they need your help with?"

"I don't know."

"Is that why you went to the library?"

"Yeah. I thought I might be able to dig something up about the cottage and its history, maybe find a clue to what they want."

He sighs and intertwines his fingers together, placing his hands on the table and looking at me. "Tell me what you found," he says.

"Are you for real? You want to help me with this? I thought you didn't believe in ghosts."

"I mean…I sort of don't, but if you're telling me that you've seen them, who am I to tell you they don't exist? You certainly sound convinced."

"Unless this is all in my head and I'm losing it."

"Do you think it's all in your head?" he asks, tilting his head to one side.

"No. I know it's not."

"Then what can I do to help?"

I nod and smile at him. "Thank you."

He smiles back at me and nods in return. "So, what did you find out at the library?"

I take about fifteen minutes to go through the little bit of information I discovered, including the basic history of the cottage—the Blackwaters, the death of Oliver, the tragedies that Lilly caused with the lantern, how she died, and how William Duxbridge bought the cottage and then died himself not long after.

"That's quite the story," he says when I'm finished.

"Yeah, but there's not much there that I didn't already know. I had bits and pieces from Emily and a few other people in town."

"It also doesn't help is figure out what they want your help with."

"Exactly."

"So, how many ghosts have you seen?"

I think about it for a moment before answering. "I think only two."

"The girl and the sailor."

"Yeah. I'm sure the girl is Lilly Blackwater."

"The one you drew in the picture."

"That's her. I think each time I've seen the sailor, it's been the same one."

Jerry frowns and then sighs. "You said the sailor said Duxbridge. Do you think he might have been talking about William Duxbridge and not the town?"

"Could be," I reply with a shrug. "And then there's this." I pull the paper out of my pocket and hand it to him.

He frowns and opens it up, studying it for a moment before looking at me. "Cave Spiritus?"

"It means beware the spirits, in Latin."

"And where did this come from?"

"Some little old lady just jammed it in my hand when I was in town earlier."

"That's creepy. Who was she?"

"No idea," I reply, shaking my head.

He hands the paper back to me, and then I look around and suddenly realize the sun has already set, and darkness is beginning to reclaim its domain over the area.

"It's starting to get late," Jerry says, looking at the quickly darkening sky. "I should probably get going."

My shoulders slump slightly. "Yeah. I guess you want to get home and get some sleep."

"Yeah, my new boss is such a slave-driver," he says, grinning at me.

"Ha-ha. So funny."

"Anyway. Let me help you clean this up," he says, standing and starting to gather the plates, silverware, and glasses.

"Don't worry about it. I can take care of it."

"You sure?" he asks, slowly setting the items back down on the table.

"I'm sure."

He looks over at the house and frowns slightly. "After what you just told me, I feel like you shouldn't be here by yourself."

I glance at the cottage and then back at him, a smile slowly building on my face. "I'm okay. Like I said, they don't seem like they want to hurt me. They just want help."

He nods, but the frown does not fade much. "I hope you're right," he says. "I'll see you tomorrow morning."

"I'll be here."

He smiles at me and starts to head toward his truck when I suddenly rush over to him and grab his arm. He stops and turns back, and I lean up and kiss him gently on the cheek.

"Thanks for tonight," I say, blushing at my own actions.

"You're more than welcome," he replies, smiling warmly at me.

He climbs into his truck, and a few moments later, the taillights vanish into the dark as he disappears down the driveway. I feel a real sense of loss as I watch the lights of his pickup get farther and farther away along the highway.

13

~13~

I wake with a start, sitting straight up in bed. My heart is racing, and sweat is beaded on my forehead. I look around the room, fully expecting to see Lilly or the sailor standing at the foot of my bed, but no one's there. I lie back down and stare at the ceiling, studying the shapes created by the moonlight coming through the windows. When I turn my head and look over, the little clock on the nightstand reads 3:27 am. I sigh quietly and close my eyes. When I open them again, I look at the clock—3:31.

"Shit," I say before throwing the covers to the side and swinging my legs off the bed.

The second I stand, I look toward the hallway, and I spot small wet footprints leading out of the room. They're not the boot steps of the sailor; they're much smaller and more delicate.

"They are going to ruin my floors," I mutter quietly to myself.

I creep along the trail, constantly searching for the maker. As I step into the kitchen, I spot the young girl, who I assume must be Lilly, standing in the living room. She's over by the fireplace, and she turns her head and stares at me. Her bright-blue eyes peer out from under her flowing black hair.

I swallow hard and let out a breath. "Lilly?" I ask.

She raises her head slightly, allowing me to fully see her face for the first time. Her skin is pale, and her lips are bright red. She's beautiful, even if she is a ghostly apparition.

"What do you want from me?" I ask when she doesn't answer or even gesture.

I glance at the mantle beside her, and my eyes lock onto the old, leather-bound journal sitting on the end of the wooden beam. I shake my head.

"Are you the one who keeps moving the journal?"

Instead of replying, she just points to the book.

"I know. It's your diary."

She slowly shakes her head, her hair moving back and forth, seemingly delayed for a few seconds. It reminds me of how Captain Salazar looked in one of the *Pirates of the Caribbean* movies, like he was constantly underwater. She points again, gesturing with more force this time.

"I don't understand."

Her shoulders seem to slump, and she stares at me

with those bright-blue eyes and takes in a breath, as if it pains her somehow to do so.

"The *key*," she says, her voice trailing off slowly.

"The key? Yeah…I need the key. I can't open it."

She points to the mantle again, and finally, it dawns on me.

"The key is hidden, just like the diary?"

Again, she nods slowly, and then suddenly, I feel incredibly tired, and my eyes begin to close. The next thing I know, I'm lying in bed and the sun is shining through the windows. I can hear Jerry talking outside with at least one other person. I glance at the clock—8:12.

"Shit!"

I jump out of bed and scramble around for my clothes, slipping into my jeans and pulling on the same shirt from yesterday, along with a pair of red tennis shoes. I run a brush through my hair a couple of times and jog out to the kitchen and then directly to the front door, pulling it open and smiling at Jerry and the guys.

"It's about time you got here," I say.

He looks at me and shakes his head. "Don't even try that," he says, grinning at me as he reaches over and plucks a sock off the underside of my right arm. "This looks like the same shirt you had on yesterday."

I snatch the sock out of his hand and grin. "Okay. You got me."

"Never bullshit a bullshitter," Jerry says, stepping past me into the house, followed by Tom and Aaron.

"How are you doing this morning, Miss Tanner?" Aaron asks with a smile.

"I'm doing good, thanks. You guys going to finish up today?"

"Hopefully," Tom replies as he lugs in a canvas bag full of supplies.

"That's awesome. Get it done and there might be another lunch in it for everyone," I say.

"We're on it."

"Is that where we're at now? Bribes?" Jerry asks.

"We all do what we have to do."

We all laugh, Tom and Aaron get to work, and I look over at Jerry.

"Can you give me a hand with something?"

"Sure," he replies with a smile.

We head into the living room, and Jerry looks around.

"I thought we weren't doing anything in here."

"We're not."

"Okay," he says, his brow furrowing slightly.

"I just need your help."

"With what?"

I put my hand on the mantle and grin at him. "I need your help in finding something."

"Finding what?"

"A key."

"A key? What kind of key?"

"The hidden kind of key," I reply, and he shakes his head.

"Does this have something to do with the ghosts," he asks, whispering the last word.

"Yeah."

"All right. Where do you think this key is hidden?"

I look at the mantle and then back at him. "Somewhere

right here," I reply, gesturing to the large wooden beam protruding from the wall above the fireplace. "Do you think this thing is original?"

He studies it for a moment and then nods. "Yeah. Pretty sure. Did they tell you it's in here?"

I nod slowly. "They've both pointed to it. It must be here."

Jerry studies the beam again and then walks back into the kitchen and retrieves a couple of items from his toolbox. He returns with a small screwdriver and a pair of needle-nose pliers.

"Look for anything that looks like a patch or some sort of seam," he says.

We both start searching, slowly going over every square inch of the beam. Jerry starts on the right side, and I begin on the left. The wood is incredibly old, and the hand-hewn ax marks help reinforce our thinking that the mantle is original to the house. I carefully run my fingers along the rough wood surface, slowly hunting for any sign of a hiding place.

"Hold on," Jerry says a few minutes later.

I stop and look over at him. He's sitting on the floor, leaning up against the fireplace and peering upward at the bottom of the beam. He's looking at a section a few inches from the end of the mantle, carefully probing the wood with the screwdriver.

"What do you got?" I ask.

"I swear there's a seam right here."

I crouch next to him and study the area he's looking at, and I can definitely see a small square that doesn't quite look like it belongs. He reaches into his pocket and retrieves a small folding knife. After opening it, he runs the edge of the blade along the seam, using the tip to scrape out a tiny bit of wax and years of accumulated dirt. When he reaches the end of the beam, he continues around the corner and then stops. Scooting over, he studies the end of the mantle for a moment and then grabs the top of the beam with his fingers and uses his thumbs to try to move the little section of wood.

At first, nothing happens, and then slowly, it begins to slide toward the end of the mantle. When it's about a quarter of an inch out, he grabs the end and pulls, wiggling the little section of wood back and forth a few times to loosen it up. Finally, the little rectangle of wood comes free of the much larger piece.

"What is it?" I ask, rushing over to him.

He's holding the little, flat section of wood in his hand. There's a small, carved-out portion where a tiny gold and silver key is resting.

"How the fuck did you know that was there?" Jerry asks, looking at me.

"I told you, ghosts," I reply in a low whisper.

I hold out my hand, and he turns the little piece over, dumping the key into my hand. The second it touches my skin, it feels colder and heavier than it should. I turn it over in my palm a couple of times, studying the little item. It's quite beautiful for a simple key. I lift it up, and I notice it's engraved with the same image of the ship that decorates the front of the journal.

"Come on," I say as I head to the bedroom with Jerry trailing just behind me.

We pass through the kitchen, where Aaron and Tom

are diligently working. I step into the bedroom and grab the diary off my dresser. Jerry stops in the doorway, looking a bit awkward as he looks at me, unwilling or perhaps unable to step across the threshold into my private space.

"What are you doing?" I ask him as I take the key and insert it into the tiny lock.

"I just didn't know if—"

"We're not in high school," I say, smiling at him. "You can come into my bedroom."

"Yeah, you're right."

I start to turn the key, but at first, it doesn't seem like it's going to move, but I press it in a little harder, and finally, the lock clicks loudly and opens. I feel a chill, and I look at Jerry. I can see from his reaction that he feels it, too. "You feel that?" I ask.

He just nods as he steps up next to me, a frown on his face. "Yeah, I do."

He looks around the room as if Lilly might suddenly appear, which she just might. I look back at the journal and slowly open it. The binding is stiff, and the leather creaks quietly as the cover is opened for the first time in more than two hundred years. I almost feel like I should be wearing gloves while touching something so old and precious. I slowly lift the first page and fold it over. I become the first person to read the words written by Lilly Blackwater two centuries ago.

"Shit," I say, shaking my head.

"What's the matter?" Jerry asks.

"It's all in French."

I scan the first page, and the only things I can make out are parts of the dates and the name Oliver Blackwater.

"Why is it in French?" Jerry asks.

"She was from France. She married Oliver Blackwater, and they moved here."

"Hmm. I guess you better get a good translation app on your phone."

"Yeah," I reply, nodding my head. I close the book again and sigh quietly.

"You okay?" he asks.

"I'm fine, just a little disappointed. I suppose I should have expected it."

"Well, thank God for the internet. It shouldn't be that hard to convert it all to English."

"I suppose not."

"I do have a question, though," Jerry says.

"What's that?"

"Why was it hidden?"

I PULL into the parking lot of the historical society, and I instantly get the same sense of foreboding I had when I was here yesterday. I take a deep breath and step out of the car, grabbing my purse and laptop bag. There's one other car parked a few spaces down, which I assume must be the curator. I stand for a moment and study the outside of the building. There's something dark and brooding about the house. Even though great pains have been taken to lighten the outside, it's still a depressing and oppressive place. I think about my little cottage on the cliff, isolated and alone, but it's full of light and seems like it used to be a happy place drowned by grief and sorrow. This place seems the opposite, a dark place covered over with a sheen of happiness.

I walk down the little path, between two rows of brightly colored pansies, to the front door. A little sign hangs on the knob announcing, "We Are Open–Come on In." I open the door and walk inside. It's obvious this building used to be someone's house that's since been converted into a museum/library. Despite the amount of light pouring in through the windows, the place still has an ominous sense about it.

The entryway is filled with ornately carved woodwork, all of it dark, continuing the moodiness of the exterior. A heavy arch beckons visitors forward, but I cannot rid myself of the urge to run away. I force myself to continue deeper into the museum, and as I step into the main room, hallways branch off in all three directions. There are a few small glass display cases filled with different artifacts from the 1800s.

I can see a room at the end of the corridor on the left that's filled even more cases, some of them lining the walls.

"Hello. Welcome to the Duxbridge Historical Society," a cheerful young woman with dark hair and bright-blue eyes says as she walks up to me before I can go any farther.

"Hi."

"My name is Linda, and if you need anything, please let me know."

"Thank you. I will."

She smiles and looks at me for a few seconds. "Are you just passing through? I don't think I've seen you around before."

"Oh. I just moved here."

"Have you? Where?"

I pause for a moment before answering. "I'm the new owner of Blackwater Cottage," I say, preparing myself for an onslaught of questions or even some sort of warning or rejection, but it doesn't come.

"*Oh*," she says with a genuine smile. "I've always admired that house...from afar."

"Why from afar?"

Now it's her turn to pause before answering. "The ghosts," she says with a sideways grin.

"Do you believe in them?"

"Oh, most certainly. All these old houses have a history, and with history comes...baggage."

"And a ghost is baggage?"

"It can be. It depends on why they're still here."

I nod silently. "I suppose you're right."

"Anyway," she says, smiling at me. "What brings you here today?"

"I'm doing some research on the house and on the town."

"Well, we certainly can help you with that."

"That's what I was hoping."

"We have quite a selection of books and historical arti-facts, as well as a trove of documents stretching all the way back to the founding of the town."

"I think that's exactly what I need."

"Wonderful," she replies, her face lighting up with excitement. "Follow me."

We turn right and walk about halfway down the hall. She stops at a small door, pulls a set of keys out of her pocket, and unlocks the door. She pushes it open and the smell of old paper and dust, very similar to the library, wafts out.

"Sorry. It's a bit musty in here," she says, apologizing.

"It's okay. I kind of like it."

She chuckles to herself and hits a button on the wall, filling the small stairwell with light. We descend the five or six steps into a massive basement. The air is cool but dry, probably due to some sort of climate control system.

She flips the switch on the wall, turning on a small overhead lamp, illuminating the shelves and shelves and shelves of books, papers, maps, and an incredible number of other documents. There's a single large table in the middle of the room, with four stools spaced at intervals around it. There are also four desk lamps on reticulating arms, one set in front of each stool.

"I'm sorry it's a bit cool down here," she says. "But it's better for the paper."

"That's fine. It feels good compared to outside."

"Well, if you need anything, just pop on up. Historical tomes are in that section," she says, pointing to the area. "Personal diaries we've been gifted are over there, legal documents on the shelves and in the cabinets on that wall, and maps and other various papers are over there."

"Wow."

"Have fun," she says before smiling and heading back

up the stairs when the sound of the front door opening drifts down the steps.

I take a moment to just look around the room, and then a chill fills the air, and it's not from the climate-controlled environment but from something much more sinister. It doesn't even feel like the same sort of "chill" that I get when one of the ghosts at the cottage appears. It seems colder somehow. I shake it off, and the goose bumps that had formed along my arms slowly fade away.

I spend the next two hours going through the massive collection of dusty books and even dustier loose documents, excerpts from personal diaries, and other various papers from people long since dead. I study some of the maps from the founding of the town, as well as the surrounding area. The entire time, I feel like someone is watching me, but there's no sign of Lilly or the sailor.

When I'm finished, I have eight pages of notes in a Word document and about two dozen pictures on my phone. It only takes me a few seconds after finishing to realize that I should have just taken pictures of everything instead of doing all that note-taking, but it is what it is. There's a lot of information to go through, but I found four names, some of which I already know and a few that are new to me—Lilly and Oliver Blackwater, William Duxbridge, Randolph Larsen, and Kitty and George Kingston.

I feel like I need to get home, read through my notes, and start putting this puzzle together, but most of all, I want to talk to Jerry. I close my computer and slip it into my bag and start to stand up when something unseen slams into me, knocking me off the stool and onto the floor.

"What the hell?" I say aloud, looking around the room.

I know I didn't trip or stumble; something definitely pushed me. I scramble to my feet and start to reach for my laptop bag when I'm knocked to the right, pushed hard into one of the dozens of bookcases. I get a feeling of dread as something akin to a shadow begins to form in the darkened corner of the room, but it's not a shadow; it's too dark. It's like a hole in the darkness, an emptiness that somehow seems full of rage. I can feel it advancing on me, the menace and fury in it filling the room, the air becoming heavy.

I feel bolted in place, unable to move, unable to flee, unable to speak. Suddenly, the door at the top of the steps opens, and Linda calls down to me.

"You okay down there?" she asks from the top of the stairs.

Instantly, the shadowy form vanishes into the air, and I can move again.

"Yeah," I say, finally recovering my voice. "I just tripped on the stool."

"Okay. Just checking."

I grab my bag, purse, and phone and dart toward the steps, leaving the collection of books and papers strewn on the table. Linda smiles at me as I climb the stairs. I look up at her and frown slightly.

"I'm sorry I left a mess on the table," I say.

She shakes her head and waves off my concerns. "Don't worry about it. It gives me something to do. The exciting life of a small-town museum curator."

I step back into the hall, and she closes the door behind me. Immediately, I feel a sense of relief, but I know I won't even start to feel better until I'm far away from this place.

"Did you find what you were looking for?" she asks as we're walking toward the entrance.

"I think so and maybe more."

~14~

"**W**hat?" Jerry asks, his expression a mix of confusion, fear, and anger.

"Something attacked me."

"Somebody or something?"

We're standing outside the cottage, far from the front door, just so Tom and Aaron don't hear us. They're busy working on the kitchen and the bathroom, but the minute I returned, Jerry saw my face and pulled me aside.

"Some*thing*."

"Was it a ghost?"

"Maybe."

"Like these two ghosts? Like Lilly and the sailor?"

"No," I reply, shaking my head. "Whatever it was, it meant me harm. I don't feel that from Lilly and the sailor."

"Jesus, Ally. Are you okay?"

"I'm fine. It just knocked me down and then into one of the shelves."

"Are you sure you didn't just trip?"

I glare at him for a moment, and he nods.

"Okay, okay," he says. "I believe you."

I sigh and release the little bit of anger I had been holding in.

"Did you find what you were looking for?" he asks, echoing Linda's question.

"I hope so. I just have to go through it all. Do you think we could start tonight after dinner?"

He pauses, and his mouth opens and then closes without saying anything, and I feel my heart sink. "I would, but...I got a call from another client, and I have to run out there."

"Where...where is it?"

"Up in Hampton."

"Where's that?"

"It's about an hour north."

My shoulders slump, and he frowns.

"I can cancel," he says.

"What? No...don't do that. You have work to do. I can't ask you to do that."

"You don't have to ask."

I smile and shake my head. "Listen, Jerry, I'm fine," I say, trying to reassure him.

"I...I just don't feel right leaving you here alone," he says, looking at the cottage behind me with deep suspicion.

"I told you. Whatever was at the historical society is not the same as the two ghosts that are here. They've never threatened me. I've never really felt scared when they're around. Startled maybe, but not scared."

He shakes his head and sighs. "You could check into a hotel for a few days."

"I'm not leaving my house," I say, pausing for a moment when he starts to protest. "And before you say it, I'm not saying 'I'm not leaving my house' like idiots say in the movies who always end up getting killed. I feel perfectly safe here, and if I don't, then I'll leave."

"You promise?" he asks.

"I promise," I reply with a warm smile.

"All right," he says with a frown still on his face. "I'm not happy about it, but I'm just your contractor."

I tilt my head to the side and smile. "You're more than that, and you know it."

"I know," he replies with a sly grin. "I just wanted to hear you say it."

I shake my head and chuckle. "You are rotten."

"Not the first time I've heard that," he says, and then he looks around for a few moments.

"What? What's the matter?"

"I don't see lunch anywhere."

"Wow. Is that where we are now? Bribes?" I ask, repeating his questions from earlier.

"You're the one who brought it up this morning."

"Fine. You do remember that I was attacked by a ghost, right?"

"No, no. You don't get to use that because you said you were fine," he replies with a wry expression.

"Burgers?"

"I think burgers would work."

I start to turn and head to my car, but I stop and look back at him. "Are they going to finish up today?" I ask.

"They should."

"Then I guess lunch comes with beer," I say.

"That works, too."

I smile and walk to my car and climb in behind the wheel.

"See you soon," he says, waving to me with a wicked grin on his face.

"Yeah…yeah."

I drive down the gravel path with a smile on my face and the last feelings of dread from my encounter slowly fade away in the bright sunshine.

I stop at the diner and order four cheeseburgers with the works (on the side), a basket of fries to go along with each one, and four slices of pie—one chocolate, one apple, one blueberry, and one lemon. The cook waves at me through the pass window and informs me that Emily is off today.

After pulling up in front of the house, I honk the horn, and the boys emerge, huge smiles on their faces when they see the large, grease-stained sacks. I look at them and frown.

"No beer?" I ask, grinning at them.

"Oh shit," Aaron says before turning and darting back inside.

I set the food on the little table, dolling out the burgers and fries and then pausing as I retrieve the little Styrofoam containers filled with the pie slices.

"I didn't know what everyone likes, so I got one of everything," I say.

Tom shakes his head and smiles at me as he opens the containers, exposing the little treasures hidden inside. "What's not to like? It's pie."

In the end, Aaron and Tom take the blueberry and lemon, leaving the apple and chocolate for Jerry and me. We decided to split them, just as we had the other night. The boys sit at the table, and we sit on the tailgate of Jerry's truck.

When we finish, Jerry and I toss all the garbage in the little dumpster.

"Thank you for that," Aaron says, patting his belly with a smile.

"Oh yeah...definitely thank you," Tom adds.

"No problem. It's my pleasure. So, when do you think you're going to be finished?"

"In about an hour or so," Jerry says. "We're just finishing up the final touches and cleaning up the mess."

"Really? Everything?"

"Everything."

"That's great."

"We aim to please," Jerry says.

Tom looks at me and smiles. "I'm sure going to miss your lunches, though," he says with a laugh.

* * *

I SIT down on the couch with my laptop on one side and my phone on the other. Lilly's journal is on the arm of the sofa, the key still inserted in the lock, now attached to the tome with a piece of string. I have a small notebook on my lap and a black fountain pen with gold trim that

Steven gave to me on our second date. When I asked him why he was giving me a pen, he said, "So you can write how great this date went in your diary."

I open my computer and pull up the document where I stored all my notes. I also pull up the pages of notes I took at the library last week. I begin carefully extracting the really important bits while leaving the less pertinent parts behind. I already know some of it, but I need all of it to try to make sense of everything that's happening.

Suddenly, the doorbell rings, and I jerk with a start. I glance at the time on the computer—8:11.

I pad down the hall to the front door, undo the two locks and pull it open.

"Nightcap?" Jerry says with a smile while holding a bottle of wine in one hand and two glasses in the other.

"Jerry, what are you doing here? I thought you had work to do."

"I did. I did it," he replies.

I shake my head and smile at him before stepping aside, letting him enter. I close the door behind him, and I fully admit that I glance at his ass for a moment, my head tilting to the side slightly. He turns suddenly and grins at me.

"Are we in the living room?"

"What? Oh…um…yeah, in the living room."

I feel a blush run across my skin at just the thought that he might have seen me checking him out. I follow him into the room, and he sets the bottle and the glasses on the little coffee table.

"Corkscrew?"

"Sure," I reply, dashing off to the kitchen and searching

through the drawers until I find one. I walk back into the living room and hand it to him.

He nods and smiles at me before slowly twisting the worm into the cork. He opens the bottle with a "pop" and then fills the two glasses, handing me the second one.

"So. Fill me in," he says, leaning back against the corner of the sofa.

"Before we start that. You didn't have to come back here after working all day."

He grins at me. "Just helping out a friend," he replies, and I know I blush this time.

"I'm glad you're here," I say, and he smiles warmly at me, setting off a flock of butterflies in my stomach,

"So. Fill me in."

"All right." I pick up my laptop and scan the notes. "The land here was purchased in 1812 by Oliver Blackwater, and the cottage itself was finished in 1815. Strangely, there was a protest lodged by William Duxbridge over the sale of the property, but the local magistrate ruled that Blackwater was the rightful owner and the sale was legal."

"Duxbridge? The town founder?"

"Yeah."

"What was he protesting?"

"I have no idea. I couldn't find any other details on it."

"Hmm. That's interesting, but what does it mean?"

"I don't know…yet." I look at him and grin. "That sounds like something you hear from a detective."

"Well, that's what we're doing here, isn't it? Solving a mystery?"

"I guess we are," I reply before turning back to my screen. "So, the Blackwaters moved into the house in June of 1815. According to some legal records, Oliver left to sail to England aboard *The Dominator* in late 1815 and returned on or around July 1816."

"Oliver was Lilly's husband?" Jerry clarified.

"Yes. Exactly."

"Okay. Then what happened?"

"There's not a whole lot of records concerning the next couple of years, except a couple of further complaints that Duxbridge filed with the local magistrate."

"He really had a hard-on for this place, didn't he?"

I laugh and shake my head. "I guess you could say that. Anyway, the next entry I could find concerning the Blackwaters is when he set sail in 1820, and then he never came back."

He frowns at me. "What happened to him?"

"Not really sure. The ship was never seen again, but a lifeboat was discovered a few weeks after it disappeared, drifting free in the ocean with the name *The Dominator* on it."

"So, the ship sank?"

"That's what everyone assumed."

"But nothing was ever found except the lifeboat?"

"Yeah."

"Who owned the ship?" he asks before taking a sip of wine.

"Not really sure. Why?"

"We might be able to find some information on the ship itself at the national archives."

"That's an interesting idea. Maybe I can find a place to

email them. You're pretty good at this," I say, smiling at him.

"I read a lot of Sherlock Holmes and Patricia Cornwell stories."

I take a drink from my glass and then set the computer on the couch between us. "As far as the rest of the story goes, you already know the rest of it; Lilly is driven crazy by her grief."

"Yeah, everybody knows the story, but it still doesn't tell us what the ghosts need your help with."

Suddenly, Lilly's diary pops open as if it has a spring-loaded opening mechanism, like a Jack-in-the-box.

"Fuck!" I shout and literally jump to the other end of the couch where Jerry is sitting.

He automatically wraps his arms around me, and we sit there for a few moments, just staring at the diary. Gradually, I realize that he's holding me, and I'm torn between moving away and staying exactly where I am. I look back at him, and he smiles warmly at me. I scoot away, instantly regretting my decision.

"Sorry," I say.

"It's fine," he replies sweetly before looking over at the journal. "Do you think that's Lilly's way of telling you something?"

"It probably is, but I have no idea what she's trying to say."

15

~15~

I watch as Jerry's truck disappears into the darkness, the light becoming dimmer and dimmer in the distance. I feel a profound sense of loss and a reminder of how alone and isolated I am. Maybe buying a tiny cottage on a cliff by the ocean was not the best choice after all. I stand outside for a few minutes, looking up at the stars.

I knew Jerry wanted to stay. Part of me wanted him to stay, but the other part…the stronger part, was too scared to have him stay…afraid of what might happen. A seagull goes flying overhead and caws loudly, jolting me out of my daydream. I sigh loudly and then head inside, closing and locking the door behind me. I stop short, sucking in a breath, when I spot Lilly standing by the end of the couch beside the journal.

I take a small step forward, and she looks up at me, her expression unreadable. She points to the book, and I nod.

"I know. I'm working on it," I say. "It's going to take me some time. I don't speak French."

She slowly shakes her head, and page after page begins flipping over until about halfway through the diary.

"I get it," I say. "You want me to read it."

She points to the book again and glares at me, but even with this misunderstanding—which is obviously annoying her—I don't feel any real animosity or anger from her. She points at it again, and I take a step closer. The air is so cold near her that goose bumps break out on my arms. She points again, and I look down at the book.

Her finger is hovering just above one of the few words that I can actually read.

Duxbridge.

When I look back at her, she says a single word, her voice quiet, gentle, and somewhat muted, as if it's echoing down a long hallway.

"*Beware*," she says, her voice trailing off, and then she looks even more tired and exhausted than before, as if speaking takes a tremendous toll on her.

"Beware of the town?"

She shakes her head, and I frown, and then, it finally dawns on me.

"You mean, William Duxbridge."

She nods, and her expression shifts dramatically, becoming dark and brooding. The chill increases, and I actually take a small step back.

"Why? Why do I need to beware of him?"

She points to my laptop, where the notes I took at the

149

historical society are on the screen. I look back and forth between her and the computer, and then my mouth drops open.

"Is that who attacked me in the basement?"

She nods slowly.

"Why? Why did he attack me?"

She points to the book again, and I look down at it before looking back at her, but she's gone, leaving me alone in the living room. I grab my laptop off the couch and sit down, my legs crossed. Leaning over, I drag the journal next to me and open my web browser. I type in a search for a French to English translation site. I flip the pages in the journal back to the beginning and type in the first few sentences.

It takes me a few tries to find a site that seems easy to use, takes more than a few words at a time, and appears to properly translate the words into sentences. After entering them and getting the English version, I copy and paste the results into a Word document.

May 14, 1812–Paris

Oliver came to see me again today. He's so handsome and charming, and he always makes me laugh. We walked through the woods, and he held my hand. It was glorious, even though it was rather cold. He gave me his jacket, which he wrapped around me, and I felt warmer.

THERE ARE some additional entries that run along in this same vein, so I skip over them.

. . .

August 9, 1812–Paris

Oliver asked Father today for my hand in marriage, and he said yes! I am to become Mrs. Oliver Blackwater. It's such a commanding name—Blackwater. I am so excited, and I acted as if it was a surprise, but Oliver had already asked me before he talked to Father. We were going to run away if Father had said no.

February 2, 1813–Paris

Now that we are married, Oliver has asked me to move to England. At first, I wasn't sure if I could leave Mother and Father, but I talked to her, and she said I should go, as she is quite fond of Oliver, and that it's time I start out on my life.

June 22ND, 1813–Portsmouth

Life is changing so fast for us. We've only been here in our little house for a few months, and Oliver has been offered the opportunity to captain his own ship. It's a fine merchant vessel with the somewhat frightening name of The Dominator. *We had dinner last night with Mr. Larsen, the owner, where he fell into conversation with Oliver about the ship. They even allowed me to join them. How did I become so lucky to have a man like Oliver fall in love with me? That night after we were alone, Oliver asked me my opinion on the matter. I told him he had to accept it; even though I know he will be gone for long periods of time, it is something he simply cannot decline.*

. . .

AUGUST 5TH, 1813–Portsmouth

It's quite lonely here with Oliver out to sea, but he's doing this for our future, and it is my duty to support him.

AGAIN, I bypass some other entries that don't seem that important, related to her life in England and visits to France to see her parents.

FEBRUARY 9TH, 1813–Portsmouth

Oliver has returned from his trip to the United States and has asked me if I might like to move there. He says that opportunity abounds in this new nation, and Mr. Larsen has offered to pay for our passage and all other expense related to the move. I'm scared, but I trust Oliver, and I love him with all my heart.

I SKIP over all the descriptions about the voyage and the arrival in America, as they don't seem pertinent. My eyes are starting to get heavy when I spot the name Duxbridge as I'm scanning through the next few pages. I back up a few paragraphs and begin translating again.

SEPTEMBER 20TH, 1813–Duxbridge

We've finally arrived in the tiny hamlet of Duxbridge, Massachusetts. It's a lovely spot, close to the ocean and surrounded by some beautiful woodlands. Oliver wants to build a house here, even though he will be sailing out of Boston on his trips back and forth to England. He thinks the city is far too crowded, which I agree. Boston is very much like London—too dirty, too smoky, and too noisy. We've started looking for properties where we can start our life together.

I SCREAM when the front door suddenly swings open, slamming against the wall and knocking over the little side table where I tend to throw my keys. "Jesus," I say, staring toward the little entryway.

I get up off the couch and move cautiously to the door.

"Must have been a gust of wind," I say to myself, even though part of me knows it probably wasn't.

I slowly put the table back in place, set my keys on top, and step onto the little porch, expecting the wind to be blowing, but the air is still as stone. I quickly move back inside and close the door, turning the lock and setting the chain.

* * *

"ALLY," I hear someone say.

I roll over and pull the covers tight up around my chin.

"Ally."

I sigh and shift onto my back and slowly open my eyes. It takes a moment for them to focus on the figure sitting on the edge of my bed.

"Steven?" I ask, starting to sit up, blinking my eyes. "What are you doing here?"

"I came to see you."

"To see me, why?"

"To tell you, it's okay."

I shake my head slowly.

"What's okay."

"To move on."

"I don't want to move on," I reply, my voice cracking.

He reaches over and takes my hand in his, gently wrapping his fingers around mine. I don't pull back. I know he's not really here, but I can feel his hand on mine, that familiar warmth of his skin.

"The only way to keep moving forward, Ally, is to move on," he says gently.

"This is all in my head, isn't it?"

"Probably," he replies with a smile.

"I don't care if it is. It's just nice to see you. I've missed you so much."

"I've missed you, too, honey."

"I wish you could stay."

"You know I can't."

"I know," I reply with a sad sigh.

He lifts his hand and cups my cheek softly in his palm. "I love you, Ally."

"I love you, too," I reply, reaching up and gently resting my hand on his arm.

He smiles at me, and suddenly, I sit straight up in bed, my heart racing. I look around the room, my eyes darting from one thing to the other in the darkened space. I take in a breath, and the next second, I'm crying uncontrollably, slumped over as tears drop onto the sheets.

The next thing I know, my alarm is going off on the nightstand. I slap the top of it and flop over onto my back, staring up at the ceiling as the sounds of birds chirping and waves breaking on the cliffs drift into the room. A smile slowly begins to bloom on my face, and then the doorbell rings. I jump out of bed, rushing down the hallway. I spot Jerry's truck in the driveway, and I tear open the door.

He's standing there, holding a small box of donuts and two cups of coffee in a cardboard holder. I'm in the long T-shirt I normally sleep in, and my hair is sticking up in all sorts of crazy directions, but he doesn't even bat an eye.

"Morning," he says, smiling warmly at me.

I step up next to him and stand on my tiptoes and kiss him on the lips as I slide my arms around his neck. At first, he doesn't respond, but a moment later, he kisses me back, awkwardly trying to hold me and not drop our breakfast all over the ground. I step back and smile at him. His expression is a mixture of surprise and confusion, all combined with a beaming smile.

"Morning," I reply.

"What was that?" he asks. "Not that I'm complaining."

"I hope not," I reply with a little chuckle. "I just wanted to check something."

"What's that?"

"If we're more than just friends."

"Are we?"

"I think we are."

"That's good," he says, grinning at me. "Can I uh…can I come in?"

"Oh yeah, sorry," I reply, taking the donuts from him and turning and walking into the kitchen.

He follows directly after me, and I set the box on the

counter. Then I glance at my reflection on the screen of the refrigerator, and I'm immediately mortified.

"Oh my God," I mutter. "I look terrible."

"You do?" Jerry asks. "I didn't notice."

"You're just saying that."

"I am saying it, but I also mean it."

"Well, so do I. I'll be right back," I say before rushing off down the hall to my bedroom.

After closing the door, the reality of what I just did hits me like a tidal wave, and I step over to the bed and sit down on the corner of the mattress. I look at myself in the mirror and shake my head.

"What did you do?" I ask myself quietly.

For a moment, my expression is one of concern, with furrowed brows and frown lines, but gradually, it evolves, and I begin laughing to myself.

"Well, I guess it's out there now," I say to myself. "Kind of hard to take it back."

"Do you want to take it back?" I ask.

"No," I reply after a short pause.

"Then stop sitting in here. Fix your hair and get out there."

I strip out of my shirt, pull on a clean pair of jeans, a light-blue T-shirt, and a pair of blue Vans. I grab the brush off the dresser and quickly run it through my hair a few times until it looks presentable. I smile and check my teeth before breathing into my hand and sniffing. I take a deep breath and hold it for a moment before heading to the door. I stop just after placing my hand on the knob.

"Here we go," I say quietly.

I exit the bedroom and walk down the short hallway

to the kitchen. Jerry is standing by the counter, one of the coffees in his hand and the other sitting a few inches from him. The little bright-blue box of donuts is open, the lid folded back. A small chocolate-covered pastry of some sort is resting on a paper towel in front of him. He looks up and smiles at me, his eyes sparkling.

"Hi, again," he says.

"Hi," I reply, unable to make direct eye contact with him.

"Coffee?" He pushes the second cup over toward me.

"Thanks."

"Donut?" He turns the box in my direction, and I look inside.

I'm not even sure if I can eat anything without vomiting from nervousness, as my stomach is flip-flopping in my belly.

"Awkward...huh?" he asks.

"Sorta," I respond.

"That's what donuts are for."

He smiles, and I laugh quietly. I pick one of the round fruit-filled ones as little bits of powdered sugar drop onto the counter.

"By the way, if that's how I get greeted for bringing donuts and coffee, I'll be by every morning," he says.

I shake my head and smile. "Awkward again."

"Oh...sorry. Too soon."

~16~

"Don't you have someplace you need to be?" I ask as we're sitting outside at the little table, finishing off the last of the pastries and coffee.

"I'm taking a day off," he replies.

"Are you?" I smile, and he responds in kind. "Do you have plans?"

"I was thinking about hanging out with a friend of mine."

"Were you?" I ask, grinning at him.

"Yeah. She's been pretty stressed lately. I think she needs a break."

"Hmm. Maybe she has other plans. Have you asked her yet?"

He looks off to the side and frowns, and then rubs his fingers on his chin. "I really didn't. I thought it would be cute if I just showed up at her place with a box of donuts and some coffee and sprung my idea on her."

I nod slowly. "That's one way to go."

"You don't think that would work?"

"Oh…I'm not saying that. I think it all depends on the friend."

"What do you suggest?"

"Well," I say, shaking my head, "I think you should just go ahead and try your plan. What's the worst that could happen?"

"She could say no."

I nod. "She could, but she might say yes. She might be so impressed with your plan."

"Okay then, I'll give it a try. Thanks for your advice."

"Not a problem," I say, downing the last bite of an amazing bear claw.

Jerry leans back in his chair and just sits for a moment before he leans forward again. "Hey, you want to go on a little road trip with me?"

"I don't know. I might have plans," I reply, and he frowns.

"Really? This is how we're going to do this?"

I start laughing and reach over to touch his hand, brushing my fingers across his; in for a penny, in for a pound, as they say.

"Do I need to change?" I ask.

"You might want some better walking shoes."

"Where are we going?"

"You'll see," he replies with a smile that sends a thrill up and down my spine, and the butterflies that have been flittering around in my stomach are now trying to break the sound barrier.

"I'll be right back," I say, and I head inside, walking to the bedroom and quickly sorting through the couple of boxes of shoes that I still haven't unpacked.

It takes me a few minutes to find the pair of Skechers I'm looking for. I slip them on and then quickly apply a bit of lipstick before heading back to the hallway. I stop in the door and look at the picture of Steven and me on the dresser, smiling as we held each other on the beach down on Anna Maria Island in Florida. I pause for a minute and then kiss the tips of my two fingers, pressing them against the glass before walking out.

When I get back outside, Jerry is standing by his truck, the little table all cleaned up. He opens the passenger door and holds it for me. He bows slightly and waits as I climb inside before gently closing the door and walking around to the driver's side. He slips in behind the wheel and starts the engine.

"Where are we going?" I ask.

He looks at me and grins. "No questions."

"No questions?" I ask.

"No questions."

"Okay. No questions."

He puts the truck into gear, and we start down the driveway. His truck is some sort of older model, with a huge bench seat that spans the entire width of the cab. I get a brief glimpse in my mind of us driving down the road with me leaning against him as he drives, but for now, I sit closer to the door than to him.

When we reach the highway, he turns toward town. I

start to say something, and he looks at me and grins, and I close my mouth. He winks at me, and I giggle quietly.

"Did you find out anything from the diary?" he asks.

"I thought we weren't asking questions."

"Oh…I get to ask questions; you don't."

"Is that so?"

"That sounds like a question."

I laugh and slap his arm playfully, and he smiles at me. "I started translating it last night. It's slow going."

"Did you discover anything?"

"Not a whole lot yet."

"Well, I can give you a hand with it later."

"I'd like that."

"Good," he says with a grin.

When we reach town, he pulls in front of the diner and climbs out. He leans back in through the window. "I'll be right back."

"Okay," I say, smiling back at him.

I watch him through my window as he walks into the restaurant and talks to Emily. She looks in my direction and waves. I wave back and smile. She leans down and retrieves a wooden picnic basket lined with blue and white linen. They talk for a few seconds and then laugh at something together, and for a brief flash of time, I feel a tiny pang of jealousy, but it fades just as quickly.

Jerry takes the basket and starts back toward the door. I look past him at Emily, who smiles at me, flashes a thumbs-up, and then makes a somewhat obscene gesture with her hips. I shake my head and laugh. Jerry comes around to his side of the truck and sets the basket in the bed, taking a moment to secure it with a couple of bungee cords. He climbs into the cab again and looks at me.

"You had this all planned, didn't you?" I ask.

"What? Emily just happened to have a picnic basket full of goodies behind the counter."

"Oh really?"

"Wow. That's two questions in a row."

"Sorry."

He starts laughing and then slips the truck into reverse and backs out of the space. We drive down a few stores, and he pulls into another spot in front of the liquor store.

"Again?" I ask.

"Didn't we just talk about this?"

I shake my head and cross my arms in a gesture of feigned anger.

"Be right back," he says, grinning at me.

After he's inside, I sit back and look up and down the street. A few other patrons are strolling along the sidewalk, including a young couple, their hands linked together as they window shop the small stores and businesses. I close my eyes for a moment, and when I open them again, I fully expect to see one of my ghosts, as I've begun thinking of them, staring at me, but there isn't. A few seconds later, Jerry emerges from the store with two small paper sacks. He walks over, slips the two bags into the bed by the basket, and climbs into the truck again.

"All right. Now we're ready," he says, smiling at me.

"Finally."

"Patience is a virtue," he says.

"Not one that I have."

"Noted."

We back out and then head down the highway away from the cottage and the town. As we drive, it's killing me not to ask any questions, but I'm trying very hard to obey the rules. After driving for about fifteen minutes, Jerry turns off the main highway and onto a much smaller road. I watch the trees and rock formations flow past us as we drive along. I look over at Jerry, who is concentrating on driving, and I study him for a moment, and I smile, knowing that I really do feel something for this kind, strong, funny man with sparkling eyes.

I reach my hand over and tentatively lay my fingers on top of his. He glances at me, and for a second, I think that he's going to pull away, but instead, he turns over his hand and interlaces his fingers with mine.

"How much farther?" I ask, noticing that we're slowly beginning to climb upward. I catch glimpses of the landscape beyond the trees as we drive, but I still can't tell where we are.

"It's not far."

"You answered my question," I say, grinning at him.

"It was only a temporary rule."

"Really? So, where are we going?"

"You'll see."

"That really doesn't answer my question."

He squeezes my fingers gently. The tickle in my stomach explodes into a series of fireworks, and I suddenly don't care about the answer anymore. We follow the road as it slowly curves to the left, and then Jerry slows the truck. We turn off the road onto a crude track through the woods that's basically nothing more than two parallel dirt lines.

"We're almost there," Jerry says as if he read my mind as we jostle our way along the trail, the truck squeaking and creaking on the rough terrain.

Finally, we emerge from the trees and into a wide-open space. I have to put my hand up to shield my eyes from the bright sunshine until I become accustomed to the glare. The sky above us is so wide and open that it feels like we're in Colorado or Wyoming.

"Where are we?" I ask as Jerry stops the truck.

"Just a little place I found a few years ago."

He smiles at me, and when our hands part so we can climb out, I experience a feeling of loss. All I want is to have his hand in mine again. We walk to the front of the truck, and Jerry steps over and stands next to me. We're up in the mountains above the city, on an overhang or rock shelf. Soft green grass, intermingled with mossy patches, covers the ground, except for the very edges of the exposed rock cliff, much like back home. I can see the tops of the trees far below us and the highway winding its way through the woods, along with the little village of Duxbridge tucked into the tiny valley. I look toward the ocean and easily spot my cottage in the distance.

"It's beautiful," I say, looking up at him.

He nods and smiles. "Yeah," he replies before turning his head, leaning down slightly, and pressing his lips to mine.

The feeling of his skin against mine sends a series of pulses of excitement through me that race up and down my arms and legs and then collide deep down in my belly. I slip my arm around his neck, and his hands gently hold me on each side, pulling me closer. A few moments later, we step apart, and I gaze into his eyes.

"This isn't too fast, right?" I ask, suddenly unsure of myself again.

"Is it?"

"No," I reply after thinking about it.

"Good," he says, taking my hand again and walking us back to the truck. "Hungry?"

"Absolutely."

He reaches into the back and gets the two bottles, handing them to me. He retrieves the basket and a large red blanket and looks at me again.

"Follow me," he says, and we walk down a little way from the truck toward a craggy tree that looks different from most of the other trees in the area.

It's not very tall, but its branches spread straight outward toward the ocean, creating a shady spot under the blazing sun high overhead in the sky. Jerry sets down the basket and opens the blanket with a flourish, carefully guiding it to the ground. He flattens it out, making sure it's smooth before extending his hand to me. I set the two bottles on the blanket, making sure they're balanced before I release them. I smile and take his hand, allowing him to help me sit. He picks up the basket and sets it just off to the side, then takes a seat opposite me.

"I'm glad you said yes," he says.

"Me too," I reply with a warm smile. "You really didn't have to do all this."

"I know." He looks at me and then begins unpacking the basket. At one point, he hands me a corkscrew. "Do you want to open the wine?"

"Of course, I do." I take the bottles out of the bags and look at the labels. "Nice."

"I do know my wine," he says as he sets a plate and silverware out for both of us along with the little containers of food, which he has yet to open.

I pull the cork on the first bottle, and he hands me the stemless glasses. I set one of them off to the side for a moment and then fill the first, followed by the second. When I look back at him, he has all the food laid out, and I start chuckling.

"Grilled cheese and chips?" I ask.

"Not just any grilled cheese—" he starts to say before I interrupt him.

"I know…it's grilled cheese with three different cheeses."

"Exactly," he says, looking slightly confused. "Emily said it was your favorite."

"It is," I reply. "Did she include grape jelly?"

"Yeah, she was going to, but I said I was getting wine, and she said that was even better," he says with a chuckle.

I hand him one of the glasses, and we clink them together above our fancy lunch of three-cheese grilled cheese sandwiches.

"Thanks for this," I say. "I needed a day away from everything."

"Anytime."

~17~

"How did you find this place?" I ask as we're sitting under the little tree, both of us leaning back against the trunk.

Everything is packed up, except for the blanket, which is still spread out on the ground under our legs. We both have our shoes and socks off, the sun warm on our skin in places where it manages to sneak through the thick foliage of the tree.

"I found it a few years ago," he says.

"You just found it, way out here?"

He sighs quietly, and I suddenly feel like I want to take my question back, but I know I can't. There's a quiet sadness that seems to fill his eyes.

"I'm sorry...I didn't mean to—"

"It's okay. I was just wandering in the woods one day. I

was lost."

"And you found your way here?"

"I don't really mean it that way. I wasn't physically lost; I was...mentally lost."

I nod slowly, knowing exactly what he's talking about, and then I gently touch his hand. He immediately wraps his fingers around mine. He smiles sadly at me.

"I think I just ruined our day," I say.

He shakes his head and looks me directly in the eyes. "No, you didn't. It's just a memory, a sad memory...but that's all it is. This place," he says, "saved me. The minute I found it, I found peace. I found a place I could come to be alone, to heal."

I look around, and I can see why he feels the way he does about this special spot. "I wish I'd had a place like this," I say quietly.

He squeezes my hand gently, and I look at him. "You do now," he says before leaning over and kissing me, the warmth of his lips slowly dispelling the dark mood.

I kiss him back, and for a few minutes, we just enjoy the thrill of gentle exploration and the excitement of discovery that something as simple as kissing can bring. Finally, we both pull back at the same moment and smile at each other.

"So, this is a good day," he says, grinning at me as the last remnants of the gloom melt away in the bright sunshine.

"Yeah, it is," I reply, gazing up at him.

We sit there for some time; I'm really not sure how long. All I do know is that it's the first time in a long time that I've felt happy, and I don't want it to end. I shift my position slightly so that I'm actually leaning more up against Jerry than I am against the tree, and he drapes his arm gently across my shoulder.

Some time passes, and then I look over at him. "Sure glad I picked your name off Google," I say.

"What?"

"I needed a contractor, and you were the fifth one I tried. The first two didn't answer, and the other two said they were busy…which I think was just an excuse after I told them where I lived."

"Well. That worked out for me, didn't it?"

"And me."

"I guess I should thank the ghosts."

"Yeah. Maybe I'll tell Lilly the next time I see her."

"That might be a good idea."

We fall back into our comfortable silence, each of us thinking about our own concerns, fears, worries, and hopes. A few minutes later, Jerry kisses the top of my head, and I can't help but smile at the tiny, intimate gesture.

"Can I ask you something?" he asks.

"Of course."

"Why the change of heart?"

I look over at him and sit up slightly. "Are you not okay with this?" I ask.

"Oh…um…no, I'm fine with all—" he starts stumbling, and I smile at him.

"I'm just messing with you."

He frowns at me and shakes his head. "That was mean…it was funny, but it was still mean."

"Sorry. I had to do it," I say, smiling at him before

pausing for a moment, my expression changing. "To answer your question, I sort of talked it out."

"Talked it out? With a friend?"

"Yeah. You could say that."

"Well, however it happened, I'm just glad it did. I wanted to say something to you about how I was feeling, but I wasn't sure how you would take it."

I smile at him again and then lean in and kiss him gently. "I'm glad it happened, too."

He touches my face, and I lean into his hand, closing my eyes for a moment. "So, what are our plans with the ghost investigation?" he asks.

"*Our* plans?"

"Yeah. I'm part of the team now."

* * *

"LET'S think about this for a minute," I say as we're sitting on the edge of the cliff, looking down at Duxbridge. "The ghosts need help."

"Yeah, but why?"

"Exactly. Why would a ghost need help?"

We're holding hands, our fingers intertwined, our glasses of wine at our sides.

"Well, if you believe what you see in the movies, it's usually because they can't move on," he suggests.

"If that's the case, why can't they?"

"Unfinished business?"

"Another movie trope."

"Yeah, but who's to say that it's not true?"

I shrug and nod slowly. "I guess you're right."

"What else do we know?"

"Just what I've translated from the diary so far, most of it doesn't apply, but I have a feeling there's a lot more to come as I get deeper into it."

"Okay. What else seems...odd?"

"The whole thing at the historical society."

Jerry nods and frowns. "That really bothers me," he says.

"What does?"

"You being alone in that house, after what happened."

I shake my head and smile at him. "You're sweet," I say, and he frowns, and then it slowly transitions into a somewhat reluctant smile. "I'll be fine."

He growls, which makes me chuckle quietly to myself. "Do you really believe it was the ghost of William Duxbridge who attacked you?" he asks.

"I don't know for sure, but Lilly does."

"I guess she would know."

"Yeah, probably."

"So, he attacked you because you were researching him."

"I mean...I wasn't necessarily researching *him*, but I was looking into all the events around the cottage and Lilly and her husband."

"You think he's hiding something?"

"Not sure that a ghost can hide something, but I don't think he's happy that I'm opening up old wounds, so to speak."

Jerry sighs and shakes his head. "This is so difficult without having any people to actually talk to."

I fall silent for a minute, and then I look at him and

smile.

"What?" he asks.

"I think there is someone."

"What? Who?"

"The Kingstons. Kitty and George Kingston."

"Who are they?"

"They owned the cottage before me, back in the fifties."

"In the fifties?" he asks, sitting up a little straighter while still holding me close. "Are you sure they're even still alive?"

"Not yet, I'm not."

I slide my phone out of my pocket and pull up Google. I type in their names and hit search. Within a second, my screen is filled with results, most of which don't mean anything, so I do another search, adding the word "Duxbridge." That seems to narrow down the results, and I quickly scan through them, stopping at an entry for Facebook featuring an older couple. I click on the link, and it opens their page on the social network system. I can't see much information, but the one thing I can see is where they live—Lindhaven, Massachusetts.

"Hmmm. You want to go on a road trip tomorrow?" I ask.

He sighs and then shakes his head, looking very concerned. "I can't. I have work."

"Work, of course," I say, "I shouldn't have even asked."

"No…I mean…I can always cancel."

"Jerry," I say, turning and looking at him, "you have to work. You can't just drop everything to go 'ghost hunting' with me."

"Ghost hunting? Is that what you're doing?" he asks with a wry grin.

"Probably not. It's more like detective work."

"Oh…yeah, so now you're a ghost-hunting detective."

I shake my head and smile at him before sitting up slightly and leaning in toward him while gazing into his eyes. "You know. You're lucky you're cute," I say.

"I know," he replies before slipping his hand behind my head and pulling me down to him, our lips pressing together.

When we finally pull away, I sit down beside him, taking up my former position, and lean against him. He drapes his arm over my shoulder again, and I reach up and wrap my hand around his.

"Can we stay here for the rest of the day?" I ask while gazing off toward the ocean.

"That was my plan."

"That's a good plan."

"That's what I thought."

We sit for another few minutes, just enjoying the peace and tranquility of our secret retreat. Finally, I look up at him and smile.

"I can see why you love this place, why it helped you," I say.

"I'm glad you like it. I've never shared it with anyone before."

"That means a lot to me," I say, squeezing his hand gently.

He nods and pulls me a little closer, and I snuggle into him.

~18~

*A*s the sun is just beginning to set, Jerry pulls to a stop next to my car in front of the cottage. A little white doggie bag from dinner at the diner is sitting to my right between me and the door. I'm leaning against him, much like I imagined I would like to do before he picked me up in the morning. He puts the truck into park and looks over at me.

"We're here," he says.

"I know."

His right arm is draped over my shoulder, his hand resting on my hip. He doesn't say anything further. We just sit and stare out the windshield at the clouds hovering above the ocean miles and miles from the edge of the cliff. I sigh, and I feel Jerry shift slightly.

"What's the matter?"

"Nothing," I reply. "It's just the end of the day."

"Yeah," he says, squeezing me gently.

"I should probably go in. You need to get home to get some rest. You have work tomorrow."

"Yeah," he says again, his voice quiet and tinged with a bit of sadness.

I use all of my willpower to sit up, pick up the little bag, and open the door. Every inch that I move away from him feels like a mile, and I miss his touch almost immediately. He climbs out as I walk around the front of his truck, and we move slowly to the cottage door. He takes my hand again as we make the short stroll. I squeeze his hand gently, and he smiles at me. When we reach the little porch, I turn and look up at him.

"It was a great day, Jerry. It was the best day I've had in a very long time."

"Me too," he replies.

He leans down, and we kiss, our lips pressing together, and I drop the little bag and wrap my arms around his neck. Our kiss intensifies, and Jerry's hands travel down my back, resting just above my ass. After a few minutes, Jerry pulls away, and I look at him.

"What's the matter?" I ask.

"We should probably stop," he says, his hands still on my hips.

"Should we?"

He nods and swallows hard. "If it keeps going, I'm not going to leave," he says, "and I don't think either one of us is ready for that."

My heart wants to say, "Who cares?" but my head is

telling me he's right. I nod slowly and take a small step back.

"You're probably right," I say, nodding.

He takes his hand and cups my chin, gently lifting my head. "Don't get me wrong, Ally. I would love nothing more than to stay here tonight and let what will happen, happen…but that's not what either of us really needs right now."

I nod and smile at him, gazing into his beautiful blue eyes, and then I sigh quietly.

"Let me revise my response…you're definitely right," I say, and he smiles back at me. "But that's not to say I would be unhappy to have you stay the night."

"Yeah. I know."

He leans his head down and kisses me again, gentler this time, more full of love than urgency or lust. When we step apart, he takes in a deep breath and holds it for a few moments before releasing it slowly.

"Are you sure you'll be okay here?" he asks, looking at the little house.

"I'll be fine. Really."

"I know you say that, and you might even believe it, but I'm still worried."

"I'll be okay," I say, gazing up at him. "I won't say I'm not worried, but I feel perfectly safe."

"All right," he says, sighing again. "I'm going to head out. I have to be up in Lincolnshire at seven tomorrow morning."

"When will you be back?"

"Probably not for a few days. It's a big job."

My heart sinks when he says that, but I cover it with a warm smile. "Make sure you call me."

"You know I will."

I nod and smile at him. "You be careful, okay?"

"I will. You too," he says before kissing me one more time.

"I will."

He turns and heads toward his truck, and I have to use every ounce of willpower not to call him back and spend the night under the covers of my bed. He turns the truck around and then stops in front of the door and leans across the seat toward me.

"I'll call you tomorrow," he says.

"You better," I reply with a smile.

He shakes his head and grins at me before heading off down the driveway, disappearing into the dark within a few minutes. I stand outside for a little while, part of me wishing he would turn around and come back. Eventually, I walk inside, closing the door behind me and locking it with both the bolt and the chain. I grab a beer out of the fridge and head to the living room, picking up Lilly's diary and slowly flipping through a few pages, but after a couple of minutes, I close it, setting it on the arm of the couch. I close my eyes and lean my head back on the pillow.

When I open my eyes again, it's dark inside the house. There's some moonlight coming through the kitchen and the living room windows. The journal is still sitting on the arm of the couch, but it's open, and I'm sure I closed it before I fell asleep. I look around the room, but there's no sign of Lilly or the sailor. I slowly get to my feet and head down the hallway, using the wall for balance, as I feel half-asleep. I crawl in under the covers and lay my head on the pillow.

The sound of glass breaking wakes me up. It takes a few seconds for my senses to calibrate—my vision, my hearing, and my coordination. I jump out of bed and creep toward the bedroom door. I peer cautiously around the corner toward the kitchen, but I can't see anything in the dim light. I slowly move down the hall, suddenly realizing about halfway there that I should have brought some sort of weapon with me in case I was being burglarized. I spot the glints of light off the shattered glass on the floor by the sink. I can't tell if it came from a window or from something else.

I glance into the living room, and when I look back, the black shadow from the historical society is floating just a few feet away from me in the middle of the kitchen. I'm frozen in fear, my heart racing and sweat breaking out on my forehead. I start to take a step back down the hallway when the shape suddenly lunges at me.

I scream and wake up, soaked in sweat, my room bathed in darkness. I sit there for a few minutes until I gather myself. I slip off the bed and walk to the door, peeking around the corner at the kitchen, and it dawns on me that I'm doing exactly what I was doing in my dream. I shake my head and then pad my way down the hall, stopping at the corner and studying the kitchen. There's no sign of any broken glass or anything else out of place. I stand in the junction between the kitchen and the living room, and then I look at the front door.

Both the chain and bolt are unlocked. I run the events

of last night through my head, trying to remember if I locked them. I think I did…I know I did.

I shake my head.

"Why would a ghost need to unlock the door?" I ask myself out loud, not even sure if I'd seen a ghost or it was all just a dream.

I walk over and turn the bolt and slide the chain in place before making my way back to the kitchen. I stop and turn, looking at the door again, just to make sure they're both still as I left them. As soon as I see that they are, I head back down the hall and into my bedroom. I slide under the covers again, and within a few minutes, I'm fast asleep.

* * *

THE EARLY MORNING sunshine is coming through the passenger's window as I drive. I reach over and flip the visor down and turn it toward the door so that it'll block some of the glare. I glance at the GPS and take the next right, heading down the gently winding two-lane highway through the trees and low hills. A few minutes later, the tiny hamlet of Lindhaven comes into view. It looks quite similar to Duxbridge, except that it's much farther inland and the ocean is nowhere in sight, and there are no mountains, just a collection of rolling hills that extend in all directions.

When I drive into town, I pull over in the quaint downtown and put the car into park. There are a few pedestrians coming and going along the sidewalks and across the streets. Most of the storefronts are filled and look to be thriving, although I can't understand how they find enough business since I didn't pass a single house on the way here. There's a couple of restaurants, a small drugstore, and a slightly larger farm supply business that looks like something out of the 1880s.

I found the address for the Kingstons after a few Google searches and by using the clues on their Facebook page. I climb out of the car and look around the little downtown. A small sign reading "Wholey Moley" with a picture of a donut draws my attention. I cross the street and walk down the sidewalk, nodding politely to some locals. When I reach the shop, I inhale the intoxicating scent of fresh donuts and pastries. I open the door and walk inside. A young woman in a blue apron speckled with flour or powdered sugar smiles at me from behind a glass case.

"Morning," she says.

"Morning."

"Can I get you something?"

"Do you have like a half-dozen box?"

"Of course," she says, gesturing to the low glass cases filled with rows and rows of a huge variety of donuts, although there are only a few of each one. "What would you like?"

"Can you just pick six of the most popular?"

"Sure." She starts plucking the little round pastries from their trays and carefully filling a small, bright-yellow box.

"Haven't seen you around before. You visiting?" she asks as she's working.

"I am. I'm actually looking for someone."

"Really?" She folds the lid down and tucks a little tab inward to lock it in place. "Who? If you don't mind me asking."

"Kitty and George Kingston."

"Can I ask you why you're looking for them?"

"I'm writing a book, and they might have some information for me."

"A book, huh? What sort of book?"

"A ghost story."

That seems to spark something in her, and I see a brief but noticeable understanding of why I'm looking for them.

"Hmmm. Well, I'm not sure I should tell you, but you're already here, which probably means you know they live nearby," she says, studying me. "Their place is down 52 a little ways—small yellow and white farmhouse. You can't miss it."

"Thanks, Sarah," I say, reading her nametag. "You have coffee, too, right?"

"What's a donut shop without coffee?" she asks, grinning at me, her concern of a few moments prior vanishing.

"Can I get three large and just toss some creamer and sugar into the bag?"

"No problem." She turns and starts filling the first of the trio of to-go cups. "By the way, if you're getting this for your visit, I would recommend getting an eclair for Kitty. That's what she loves."

"Oh. Okay. Throw one of those in," I say before looking down at the chocolate pastry behind the glass. "Make it two."

A few minutes later, I walk out of the little shop and head back to my car, carrying the donuts in one hand, the little bag with the two eclairs on top. I have the coffees in a cardboard carrier, in the other. I set the drinks on the roof, place the donuts on the passenger seat, and then set the coffees on the floor, using my laptop bag to hold them in place against the side of the central console.

I back out of the space and follow the GPS down to the intersection for Route 52 and turn left. I pass a small cluster of newer houses, and when I say newer, I mean built sometime in the fifties or sixties. A few minutes later, I'm driving through low farmlands dotted with trees. It's not long before a small yellow and white farmhouse comes into view on the right side of the road. A white picket fence encloses the small front yard, and a yellow labrador is lying in the shade of a large oak tree.

I stop beside the mailbox with the name Kingston hand-painted in a lovely, flowing script. The dog looks up at me and wags his tail but doesn't bother getting up. I pull over to the side of the road in front of the fence, a few feet past the mailbox and the driveway. I step out of the car and close the door, looking across the roof toward the little house. I can see a couple of chickens wandering around in the yard near the dog, as well as a few cows in the fields behind the house.

The house is small but well maintained and looks like it was probably built sometime in the late 1800s to early 1900s. I grab my laptop bag and sling it over my shoulder before picking up the coffee and the pastries. I walk down the dirt driveway along the fence while the dog and the chickens watch. When I reach the little gate just before the house, I use the edge of the coffee carrier to open the latch and then step through, making sure it's locked behind me.

Again, the dog watches me but makes no attempt to get up. I walk up the two steps onto the small porch. There are two rocking chairs to the right of the door with a small table in between. I use my hand holding the donuts and gently knock on the screen door. The inner door is already open, and I can see all the way to the little kitchen at the back of the house. I wait, but no one comes to the door. I stand for a moment, trying to decide what to do when an elderly lady comes around the side of the house.

"Hello," she says with a heavy New England accent and a warm and welcoming smile.

She's dressed in blue jean overalls, a blue and white checked flannel shirt, brown cowboy boots, worn leather gloves, and a felt hat that resembles the fedora Indiana Jones wears.

"Oh, hello." I turn and walk back down the two steps as she comes through the gate.

"Can I help you?"

"Um…this may sound odd, but I was wondering if we could talk…if you have a couple of minutes."

She studies me for a moment, her light-brown eyes scanning me up and down. I'm not sure how old she is, but I wouldn't peg her at more than late sixties, but I know she must be older.

"What did you want to talk about, dear?"

"Ghosts."

~19~

"Obviously, you must have talked to Sarah," she says as we walk into her kitchen, and she points to the little bag.

"She did mention that these might be a way to encourage you to speak to me."

She smiles and gestures toward the table. "Have a seat, honey."

I set the donuts and eclairs on the table and pull out the chair closest to me. She retrieves two small plates from one of the cabinets, two forks from a drawer, and then joins me.

"She knows the way to my heart, that girl," she says, sliding one of the dishes and fork across to me. She pulls two napkins from the little holder in the middle of the table and hands me one.

I open the box of donuts and then pull the two carefully wrapped eclairs from the bag and set them on top of the folded paper sack.

"I wasn't sure what your husband likes," I say.

She smiles warmly at me, and a tiny flash of sorrow passes across her face and then dissipates just as quickly. "Oh. My George passed close to five years ago."

"I'm so sorry. I didn't know," I say, and she reaches across the table and gently pats the back of my hand.

"It's all right, dear. How could you have known? Besides, that leaves more for me," she says, grinning at me.

"That's true."

"So? You bought the old cottage?"

She takes one of the éclairs and places it on her dish. She picks up her fork, cuts off a portion of the pastry, and lifts it to her mouth. I take one of the chocolate-covered donuts and take a bite before setting it down on my dish.

"Yes. About a month ago, or so."

"It's a lovely little house."

"It is," I say before pausing for a moment. "Can you tell me why you guys sold it? You weren't there for very long, were you?"

"No. Not really. We bought it in…1947, I think it was, just after George got back from overseas, and we sold it in 1952. When we first moved in, the place was a mess. No one had lived in it since around 1820 or something like that. It took a lot of work and a lot of love to make it livable, and a lot more to make it beautiful again."

"That's what I mean. After all that work, why didn't you stay?"

"I think you already know," she says before taking another bite of her éclair.

"The ghosts."

She nods slowly while wiping her mouth with one of the little paper napkins. "You've seen her?" she asks before removing the top on the coffee and pouring in two of the creamers and two packets of sugar.

"I've seen *them*," I reply.

"Who's them?" she asks while stirring the cup with her fork.

"Lilly and the sailor."

She takes of sip from the cardboard cup and then sets it back on the table. "What about the other one?"

"The other one?"

"Yes. The dark one."

A chill runs up and down my arms, and I pause.

"You've seen it, haven't you?" she asks.

I nod. "I've seen it."

She shakes her head and sighs quietly. "You asked why we left. It wasn't long after we moved in that we first encountered Lilly. We were shocked, of course, but neither of us ever felt...in danger, and then the first of the sailors appeared to George one night."

"The first?"

"Oh yes, dear. There are many sailors," she replies.

I'm a little shocked by the news as I thought there was only one of them. "What did they do...did they talk to you?"

"Oh no," she says, shaking her head. "They would just point at things, like the old fireplace in the kitchen and the fireplace in the living room. We never could figure out what they wanted." She looks at me and tilts her head to the side. "They did the same thing to you, didn't they?"

"Yeah."

"Did you ever find out what they wanted?"

"Yeah…after a while."

"What was it?"

I open up my laptop bag and retrieve Lilly's journal, setting it on the table. "It's Lilly's diary."

She looks at the book, and she starts to reach for it but then pulls her hand back. "Where was it?"

"The book was hidden in the kitchen fireplace, and the key to open it was in the living room mantle."

"That's interesting. George would have liked to have known that," she says, smiling about some private memory. "Anyway…we were never scared of Lilly and the others, but then, it arrived."

"The dark shadow."

"Exactly," she replies, looking around the room, as if it might suddenly appear…and honestly, I'm a little nervous about it as well.

"What happened?"

She sighs and begins rubbing her hands together.

"The first time it appeared, George and I had started doing some research on the house, and we had just returned home from this little museum in town that they had just opened. We had a whole bunch of notes about the history of the cottage when this…thing suddenly materialized in the kitchen and attacked us."

"Attacked you? How?"

"It knocked me down, and I cut my head on the side of the kitchen counter. George tried to defend me, but it pushed him back and then flung a knife at him from the block."

"Oh my God. That's why you moved out."

"Yeah. Exactly."

"What do you think the shadow is?"

"I don't think…I know. It's William Duxbridge."

* * *

"WHY DO YOU THINK THAT? Why do you think that it's Duxbridge?"

"Because of what we found," she says, peering into the donut box.

"What did you find?"

"Apparently, he was obsessed with the house," she replies as she picks up one of the remaining donuts covered in white frosting and bright-colored sprinkles.

"Yeah," I say, my excitement slowly fading. "I found out about that."

She looks at me for a moment and then grins. "There's more to it, dear."

"What do you mean?"

"He was more than just obsessed. He was willing to kill to get it."

"How do you know that?"

"From the notes we took and the research George did, there were allegations that he had murdered the previous owner of the property before Lilly and her husband bought it."

"How were they able to buy it if the owner was dead?"

"From what we found, there was a will that Duxbridge

didn't know about that gave the property to one of the owner's nephews. They're the ones who sold it to Blackwater."

"That connects a few dots," I say, thinking about the cryptic notes about the case Duxbridge filed about the sale of the property.

Kitty takes a bite from the donut and smiles at me. "There was one person we couldn't figure out, though. He had dealings with Duxbridge just before Lilly died, but we could never put it all together."

"Who was it?"

"I can't remember," she says, frowning.

"Do you have those notes?"

"I think so," she says, tilting her head upward as if in thought.

I sit back in my chair and wait, hoping she'll remember where they are. After a few seconds, she smiles at me again.

"Come on with me," she says, standing up from her chair after finishing off the last of her donut.

I follow her out of the kitchen and through the back door, the long spring on the screen door groaning as it's stretched. We walk across the low grass at the rear of the house, toward a white and yellow, two-car garage. She opens a side door, we walk inside, and she hits a switch on the wall. The large wooden garage door slowly opens, flooding the space with light. There are two cars parked in the middle of the room, one of them a newer model red Subaru Forester, but the other is what I think is a 1967 Chevrolet Corvette in bright blue.

"Wow," I say quietly. "That's nice."

"Oh," she replies, stopping in her tracks and looking at the convertible sports cars and smiling. "That was George's baby. He bought it straight off the showroom floor in 1966."

"It's beautiful."

"Thank you. He would be happy you like it."

There doesn't seem to be a speck of dust or dirt on it, and I'm sure that she probably cares for it, keeping it clean and maintained. We walk to the back of the garage to a pair of old metal file cabinets. She opens the top drawer of the right-hand cabinet and begins rifling through some of the folders. After a few minutes of searching, she pulls out a file and lays it on top of the cabinet, then continues searching.

By the time she's done, there are four dark-green folders stacked in my arms as well as a cardboard box, the same dimensions as a sheet of paper. We head back to the house, stopping on the rear porch.

"Can you give me a minute?" she asks. "I need to give the horses some water."

"I can give you a hand."

She looks me up and down as if she's trying to decide if a city-slicker like me would have any idea what to do with a real live horse. "If you want. That would be nice."

I set the files and the box on one of the two chairs to the left of the door. We cross the small backyard to the fence. She opens the metal gate and then closes it after I step through into the field. The fence is close enough to the house that someone might even be able to feed one of the horses while sitting on a rocking chair. A large horse barn looms in the distance.

"You work around horses before?" Kitty asks.

"I've been around a few. My grandparents had a farm out in Nebraska."

She nods approvingly. "That's good. We're not doing anything but water at the moment, but some people are scared of horses when they realize how big they are," she says, chuckling to herself.

"Not a problem for me."

She suddenly whistles, louder than anyone I have ever heard, just as we reach the huge sliding doors of the barn. She pushes them open, the wheels siding easily along the well-maintained tracks. The aroma of hay, feed, and horse manure drift out, and I inhale deeply, my mind filling with memories of my grandparent's farm. When we're about halfway down the line of six stalls, four horses come through the open doors at the far end of the barn, each one heading to its own private space.

"Get the hose," she says, pointing to a coiled-up green hose hanging on the wall by the doors.

I walk over and take it down, unspooling it as I walk after turning on the spicket. There's an old-fashioned straight twist nozzle attached to the end that's slowly dripping water.

"If you don't mind, fill each of the corner troughs while I give them a scoop of food," Kitty says.

"No problem."

I drag the hose over to each stall in turn and fill the black plastic troughs while the horses stand and watch me with their big, beautiful eyes. One of them, a very large white stallion, walks over and nudges me with his head.

Kitty laughs and smiles at me. "Blizzard likes to have water sprayed on his head," she says.

"Oh...okay."

I turn on the water and spray him gently. He turns his head from right to left and then shakes it back and forth. I take this as a signal that that's enough, and I turn off the water and move to the last stall to fill the container. I walk back over and replace the hose, being sure that it's as neat as it was before I took it off the hanger. When I turn around, Kitty is smiling at me.

"You remind me of our daughter," she says.

"What's her name?"

"Ashley."

"What does she do?"

She sighs, and a sad expression takes hold and then quickly fades. "She passed a year before George," she says.

"I'm so sorry."

"No need to be, honey. She had cancer. It was a blessing. The worst part of it was that I think it sort of drained George of his will to live."

"I know what that's like," I say quietly, and she walks over and takes my hand.

"We all do, dear. We all do."

"I guess you just try to keep moving forward, right?" I ask, maybe trying to get some sort of confirmation of my thought.

She nods slowly, and we walk to the open doors at the far end of the barn, where the horses had entered. The field beyond stretches out of sight across the low, gently rolling hills. I can see a few cows in the distance, grazing with their heads down under the bright, late morning sun.

A couple of chickens wander past us, their heads bobbing forward as they walk.

"Yes. You don't really have much choice," she says as we stand just looking into the distance.

I look around at the horses, the cows, and the rest of the farm, and I smile.

"Is that what you're trying to do here? Move forward?"

"I think so," she replies with a sad smile. "There ain't much else you can do. Livin' is hard, even when you have someone to bear the burden with you."

I nod slowly. "Yeah. That's the truth."

She looks over at me, and I can tell she knows I'm speaking from experience, even if she doesn't outright say it. It feels like a bond between two people who've been through trauma together; even if they don't really know each other, they're still kindred spirits.

"Is that what you're doing, too, honey?"

"Trying to move forward? Yeah," I say quietly.

"That's good."

We stand for another few minutes in silence, the only sound coming from the horses behind us, drinking water, moving around in their stalls, or chuffing and snorting.

"Come on," she finally says. "Let's go look at what we got, and I can make some lunch for us."

2 0

~20~

Most of the notes that she and George took contain much of the same information I'd already discovered. I'm flipping through some loose pages while Kitty is at the stove, making us a couple of egg and cheese sandwiches in a cast-iron skillet. I can hear the sizzling of the thick, buttered bread as she carefully flips them over and then lightly presses them down.

"I still don't see much more than I found out," I say.

"I'm sure," she replies as she walks to the table, a plate in each hand.

She sets them down, and immediately, the aroma drifting up from the sandwiches almost makes me forget why I'm even here.

"Do you want me to cut that in half for you?" she asks.

"It's okay. Thanks. It smells delicious."

"I'm glad."

"You didn't have to do this."

"Don't be silly, dear. Having someone to cook for makes me feel useful again," she says with a warm smile before picking up her sandwich and taking a bite.

"Well, I appreciate it."

She nods and smiles at me again, watching me as I take my first taste and then groan in appreciation. "Good?" she asks.

"Better than good," I reply while breaking a long string of cheese that was stubbornly clinging from the bread to my mouth.

We eat for a few minutes, just enjoying each other's company. When we're both about halfway done, Kitty starts looking through some of the documents as if she's searching for something in particular, setting most of them to the side.

"I know it has to be here, somewhere," she mutters quietly.

"What are you looking for?"

"There are a couple of papers we found that contained an entry from a diary someone discovered in one of the old houses when they were remodeling near Duxbridge. It talked about William Duxbridge and another man, who were being rather 'secretive,' as the writer states, but I can't remember his name," she says, as she's searching through the dusty old documents.

I continue to sift through the pile, scanning the papers for any names or dates that seem familiar or might fall within the range that we're looking at. Suddenly, she snatches a small yellowish scrap of parchment out of the stack and holds it up.

"I got it!" she shouts victoriously.

She slaps it down on the table and turns it toward me, with a wide smile and a look of satisfaction on her face. I read through it quickly and then pause, just staring at the passage for a minute.

"What's wrong?" Kitty asks.

"Larsen," I say, staring at the name. "He knew Larsen. This says the two of them seemed to be meeting secretly at the local pub, sitting in the shadows and discussing 'dark things.'"

"I don't understand."

"Where's my computer?" I ask, looking around and spotting my bag by the front door where I left it.

I jump up from my chair and rush over to it, pulling the laptop out of the bag and letting the case drop to the floor. I dart back to the table, hit the power button, and wait the five seconds or so for the unit to boot up. My leg is jumping up and down as I wait for the screen to load. Kitty is sitting across from me, watching with a slightly bemused expression on her face. I search for my note file and immediately do a search for 'Larsen.'

"What did you find, dear?"

"Larsen. He was the owner of the ship that Oliver Blackwater captained."

She thinks for a minute and then frowns. "The ship sank, right?" she asks.

"That's what people thought," I say, "but what if it didn't?"

"What do you mean?"

"Follow me on this. Duxbridge knew Larsen," I say before referring to the date on the diary entry. "And this date is the same year *The Dominator* disappeared. And at the same time, this person witnessed them meeting secretly."

"You're saying that you think the ship didn't actually disappear."

"Exactly, but Lilly did."

"Do you think he killed Oliver?"

"I don't know about that yet, but I'm pretty sure he probably paid Larsen to fake the loss of the ship."

"Hmmm," Kitty says, frowning. "How can you possibly prove it?"

"The national archives."

"They would know?"

I nod. "They have information on every ship, the owners, and what it was used for."

"All the way back to the 1800s?"

"They should." I sit back for a moment, thinking about this new discovery, my arms crossed.

"What's the matter?" Kitty asks.

"There has to be more," I reply. "The ghosts keep telling me they need help. It can't be just this. I don't see how this helps them."

Kitty nods and furrows her brow. "I think this is part of it," she says, "but it's not all of it."

"If Duxbridge had something to do with Blackwater's death, how would that benefit him?"

"He wants the cottage, right?"

"Right."

"With Oliver dead, I'm sure Lilly would have no way to afford the house."

"Not necessarily. Things were different back then. I'm sure Oliver would have left money for Lilly, and they probably would have bought the house outright, so she wouldn't have a mortgage payment to worry about."

"So, the only way for Duxbridge to get the property and the house would be to force her to sell, marry her—"

"Or kill her," I say, and a chill runs up and down my arms.

Kitty sits back and shakes her head. "It's not like we can really prove any of this," she says.

"I'm not really trying to *prove* anything. What would be the point? It wouldn't change anything. All I care about is helping Lilly and the sailors."

"But we still don't know what they need."

I nod in agreement and sigh. "Not yet, but I think we're getting closer."

* * *

KITTY WAVES to me as I'm backing out of her driveway after having driven down it a few feet so I could turn around. "Come back to visit anytime, dear," she calls to me.

"I will," I reply, waving and smiling at her.

My laptop bag, along with the box we pulled out of the cabinet in the garage, is sitting on the passenger seat. I pull back onto the highway and set out for home. As I drive, I think about the information I uncovered about

Larsen and Duxbridge, but after a few minutes, I shake my head in frustration.

"None of this is helping," I say to myself.

It's starting to get dark by the time I pull back into town. I'm driving down Main Street when I spot the lights for the diner, and I pull over to the curb and put the car into park. I sit for a few minutes, just staring straight ahead through the windshield. I can hear people passing by on the sidewalk, but to be honest, I'm not paying any attention to them.

After a few minutes, I take in a deep breath and hold it for a second and then release it. I climb out of the car and close the door, locking it, before heading to the café. The second I step inside, Emily looks up from where she's pouring coffee for a patron and smiles at me. She points to one of the empty stools near the door, and I sit down. She walks over, a huge smile on her face, and looks toward the door and then back at me.

"Where's your man?" she asks. "Is he parking the car?"

I shake my head and sigh while grinning at her. "He's working. It's just me."

"Aww. I was hoping to see his sweet ass."

"You are terrible," I say, and she nods.

"I'm aware. What can I get you?"

"Burger and fries."

"With everything?"

"Everything."

"Milkshake?"

"What else?"

"Chocolate?"

"I think that should be the only flavor they come in."

"Gotcha," she says with a grin. She turns around and drops the ticket through the window, and then returns her attention to me. "So? How's your day going?" she asks.

"Not too bad."

She frowns at me. "It doesn't seem that way."

I sigh quietly and look at her. "I just feel like I'm getting nowhere with my 'ghost' problem," I say, whispering the g-word.

"Well, how easy did you think it was going to be, solving a two-hundred-year-old mystery?"

I look at her and nod. "I didn't think about that."

"See," she says, pointing at me. "I know things."

I shake my head and smile at her. "I should have known you would have some wise words for me."

"That's right, you should have. How did you like your picnic the other day?"

"You had that all set up with him, didn't you?"

"I didn't do anything," she says, holding up her hands in surrender. "He just stopped in here that morning and dropped off the basket with a request for some things to fill it."

"I didn't know you two were so close."

"We're not close, but he was so sweet and was so excited to surprise you that day, I had to help him. So, it went well, I take it."

"It went very well. It was the best day I've had in a long, long time."

She smiles and claps her hands together a few times. "I'm so glad," she says. "So, did you do it?"

My mouth drops open, and I shake my head. "Oh my God, Emily."

"Yeah, yeah. It's so shocking to hear me talking like that. So, what's your answer?"

"No, we didn't *do it*."

"Aww," she replies, looking quite sad at my answer.

"Is my food ready yet?" I ask, purposely trying to look behind her.

She shakes her head. "Not yet."

Someone at the other end of the counter signals for her, and she frowns.

"I'll be right back," she says, turning just as the little bell in the window rings. She stops and retrieves my plate and sets it in front of me. "Here you go, ma'am."

"Thanks," I reply with a shake of my head.

She heads down to see what her other customer needs, and I pick up the burger after salting it and the fries. The minute I have it raised to my mouth, I look over toward the door, and the sailor is standing there, staring at me. I put the burger on the plate and look back at him.

"I'm working on it," I say while watching the rest of the diner. "Can I just have my dinner?"

He doesn't respond. He just stands by the door and stares, so I turn back to my meal and begin eating. When Emily walks back over, she frowns at me.

"What's wrong?" she asks. "Not good?"

"No. It's fine. One of the ghosts is right there, watching me," I reply before taking a bite of a couple of fries.

"Really? Where?"

"By the door," I say, turning and looking, but he's gone.

"You sure you're okay?"

"Honestly? No."

~21~

As soon as I walk through the front door, I head directly to the couch, kicking off my shoes and sitting down with my laptop. I pick up Lilly's journal and begin flipping through the pages, looking for the names of people I know—William, Oliver, Larsen. It doesn't take long before I find the next entry that looks like it might be useful.

MARCH 20TH, 1815—Duxbridge

Construction is underway on our new house. Oliver is helping set the foundation stones, while many talented wood-workers and carpenters are preparing the "bones of the house," as Oliver calls it. We've been staying at the local inn, but I am growing tired of living like a vagabond. I want to put down roots.

April 30ᵀᴴ, 1815—Duxbridge

The house is nearly finished. Oliver says we can move in next week. He took me on a tour, and I was thrilled to see the two large fireplaces. I can picture myself cooking wonderful meals for him in the kitchen that rivals anything I've seen in the fanciest houses in France or England. Oliver was right. Living here in the new states is a wonderful opportunity for us.

June 2ᴺᴰ, 1815—Duxbridge

Oliver is away on his first trip back to England since our move. He should be back sometime around Christmas. I am making the best of things, trying to make the house as nice as I can, and keeping up with all the daily chores without much trouble.

August 9ᵀᴴ, 1815—Duxbridge

Summer has been so hot this year, far hotter than I can ever remember in England or France. Thankfully, the wind off the ocean helps cool things down within the cottage. I had a strange visit today from a man who called himself William Duxbridge. He introduced himself politely enough, but when he took my hand to offer a kiss, I felt quite uncomfortable. He kept looking at the house as if it was something he coveted, but his horse and garments seem to indicate that he was quite wealthy and could *afford much larger accommodations. I hope he does not visit again.*

December 15ᵀᴴ, 1815—Duxbridge

Oliver returned today! I am so excited to have him home, and he seems just as happy to see me. It's bitterly cold, but our little house is a warm retreat from the weather outside. He says that he will not have to leave again until next year in February or March, so I have him here for at least two months!

December 25ᵀᴴ, 1815—Duxbridge

Christmas is here! It was a wonderful day, full of laughter and love, and friends and good food. Some of the members of his crew came for dinner, and they are all the most fascinating people, replete with stories from all over the world. His first mate, Avery Hawkins, and boatswain, Charlie Vertes, stand out amongst their fellow sailors.

I stop for a moment and make a note of the two names, and then a thought strikes me.

"If the ship sank, they were killed, too, right?" I ask out loud to the empty cottage. "Maybe I can find a living relative and see what they know."

I nod, and a little smile sneaks out. Inch by inch, I know we're getting closer to finding the answer. I look up from the screen and jump back when I'm instantly face-to-face with the sailor.

"Fuck!" I shout as I start scrambling backward on the couch for a moment.

Water is dripping off his slowly moving hair, and he stands and stares at me.

"You need to give me a break," I say. "I told you, I'm working on it."

He suddenly thrusts out his hand and grasps my wrist, holding it firmly. His touch is cold as ice, and I can feel the chill slowly spreading down my arm.

"What are you doing?" I ask.

His head tilts to the side, and he leans in closer. "*See* what I *see*," he says, his voice deep, echoey, and distant but filled with a strange power.

Instantly, I'm on the deck of a ship in the pitch blackness with the waves and the rain lashing all around me. Sailors are rushing in all directions, shouting orders, and carrying out commands. The ship rocks to the left, and I grab a rope to keep from tumbling across the deck. I look toward the ship's rear and spot a tall man in a long coat and one of those odd, high-crested captain's hats, standing beside the large wooden wheel. A second man struggles to hold the boat's wheel steady amidst the raging storm. It's raining so hard that it's nearly impossible to see more than a few feet in front of your face.

There are dozens of sailors high up in the rigging, clinging for their very lives as the ship is battered by the storm. No one is paying any attention to me as they rush about. I make my way toward the captain, using the ropes, railings, and other items to keep my balance on the ever-shifting deck.

"We should turn back, Captain," one of the other men standing on the upper deck shouts, to be heard over the ocean and the storm.

"Turn back where, Mr. Wilson? We're not even sure where we are!" the captain replies.

"I'm afraid we might run aground!"

"If we could only get a little light, but these damn clouds!"

"The sailing master says we should be close!"

The captain shakes his head as water runs off his hat. "He hasn't been able to take a reading for close to two days. We could be anywhere!"

Suddenly, someone in the rigging shouts. "Light! Light!"

We look forward across the ship's bow and immediately spot a small light in the distance. It's up high, compared to our position and some distance off to our right.

"That seems faint for a lighthouse signal!" the man standing opposite the captain says.

"It could just be the storm dimming the light. Make for the signal!"

The man behind the wheel begins turning it, struggling against the wind and the waves. He suddenly turns and looks at me, and I immediately recognize him as the sailor. The ship begins turning, and I hold the railing as we tilt to the left.

"Rocks! Dead ahead!" someone shouts from high above.

I stare up at the rocky cliff. It looks like the one near

the cottage, but there's a second rocky outcropping a hundred yards away or so, and I swear that's where the brighter light is coming from. I look back and forth, and I can definitely see two distinct points of illumination; the closer one is barely visible, but the other one is far brighter.

"Hard over starboard!" the captain shouts, and the sailor turns the wheel as fast as he can, the old wooden ship groaning as it slowly begins changing course, but it's obvious it's too little, too late.

The bow slams into the rocks. The sound of wood cracking and splintering combines with the screams of the men as the ship breaks apart. The ocean comes rushing up, and the last thing I see is the light going out on top of the cliff.

I wake up on the floor in front of the couch, clutching my chest and screaming. It takes me a few minutes to realize where I am. I look down at my arm where the sailor grabbed me, and I can see faint finger marks that slowly fade away.

"Jesus," I mutter quietly, and then I start crying.

* * *

SOME SORT of chirping bird outside the window wakes me up, and I stare at the ceiling, the fan turning slowly above my head.

"How did I…"

I look around. I'm in my bed, under the sheets, but I can't remember coming in here last night. I try to recall what happened, but I can't. I remember coming home and working on the journal and the sailor grabbing my arm… and then it's all just a blur. I sigh, close my eyes again, and breathe in slowly through my nose and out through my mouth, trying to relax and shut out everything else.

Slowly, images begin to fill my head—the ship, the storm, and the crash of the vessel upon the rocks at the base of the cliff. It feels like a dream, but I know it wasn't. Suddenly, my eyes pop open, and I sit straight up.

"Two lanterns," I say out loud. "There were two lanterns."

The doorbell rings, and I hop out of bed, still dressed in the same clothes I was in when I got home last night. I rush down the hallway and pull the door open. Jerry is standing there, two white paper sacks in his hands and a warm smile on his face.

"There were two lanterns!" I say excitedly before he even has a chance to say anything.

"Pardon?" he asks, a confused expression on his face.

"When the ship crashed into the rocks, there were two lanterns up on the cliffs."

"How do you know?"

"Because I saw it."

That seems to stun him, and he stands there just staring at me. "How…how did you see it?"

"The sailor showed me."

He shakes his head. "Okay," he replies, sounding rather unsure. "Can I come in?" He lifts his hands and shows me the two sacks again.

"Oh my God," I say. "I'm so sorry." I step aside and let

him pass, leaning up and kissing him on the cheek as he does. "Morning," I say, and he grins at me.

"Morning." He sets the bags on the counter and looks at me.

"So? Should we talk about this?"

"After breakfast," I say, stepping up to him and wrapping my arms around his neck. "I'm sorry. It can wait."

"You sounded rather excited about it."

"I am, but there's something I'm more excited about."

"What's that?"

"Having you here this morning."

He smiles, and I swear, a little blush flows across his face, but he covers it well. "I'm glad."

He unpacks the bags, setting two breakfast sandwiches wrapped in grease-stained paper on one of the flattened-out bags, and then pulls two coffees from the other bag.

"Outside?" I ask.

"That sounds perfect."

I grab the coffee, he picks up the food, and we head back to the front door. We sit down at the little table, side by side instead of across from each other this time. He unwraps his sandwich and then looks at me.

"You're awfully dressed up for so early in the morning," he says before taking a bite.

I look down at my clothes. "Um…I never got undressed from yesterday."

"Really?" he asks, his mouth partially filled with egg, cheese, and sausage.

I nod, feeling rather embarrassed by my admission. "It's sort of a long story." I pick up my food and unwrap it, and I'm about to take a bite when he responds.

"Well, we have all morning and part of the day."

I sit back slightly, my mouth still open and the sandwich between my teeth. "We do?"

"Yeah."

"I thought you had that big job to take care of."

"I got the guys working on it. I told the client I had another job to check on."

"You lied to her?" I ask, grinning at him.

"I wouldn't call it lying…exactly. I do have another job to check on."

"Do you?' I ask, immediately disappointed.

"Yeah. I have to check to make sure that everything is okay with your foundation," he replies.

"What? Is there something wrong with it?"

He looks over at the cottage for about ten seconds and then back at me. "It looks like it was a false alarm. Everything looks good."

I grin and shake my head. "You suck," I say, laughing, and he smiles at me.

"Sometimes."

I finally take a bite of my sandwich and groan at the wonderful combination of cheese, egg, and sausage. Jerry starts in on his breakfast, and we just sit, both of us simply enjoying the beautiful morning air and the company. When we're finished, Jerry looks at me and then slides his hand along the table and wraps his fingers around mine.

"So, is this when we have the conversation about how you were able to see the two lanterns you're so excited about?"

"That pretty much sums it up."

"Hardly. How did you see them?"

"I told you, the sailor showed me."

"Yeah, you said that. What exactly does that mean?"

"He sorta grabbed my arm and took me there."

"He grabbed you?" he asks, frowning at me.

"Yeah," I say. "He didn't hurt me."

He nods, but I can tell he's not a happy camper. "So, what exactly happened?"

"He whispered something to me. He said, 'See what I see,' and then he sort of grabbed my arm, and when he did, I was instantly standing on the deck of one of those old sailing ships, in the middle of the storm, in pitch-black darkness."

"Holy shit."

"Yeah. Tell me about it."

"Could you feel it?"

"Like the rain and stuff?"

"Yeah."

"I could feel it."

"Jesus," he says, swallowing hard. "So, what about the lanterns?"

"I saw one, at first, and from what I could tell, it was on the cliff," I say, pointing to the spot, "but that light was very faint; you could barely see it."

I pause for a moment as I feel like I'm being flung back to the moment, even though I'm sitting right next to Jerry. I'm not sure if he senses my distress, but he reaches out and places his hand on top of mine, and it seems to ground me.

"What about the other lamp?" he asks.

"I spotted it just a few seconds after the fainter one. It was farther down the coast but up at the same height, and that lantern was much brighter. That's the one the ship turned toward."

"And then ended up crashing on the rocks."

"Exactly."

"So, maybe Lilly didn't have anything to do with the sinking of the ships."

I nod slowly. "Maybe."

~22~

"So, how long do I have you today?" I ask as we're cleaning up from breakfast.

"Most of the day. I do have to head out in the late afternoon to check on the job site."

I nod and smile at him, and he leans down slightly to kiss me on the lips. I sigh quietly and kiss him back.

"What's our next step?" he asks.

"We need to translate more of Lilly's diary. I think the key to everything is in there."

"It's sort of slow going, isn't it?" He picks up the old book and flips through a few pages, then gently closes it and replaces it on the arm of the couch.

"Yeah."

"How could we make it go faster?"

"Honestly, I think the only way is to find someone

who speaks French and can directly translate it. Know anyone?"

"Who speaks French?"

"Yes."

"Not that I know of."

I frown and shake my head.

"What else do you have?"

"I don't think *The Dominator* actually sank."

"Oliver Blackwater's ship?"

"Yes," I say, heading toward the front door.

"Where are you going?" Jerry asks, from his position by the couch.

"I'm taking a walk."

"Right now?"

"Yeah," I reply. "It helps me think."

"Do you want company?"

"Only if you want to come," I say, grinning at him.

He smiles and darts over to me, then we walk outside. The bright morning sun is shining down on us, and I look at Jerry, turn to the left, and walk around the side of the house, heading north. Less than a minute later, he takes my hand, and I quickly slip my fingers between his, squeezing gently.

"So? What do we know?" Jerry asks.

"We've been over this so many times; it almost feels like everything is starting to blur together."

"I feel like we should get a big whiteboard, magnets, and some sticky notes and make up something like you see in the movies."

I pause for a minute and look at him. "That might not be a bad idea."

"Really?" he asks excitedly.

"I knew you'd make a good assistant ghost-hunting detective."

He smiles at me and then leans over and kisses me gently on the cheek.

"Anyway. We both already know some of the stuff, but what new things have you come up with that we haven't talked about?"

We're approaching the peak of the cliff, where the bare rocks peek out beneath the dirt and scruffy little grasses.

"I found out that Duxbridge definitely knew Randolph Larsen."

"And Larsen owned *The Dominator*."

"Exactly."

"Which is why you don't think it actually sank."

"Yeah."

Jerry nods, and we stop at the edge of the cliff, looking down at the massive waves smashing against the rocks.

"That little entry in that journal from the historical society seemed to suggest that they were up to something."

"We just have to figure out what it was."

"I've been thinking about that," I say, looking out across the ocean while leaning up against Jerry.

He tilts his head down and kisses the top of my head. "What have you been thinking?"

"I found some information in Lilly's diary. There was a passage where two of Oliver's crew members came for Christmas dinner."

"How does that help us?"

"If we could track down some of their relatives and

talk to them," I say, and suddenly, the light bulb seems to go off in Jerry's head.

"That would prove *The Dominator* didn't actually sink."

"Exactly. There was also a short note about a visit Duxbridge paid to Lilly when Oliver was off on one of his voyages."

"What did it say?"

"She apparently didn't appreciate his attention and felt very uncomfortable."

"Do you think she might have mentioned that to her husband when he got back?"

I nod slowly. "I think she probably would, but I haven't gotten that far yet, which is another reason we need to find some who speaks French so we can get the whole thing translated faster."

"Yeah. That's going to be one of our hardest tasks."

I nod and then look past him at a couple of seagulls wheeling around one another in the sky about a hundred yards away. I frown when I look down at the cliff below them and take a small step past Jerry.

"What is it? What's the matter?" he asks, but I don't answer right away.

"That's the place," I finally reply, pointing to the rocky outcropping in the distance.

"What place?"

"That's where the other lantern was."

"Are you sure?" he asks, looking over where I'm pointing.

"I'm sure."

He looks at me, and I can tell immediately that he believes me beyond any doubt.

"Come on," I say, taking his hand again and we head back down in the direction of the cottage and then turn north, following the coast as we make our way toward the spot.

Several times, we are forced to stop and then back-track due to gaping chasms between sections of the rocky coastline until we can find a place where we can cross. By the time we reach the cliff, the sun is high in the sky, and I have sweat running down my neck and soaking into my shirt. Jerry pulls me up onto one final large, rocky outcropping, and then we walk slowly to the edge of the cliff. I look down at the waves, and suddenly, everything around me vanishes, and I'm standing alone in the dark as a storm rages overhead.

"Jerry!" I shout, turning around and around, but he's nowhere to be seen. "Jerry!"

The sounds of screams and the splintering of wood rise from the turbulent waters far below. I peer over the edge, and I see the ship breaking up as the waves batter the wooden vessel against the cliff wall. Men are in the water, but I only see them briefly before they vanish beneath the waves. I look back down the hill, and I spot a figure dressed in a dark cloak and boots heading away from me. Lightning flashes in the sky, illuminating the surrounding area, and I catch a glimpse of the corner of a lantern carried by the figure before he flings his cloak over it and vanishes into the darkness beyond.

I stand for a moment, rain soaking me, as I try to block out the screams of agony from the men dying in the ocean below. I drop to my knees, covering my ears with my hands, and then suddenly, I'm back on the cliff, brilliant sunshine beaming down. Jerry is crouched in front of me, a terrified expression on his face. Instantly, I start crying, the tears flowing out of me like a flood.

"Ally!" he says, holding me with both hands. "Can you hear me?"

Slowly, I raise my head, trying to stem the tide, and I finally make eye contact with him. "I can hear you," I manage to mutter between the sobs.

"What happened?"

"They were dying…. They were screaming." My heart is racing, threatening to burst out of my chest, and my throat is so dry that it feels like I haven't had a drink for days.

"Who was dying?"

"The sailors…. I saw the ship crashing and sinking and the sailors…in the ocean…just…drowning."

Jerry shakes his head and then pulls me close, wrapping his arms around me. I don't know how long it is before I finally sit up, looking him in the eyes.

"What happened to you?" he asks. "You just stopped talking, and you were standing on the edge of the cliff, not moving."

"What? Was I? For how long?"

He nods, his face furrowed in worry. "For like five minutes. Are you sure you're okay?"

"I think so," I reply, and then I grab his arm.

"I saw him, Jerry."

"Saw who?"

"The man with the lantern."

* * *

"Was it Duxbridge?" Jerry asks as we sit in the short, stubby grasses a few feet from the cliff edge.

"I don't know for sure. I didn't see his face…. And honestly, even if I did, I don't know if I could identify him anyway."

Jerry sighs and shakes his head. "This is scaring me," he says, holding my hand firmly in his.

"To be honest…me too."

"Maybe we should leave this alone."

I shake my head. "I can't. Lilly needs my help, and I don't think it's going to stop until we solve this."

He nods and sighs. "You're probably right."

I manage a weak smile and reach out and touch his cheek, enjoying the feel of his skin against mine. The sun glints off something half-buried on the dirt, and I look down.

"What? What is it?" Jerry asks.

"Not sure," I reply before leaning down a little closer.

There's definitely something metallic sticking out of the earth. I scrape away some of the dirt, tiny stones, and grass roots, and eventually, I pull it out. I hold it in my hand for a moment, turning it over a few times. I rub the stubborn bits of debris off it and hold it up in the sun.

"Looks like a coin," Jerry says, peering at the little brass circle.

"I think it's a button," I reply, turning it over and looking at the little loop of metal attached to the back.

I turn it back over, and using my thumb, I dig out some more of the dirt and sand and salt, finally revealing the face of an ornately engraved brass button with the letter *D* in the center.

"Is that a *D*?" Jerry asks.

"I think so." I sit for a minute, and Jerry looks at me and frowns.

"You okay?"

"Yeah…I'm fine. I'm just trying to remember something."

"What?"

"Where I've seen that button before."

He nods and waits for a few seconds before slowly standing and offering me his hand. "You about ready to head back?" he asks.

"Sure," I reply, grasping his fingers and pulling myself up with his help.

I lean against him as we head back down the hill, moving slowly through the scattered rocks and uneven terrain. About halfway to the bottom of the steeply sloped landscape, I stop suddenly.

"I saw it at the museum," I say, pulling the button out of my pocket and looking at it again.

"At the historical society?"

"Yes. There was a coat on display in a glass case. It had the same buttons."

"That could have come from any place," Jerry says. "Was it missing a button?"

"Not that I remember, but I didn't really look at it that closely."

We start walking again, hand in hand.

"Are you sure about this?"

"Sure as I can be without checking it."

"Wait," he says, pulling us to a stop. "You're not thinking about going back there, are you?"

"I have to look at the coat."

He doesn't respond for a few seconds, but I can tell he's not happy. "All right," he finally says. "I'm going to do with you this time."

"To protect me from a ghost?" I ask, grinning at him.

"If I have to."

"So, you're my personal ghostbuster?"

He shakes his head and chuckles. "I thought I was your assistant ghost-hunting detective."

"Either way. We'll figure out the details later."

"That works for me," he says as we begin climbing the slope toward the cottage.

By the time we get there, the sun is already starting to move past the midpoint in the sky.

"Wait," I say as we're walking around the side of the house. "I thought you had to head out this afternoon."

He sighs and frowns, and I shake my head.

"Jerry. Don't do that. I've already told you. You have work; you can't just ignore it. I'll be fine. I'm certainly not going into the basement of that place again."

He grumbles quietly, and I reach out and touch his cheek.

"I'm touched that you're worried about me, and that gives me the courage I need to do this...to keep doing all this."

"I still don't like it," he replies, leaning his head against my hand.

"I know, but it is what it is."

"Oh, is it?"

"Yes. It is."

He takes my hand, kisses it gently, and then smiles at

me, although I can tell there's still some worry buried under the surface.

"Fine," he says, seeming to relent. "What do you think about lunch before I head out?"

"I think I could eat some."

"All right then," he replies with a quick smile.

We walk around the front of the cottage and over to his truck. I stop suddenly.

"Hold on," I say, "let me grab Lilly's diary, just in case we think of someone who might be able to help us."

He nods and smiles, then continues over to his truck while I run inside. The moment I step across the threshold, I get a chill, but it's a dark cold, unlike the feeling I get when Lilly or the sailor is nearby. I look around. I can't see the black shadow, but I know it's close. I dart over to the couch, grab the journal and my laptop bag, and rush for the door. As soon as I get outside, Jerry looks over at me and frowns.

"What's the matter?" he asks, his brow deeply furrowed with worry and concern.

"I felt it. The shadow. It was watching me."

He shakes his head, opens the passenger door to his truck, and holds it until I'm inside.

He closes the door carefully and stands outside the truck for a moment, staring at the cottage, before walking around and opening his door. After slipping into his seat, he leans over and kisses me, gently holding my face with his hand.

"Are you okay?"

"I'm all right," I reply with a small smile.

He nods and then starts up the truck while keeping his eye on the little house.

"I don't like this," he says. "This is getting more dangerous with every passing moment."

"Which is exactly why we have to solve this mystery and help Lilly."

"Do you think that's going to get rid of the dark shadow?"

"I hope so."

He grumbles something under his breath and shakes his head, but I reach out and touch his face.

"It'll be okay," I say, smiling at him, already feeling better knowing that he's right beside me.

He nods, but I can tell he's not quite convinced.

"Let's go eat, honey," I say, stopping suddenly when the last word just popped out of my mouth without thinking about it.

He smiles at me, and the dark pall that had been hanging over us seems to dissipate like so much smoke on a windy day.

"The diner?" he asks.

"Where else?"

He shrugs and then grins at me. "Good point…honey."

I smile at him and shake my head before reaching over and placing my hand on top of his.

He puts the truck into gear, and we head down the winding driveway and out onto the highway, turning right toward town. A few minutes later, we're parked in front of the diner. Jerry hops out and opens my door, holding it for me as I step out. I give him a warm smile, and he smiles back.

"Thank you," I say.

"My pleasure."

He takes my hand, and we step over to the diner's entrance, and again, he opens the door for me.

"You know. You don't have to get every door," I say.

"My mother told me to always act like a gentleman."

"And opening doors is part of it?"

"Of course, it's one of the pillars of gentlemanhood."

The minute we step inside, Emily comes rushing over and throws her arms around my neck and then immediately does the same to Jerry, who seems a little shocked at the gesture, but takes it all in stride.

"How are you guys?" she asks, grinning at me as she moves behind the counter and guides us to our two regular stools near the door.

"We're good," I reply with a smile that I can't seem to control every time I'm with Jerry.

"It looks like it," she responds.

She gives me a little wink, and I wink back, which makes her grin even wider at me. "So, what'll it be?" she asks.

"Surprise us," I reply, looking over at Jerry, who nods his agreement.

"That works for me," he says.

"All right then." She turns and heads to the kitchen through the swinging, silver door, and I turn to Jerry.

"I think we're getting close," I say.

He looks at me and frowns., looking a little confused. "Um...I think we are, too," he replies, taking my hand and squeezing my fingers gently.

"Oh, yeah...that, too," I say, smiling at him. "I was

really talking about the ghost mystery, but it applies to us, too, I suppose."

"I think it does."

I look toward the kitchen, and Emily watches us via the pass-through window. She smiles, and I shake my head, a grin on my face as well.

"As far as the ghost thing goes, I think we need to get the diary translated as soon as we can," I say.

"I agree. I think the key to this whole thing might be in there."

"The problem is, how are we going to find someone who speaks French around here?"

"I speak French," Emily says as she walks over to us with two glasses filled with Coke.

"What's that now?" I ask.

~23~

"*I* speak French," he repeats. "I took four years in high school and four more in college," she answers. "I'm more than just an amazing waitress."

"Well, that's convenient," Jerry says with a grin.

"I had no idea you spoke French," I say, and she leans on the counter and smiles.

"Not many people do."

"If you went to school for it, what are you doing here?" Jerry asks.

"After I graduated, I was offered a job with the state department as a translator for the U.S. Embassy in Paris."

"And?" I ask. The minute I speak the word, her expression darkens, and I immediately regret asking.

"Just before I was supposed to start, my dad had a

heart attack. My mom really couldn't take care of him, she was sick with cancer, so I decided to come home."

"I'm sorry," I say, reaching across the counter and taking her hand, before realizing that I'm doing the same thing to her that everyone did to me at Steven's funeral—saying sorry—but now I understand…. What else do you say?

"It's okay," she replies with a bright smile. "That's how I ended up owning this place."

"Wait. What? You own this place?" Jerry asks, looking over at me as if we had been keeping a huge secret from him.

"Don't look at me," I say, laughing and smiling. "I had no idea."

"Of course, I own this place," she says. "Did you think I'm just a waitress?"

"Honestly…yeah. I don't mean 'just a waitress;' I mean, I thought you were a waitress."

"I am a waitress. What don't you understand about this?" she asks, grinning at him.

He shakes his head and sighs. "You're just messing with me, aren't you?"

She touches her nose with the tip of her finger and then points at him. "*Oh*, you're a smart one, aren't you? But I still do own this place."

I'm just sitting and watching them, a bemused expression on my face.

"Are we going to be able to order food?" I ask, grinning at her.

"Hmm. Let me check with your waitress. Oh wait, that's me. What can I get you?"

"I don't know if I like your attitude. Can I speak to the manager?"

"Of course," she says, pausing for a moment before continuing. "What can I help you with?"

"Your waitress is rather rude. We've been here for almost ten minutes, and no one has taken our order."

"My apologies, ma'am. We've been thinking about letting her go. I think this is the last straw."

"You two are so weird," Jerry says, shaking his head.

"That's the way we like it," I say, leaning over and bumping into his side.

Emily does not fail to notice the little gesture, and she grins wickedly at me. "Anyway. What can I get you?"

"I'm not sure," I say. "We've had your burgers, your grilled cheese, and your breakfast sandwiches."

"Don't forget the steaks," Jerry adds.

"Oh yeah, steaks, too."

"Hmm," Emily says, tapping the end of her pen against her lower lip before suddenly smiling. "I got it."

"Got what?" I ask.

"I'm not telling. It'll be a surprise."

"Not sure that's a good idea," Jerry says.

"Watch it, Romeo," Emily shoots back before heading to the kitchen.

I look over at Jerry, and he smiles at me.

"What's up, beautiful?" he asks, and I get a thrill of excitement in my belly.

"Nothing. I'm just glad I had you all to myself for so long today."

"Me too."

I reach over and take his hand, slipping my fingers

between his and squeezing gently. "What about tomorrow?" I ask.

He frowns, and I know what he's going to say.

"It's okay. Like I said before, you need to work, so don't feel bad."

He nods, but I can tell in his expression that it doesn't matter what I say.

"What are you going to do about the relatives of the two sailors you mentioned?"

"I guess I'll do some sort of Google search and see what I can find. If they're not too far, I might take another road trip."

He nods and then frowns. "That sounds good, but are you sure about going back to the historical society?"

"I am. I need to see if that button matches. If it does, it means Duxbridge was up there, and it might mean that he was the man with the bigger lantern."

Jerry starts to reply when Emily returns, setting two bright-red plastic baskets in front of us, filled with the most delicious-looking fried chicken I have ever seen. There are also two tall wire holders, each with a cone of white paper, filled with French fries.

"Enjoy," she says while setting two glasses of Coke in front of us.

"Thanks. This looks amazing."

"Of course, it does."

I pick up the breast and take a bite. The skin is crispy but light, and the meat is hot, juicy, and packed with flavor. I glance over at Jerry, and he seems to be experiencing the same moment of Zen that I am.

"Try the fries," Emily says, standing and watching us eat.

I pick one of the wedges out of the little cone of paper and bite down, and then I look at her and moan.

"Good, right? We fry them twice in the same oil as the chicken. It gives them that something special, don't you think?"

"They're amazing."

"Thanks. My dad's recipe."

"Well, you've done him proud," Jerry says, smiling at her.

She nods, and the tiniest shadow of sadness seems to pass over her face, and then it's gone almost as quickly. She smiles again and looks at me. "Now, where's this journal you need to have translated?"

* * *

"THIS SHOULDN'T TAKE me more than a few days, maybe less," she says, after flipping through about half the diary.

"Are you serious?"

The empty baskets and French fry holders are off to the side, while the half-full glasses of Coke are in front of Jerry and me.

"Absolutely."

"Oh my God. It took me forever to even get a few pages done, and I was skipping a lot of it."

"Yeah, it's hard going when you have to look up every word, but if you don't mind a recording rather than something written down, it shouldn't be a problem."

"That would be great."

"All right then. I'll start working on it tonight, and I'll bring it by in a couple of days, or maybe less."

"You're the best," I say.

"Yeah, I know, but it's nice to hear every now and then."

"Or every day," Jerry adds.

"See?" she says, pointing to him. "You are a smart one."

"All right. What's next?" I ask, turning and looking at Jerry.

He looks at his watch and frowns. "Next, I have to run to the job site to check on the progress."

"Oh, that's right," I say, trying not to sound too disappointed, even though I am, and even though I'm the one who's insisting he go.

"Are you still planning on going to the museum?" he asks.

"Yeah. I have to."

He frowns and sighs, looking as unhappy and worried as he did before we came for lunch. "I really don't like you going alone."

"I know, but I don't have a choice."

He continues frowning, and then Emily chimes in.

"I can go with her," she says.

We both look at her.

"Really? You can just leave?" I ask.

"I'm the owner. Remember?"

I look at Jerry. "What do you think? Is that better?"

"It's not ideal, but it's the best I'm going to get, I think," he says, his frown lessening slightly.

"I think that's probably true."

He sighs and then manages a small smile. "Listen, how about I stop by tonight for a late-night dessert?"

"That works for me," I reply, smiling back at him.

I glance over at Emily, and she grins at me and then raises and lowers her eyebrows a few times. I just shake my head in response.

"Do you want me to drive you home to get your car?" he asks.

"I can walk."

"Or I can give her a ride on my bike," Emily says.

"All right," he says, leaning down and kissing me on the cheek. "I'll see you later tonight."

"Okay."

"Bye."

"Bye," I say with a warm smile.

"Bye, Emily," Jerry says as he heads for the door.

"Bye, Jerry," she replies with a wink and a wave.

As soon as he's outside, she looks at me and starts giggling.

"You are smitten."

"What are you talking about?" I ask.

"Don't deny it."

I sit for a moment, and then I just start giggling along with her. "I so am. Oh my God, I so am."

She leans on the counter and takes my hand. "I'm glad. He seems like one of the good ones."

"He is. He really is." I know I only met her a few weeks ago, but it makes me feel remarkably good knowing that she approves of him.

"When did you want to head over there?" she asks.

"Whenever you can."

"We can go right now."

"Are you sure?"

"Like I said, I'm the owner."

"All right," I reply. "Let's get this over with."

"Meet me around front in about five minutes."

"Okay."

I head out, stepping onto the sidewalk. The heat hits me almost immediately. It feels like the temperature went up by twenty degrees since Jerry and I walked into the diner. A few seconds later, I hear the drone of Emily's motorcycle, and she drives out of the alley at the end of the block. She revs the engine and then races down the street, skidding to a stop in front of me.

She's still dressed in her waitress uniform, but she's also wearing her black and red helmet, creating an interesting fashion statement. She flips up the visor and smiles at me. A second helmet is resting on the rear of the seat. She picks it up and hands it to me.

"Slip this on," she says.

I pull the helmet over my head and click the chinstrap closed after adjusting the length.

"Hold on tight," she says, turning her head to look at me for a moment.

I wrap my arms around her waist and lean against her back. "Take it easy. First time on the back of a motorcycle," I say.

"I'll be gentle. Just remember, when we turn, don't fight the turn, so don't lean away, and also…don't lean into the turn."

"Okay, that's confusing."

"I know. It sounds harder than it actually is. Just sort of go with it, I guess."

"I gotcha…I think."

She nods, then kicks the bike back into gear, and we pull away from the curb. I squeeze her a little tighter, and she tilts her head back.

"Not so tight," she says with a chuckle.

"Sorry."

"It's cool."

We head out of town, heading toward my place, the wind and the landscape rushing by us. It only takes a few seconds for me to relax and begin to enjoy the ride. We zip by the entrance to my house, and for a moment, I want to suggest that she just drive up to the cottage and we can get my car, but then, I decide against it. A few minutes later, I spot the museum in the distance, and I immediately get the same feeling of dread I experienced the last two times I was here.

Emily pulls into the parking lot and stops the bike in one of the spots a few down from the same car that was here last time. She puts the kickstand down and looks back at me.

"You first," she says, her voice sounding strangely muffled by the helmet.

"Oh."

I slip off the seat and remove the helmet, tucking it under my arm and looking at the building. The feeling of dread only seems to intensify the longer I stand there. Emily steps up next to me and takes my helmet, hanging them both on the bike's handlebars.

"Do you feel that?" I ask.

"I feel it," she replies, frowning for the first time since I've known her. "What the hell is it?"

"I don't know, but there's something…dark here."

"Yeah, that's for sure. Is that why Jerry didn't want you coming here by yourself?"

"Yeah. The last time I was here, I was attacked."

"What? Attacked by who?"

"Some sort of spirit. I think it was Duxbridge."

"That seems like something you might have mentioned before I volunteered to come with you," she says, grinning crookedly at me.

"Sorry."

"Oh, well. As far as you thinking it's Duxbridge, that makes sense. This was his house," she says while looking at the gloomy stone mansion.

"Are you serious?"

"You didn't know that?"

"Does this look like the face of someone in the know?" I ask, grinning at her.

"I guess not. Yeah, this was his house."

We stand outside the building for a while.

"How much do you know about him?"

"Not that much, but having grown up around here, you didn't really have a choice but to learn about him a little in school. I mean, everywhere you go, there's his name."

"From what I've discovered, he seems like a bit of an asshole."

She nods and grins at me. "I'm not surprised."

"Why do you say that?"

"Because, even though he was the son of the founder

of the town, when it came to ensuring that it was prosperous, he was more concerned with his own wealth than with the wealth and fortunes of the town."

"What does that mean?"

"Well, the minute the factory that his family opened was offered a cheaper location closer to Boston, he took it. The place closed, and it almost killed the town."

"Sounds like he could have been a man of our times," I say, shaking my head.

"Yeah. Absolutely."

"What sort of factory was it?" I ask as we're walking slowly toward the front door.

"They made stuff like lanterns."

~24~

$\mathcal{I}$ shake my head, and we come to an abrupt stop. "You are just full of surprises today, aren't you?"

"What do you mean?"

"You know the legend about Lilly Blackwater and how she caused all those ships to wreck on the rocks?"

"Of course."

"I don't think she did it."

"Then who did?"

"I think it was Duxbridge. I think he had a much larger lantern than Lilly, something that could have been seen by a passing ship."

"Damn. How do you know all this?"

I pause for a moment and then frown. "I've seen it," I reply, and her brow furrows.

"I think we need to expand on that."

"Let's talk about it later. I want to get this over with."

"I'm with you."

I open the door, and we walk inside. I immediately feel like we're being watched as soon as we step into the foyer.

"What are we looking for?" Emily asks, gazing around warily.

"There's a coat, which I assume belonged to Duxbridge, that had buttons like this," I say, pulling the little brass circle out of my pocket.

"Where did you find that?"

"Up on a cliff adjacent to the one my house sits on."

"And what will that prove?"

"That he was there, and that maybe Lilly wasn't guilty of what everyone thought she was."

"I really need to read that diary," she says, and I nod.

"Yeah, you do."

"So, where did you see the coat?"

"I can't remember," I reply, looking around.

"You're back," I hear Linda say as she comes out of the large, former living room off to our left.

"Yeah. I uh…I found something that I thought you might be able to identify."

"Oh really?" she asks, her face lighting up.

"It's nothing big, just a little button." I hand her my discovery, and she turns it over in her hand a few times and then smiles.

"It looks familiar," she says. "It's definitely a button from an overcoat."

"Do you think it may have belonged to Duxbridge? I'm only saying that because of the *D*."

"It could be." She seems to think for a minute and then looks at me. "Follow me."

She heads us back into the living room and stops in front of a tall glass case set against the wall. Inside is a long dark-blue coat with a column of bright brass buttons, but it looks as if the third one down from the top is missing. After unlocking it with a key on her ring, Linda opens the door and holds my little button beside one of the ones attached to the coat.

"It looks like a perfect match," she says.

"It sure does," I reply, and then suddenly, a chill runs across my skin, and I shiver.

I look over at Emily, and she's frowning. I run my hand up and down my arm, and she nods, a slightly worried expression on her face.

"So, you think this is from that coat?" I ask Linda.

She closes the door and then nods. "I'm pretty sure it is. I can't be one hundred percent positive, but I'd say ninety-five." She starts to hand it back to me, and I shake my head.

"Consider it a donation to your collection."

She smiles at me. "Thank you so much," she says, and then a phone rings from somewhere deeper inside the museum. "Excuse me. I'll be right back."

"Sure."

Emily and I slowly wander around the displays, peering through the glass at the thousands of carefully displayed and preserved artifacts. I look up at the ceiling and spot the dozens of lanterns hanging from the rafters.

"I'm assuming those are some of the lanterns his factory made," I say.

Emily looks at them and nods. "I suppose."

My eyes pass over a particularly large example, coated with black paint, and then my breath catches in my throat. A tall figure dressed in a long black coat is standing in the hallway that leads deeper into the house. My throat is instantly dry, and my heart is racing. I'm used to Lilly and the sailor, but this is something different, something...terrifying.

"What the hell?" Emily says, and I finally manage to look over at her. She's staring at the creature, a look of horror on her face.

"It's Duxbridge," I mutter, and I start moving back, but before I take more than two steps, he suddenly lunges, slamming into me and sending me sprawling onto the floor.

Emily shouts and rushes the ghost, but he raises his right arm and flicks his wrist. She lifts off the floor and then is thrown against the far wall, striking a bookcase and slumping to the carpet. He turns his gaze back to me, his eyes a blazing red hue full of hate and rage. Instantly, I can't breathe, and I grasp my throat, trying desperately to draw in air as the oxygen in my lungs is slowly consumed.

"Is everything okay out there?" Linda calls from the other room.

Duxbridge spins and stares down the hall where her voice came from, and then as quickly as he had appeared, he vanishes, and I can breathe again. I suck in mouthfuls of air as I struggle to my feet. I dart over to Emily and help her up. She has a gash on her elbow and a nasty bruise beginning to form on her forehead.

"Are you okay?" I ask, checking her for other injuries.

"I'm okay," she replies. "Let's get the fuck out of here!"

We head toward the door just as Linda walks out of the back, a curious expression on her face.

"Leaving already?" she asks. "Is everything okay?"

"It's fine. My friend is just not feeling good. Probably something she ate."

"Oh my. Well, take care, and I'll see you next time," she says with a smile and a little wave.

We burst out through the front door and into the sunshine, then race to the bike, both of us glancing back at the house multiple times to ensure we're not being followed. We grab our helmets and pull them on while Emily starts the cycle and quickly backs us out of the spot. She puts the bike in gear and guns the engine, the rear wheel screeching and throwing up a cloud of gray smoke behind us as we tear out of the parking lot. Emily races back onto the highway, and I hold tightly to her, sort of going with the bike as we zip around the turns in the road until we reach the entrance to my house.

She hits the brakes, and the bike skids to the side for a second or two before she makes the turn into my driveway. We literally fly up the gravel path, and she comes to a stop just next to my car. She quickly puts the kickstand down, and I climb off, removing my helmet. She jumps off the bike, rips her helmet off, and drops it on the ground, staring at me.

"What in the mother-hell was that?" she asks.

"That was a ghost."

"How are you okay with this?" she asks.

"I've had some experience," I reply. "I thought you didn't think ghosts existed."

"Well, obviously they do, and they're fucking scary!" she shouts as she paces back and forth behind her bike.

"They're not all like that," I say.

"They're not all like that. What does that even mean?"

"Let's have a drink," I say, walking over and taking her hand.

She follows after me, shaking her head as we walk. "I'm going to need more than one drink."

"I understand."

* * *

"You said not all the ghosts are not like that," Emily says as we're sitting outside at the little table, drinking vodka from juice glasses.

She has a bandage on her elbow, and she's holding a small icepack against her forehead. I pick up the bottle and fill her tumbler again.

"They're not. Lilly and the sailor just sort of stand and look at me, except the time that he grabbed my arm."

"He grabbed you?"

"Yeah. That's how I found out about the second lantern."

"Right," she says, downing her third glass. "I thought we were going to expand on that."

"You sure you're ready for that?"

"After what just happened, I think I'm ready for anything."

I nod and then take a swig of vodka and hold it in my mouth for a moment before swallowing. I take the next twenty minutes or so to relate the tale of the sailor, the ship, the wreck on the rocks, the lanterns, and then the vision I had earlier this morning before discovering the button.

"Holy shit," Emily says, filling her glass again. "This is some crazy ass shit going on."

"Yeah, who knew?"

"You said Duxbridge attacked you the last time you were at the museum."

"Yeah, but he didn't look like that. He was more like a shadow, even darker than a shadow, actually, but he was formless…like a cloud."

"So, what do you think it means that he's taken shape…so to speak."

"I have no idea."

"It's creepy."

"You can say that again."

"Well, at least we got away from him."

I frown, and she leans forward, setting her icepack on the table.

"What?" she asks.

"He's been here."

"That thing has been here?" She looks around as if he might suddenly appear…which honestly, he might.

"I felt it this morning. I didn't see him, but I could tell he was watching me."

"Okay, that's super creepy and very concerning."

"I agree."

"What are we going to do about it?"

"I'm not sure, but I think if we can help Lilly and the sailor, that will end all of this, or at least, I hope it will."

"So, you need the diary translated."

"Yes. I think there may be some other important information about Duxbridge, Randolph Larsen, and Oliver Blackwater in it. I also think it might explain why Lilly stood on the cliff with her lantern."

"And I'm guessing it's not what we've always thought it was."

"That's what I'm thinking."

My phone suddenly rings, and I pick it up off the table. "It's Jerry," I say, and Emily smiles at me. "We're not mentioning this to him, right?"

She nods, I swipe the screen, and the video connects.

"Hey!" I say, putting on the most genuine smile I can manage.

"How's it going?" he asks.

"Pretty good."

"Did you find what you needed at the museum?"

"Yeah. It's definitely a button from Duxbridge's coat," I reply.

"And he attacked us," Emily blurts out after coming around and showing herself on the video.

My eyes go wide, and I glare at her, lifting my hand in a gesture that says, "What the hell?"

"You were attacked again?" he asks, frowning at me.

I sigh and nod slowly. "Yeah."

"Are you okay?"

"We're fine."

He looks at me sideways, and I put on another smile.

"I'm telling you, we're fine."

"Are you telling me the truth?"

"I am."

"Emily," he says, "is she telling the truth?"

"Yeah," she says from the other side of the table. "We're fine."

"If you're fine, why didn't you just tell me about it?" he asks.

"I didn't want to worry you."

"Well, so much for that."

My shoulders slump. "Jerry, we're really okay. Please, don't worry."

He sighs and shakes his head. "Fine," he says, sounding both annoyed and a little bit worried and a little bit angry.

The conversation stumbles into an uncomfortable silence. I glance at Emily and shoot her a dirty look.

"I'm not going to be able to make it back tonight," he says. "Too many problems here."

"That's okay," I reply. "I'll be fine."

"Stop saying fine. I don't want you staying there tonight."

"We talked about this already. I'm not going to let this run me out of my own house."

He shakes his head. "I know we did, but now things have changed."

"They really haven't."

"Is that so? Emily has a mark on her head and a bloody bandage on her elbow. Are you going to tell me that didn't happen today?"

"No," I reply. "It did."

He takes in a deep breath and lets it out slowly. "You can check into a hotel or something. Please do this for me," he says, his tone softening and his expression altering to match.

"You can stay with me tonight," Emily says before

sitting back down in her seat and filling her glass again.

"Would that be all right?" I ask him.

"Yeah. Anything to get you out of the house, even staying at Emily's place."

"Hey!" she says, protesting and then folding her arms across her chest.

"You sort of deserve that," I say, and she shrugs before downing another glassful.

I hear someone call Jerry's name in the background, and he turns away from the video.

"Hold on!" he shouts and then looks back at me. "I gotta go. I'm sorry…and I'm sorry I got upset."

I smile at him and shake my head. "You don't have to apologize. It was my fault. I should have told you everything right away. I'm sorry."

He smiles back at me. "It's okay. Nothing but the truth from now on. Agreed?"

"Agreed."

That same person shouts again, and Jerry shakes his head.

"Sorry, I gotta go."

"Okay. Bye, Jerry. See you tomorrow."

"Yeah. Tomorrow. I'll try to call you later."

"Okay," I reply, and then the video goes black.

I turn and look at Emily. "You know, you're a troublemaker."

She just shrugs. "Not the first time I've heard that. Come on, let's get your stuff and head over to my place. Sleepover!"

"Oh my God…what have I gotten myself into?" I ask out loud, and she just smiles at me.

~25~

"*A*re you going to make it?" I ask as we're climbing the steps up to Emily's loft.

She's leaning against the wall and nodding. "Yeah, I got this," she replies. "That was some good vodka."

"Yeah, maybe it was too good."

"I'm thinking that day drinking is not for me."

"I would agree."

We come to the landing at the top of the stairs, and Emily reaches into her pocket to retrieve her keys. The building looks like a converted warehouse or factory divided up into apartments. Emily's place is on the top floor, of course.

"There's no elevator?" I ask.

"There is, but they've been working on it for the last year, and I don't trust it."

"That's probably a good way to go."

Finally, she fishes out the keys, unlocks the door without too much trouble, and we walk inside.

"Holy crap," I say, looking around at the expansive space, with its skylights, huge wall of windows, exposed brick and ductwork, and original hardwood floors. "This place is bigger than my house."

There's a small sectional, love seat, and two chairs off to one side, forming a living room area, a kitchen with glass-fronted cabinets, floating shelves, granite counter-tops, and an impressive assortment of appliances. A short hallway leads to what I can only assume is probably the bedroom and bathroom.

I set my bags by the door and close it behind me. Emily places her keys and the diary on the small table in the entryway.

"This looks like something out of *Architectural Digest*. Are you loaded?" I ask her, grinning widely.

"I'm not loaded, not by any means. This place was remarkably cheap when you compare it to a similar loft in New York or even Boston."

"Well, in any case, it's awesome."

"Thanks," she says, walking slowly over to the couch and flopping down onto it. "Why didn't you tell me not to drink all that?"

"I'm not your mom," I reply, stepping over to the wall of windows where a small desk and computer are set against the glass.

The view isn't the greatest one I've ever seen, but it's not bad. You can see most of the little town and the ocean far off in the distance.

"I wouldn't have listened to her anyway," she says, chuckling quietly to herself.

I move back over to the couch and sit down on the other side and look at her. "I guess I'm on the couch?" I ask.

"Pfft. Do you think that's how I treat my guests?"

She rolls off the sofa and gets to her feet, already looking more stable than just a few minutes before.

"You recover quickly," I say.

"A remnant from my college days. When you major in French, there's a lot of wine involved during study sessions...you know, for authenticity's sake."

I nod and smile at her. "Of course...for authenticity."

"Follow me," she says, and I dart over to the door and grab my bag. She waits for me at the beginning of the hallway.

As soon as I rejoin her, we head down the hall. We stop at the first door on the right and walk inside. The bedroom is nearly as large as my living room at the cottage. Windows flank one side, flooding the room with light, making it feel airy and fresh. A sliding barn door on the wall to the left of the entrance leads to a large bathroom, complete with a toilet, massive walk-in shower, and soaker tub.

"Damn, girl," I say, grinning at her.

"*Lifestyles of the Rich and Famous*," she says.

"I thought you said you weren't loaded," I say, setting my bag on the bed.

"Did I? Well, as I said...I'm Duxbridge rich, but not New York rich...if you know what I mean."

"You should have just said you're rich. It saves a lot of time."

She shrugs and smiles at me. "Yeah, but it's boring to talk about it."

We walk back out into the living room and take a seat on the couch.

"Something to drink?" she asks.

"Is that a good idea?"

"I meant soda or water or something like that."

"I'm good," I say, pulling my laptop out of my bag and opening the lid.

She walks over and picks up the diary from the little table and then returns to the couch. She opens the journal and snuggles down into the cushions.

"All right," she says. "Let's solve this damn thing."

A few seconds later, she looks over at me. "Hey, where do you want me to start? How far did you get?" she asks.

I scoot over and hold out my hand. She hands me the leather-bound book. I flip through about the first half of the pages and then stop, leaving the diary open and handing it back to her.

"You can start right there."

"Perfect," she says with a smile.

She grabs her phone, opens some sort of app, and then sets the phone on the couch next to her knee. She begins dictating into it, and I start doing a search for any relatives of the two members of Blackwater's crew. It takes me nearly an hour to narrow down my results for Charlie Vertes to the point that I can begin searching for possible addresses or other contact information. After an additional hour, I haven't located anything on Avery Hawkins.

I stretch my back and roll my head from side to side, my neck popping at least once.

I look up and out one of the windows and then glance at the clock on my computer and look over at Emily. She's studying the diary intently.

"Stuck?" I ask, closing the lid on my computer.

"No...I just can't stop thinking about food," she replies with a grin.

"Hmmm. Well, I wonder where we can get something to eat?"

"Not sure. Do you know any place good?"

"Yeah, there's a little diner not far from here. Food's really good, not so sure about the service."

"Well," she says, "maybe if you left a decent tip."

"Is that so?"

"Hey, sometimes that helps."

"I can run out and get something for us."

She waves off my comment and smiles. "Don't be silly. I have an in with the owner," she says, getting up and heading to the door.

"Wait, you don't have your bike. It's still at my house."

"The diner is just around the corner. I'll be right back."

"What are you getting?"

"That's for me to know and you to find out," she says, grinning at me before she opens the front door.

"You are such a brat."

"I know you are, but what am I?" she says as she slips out the door.

* * *

I OPEN up my laptop again and let the system boot up. I pull up the website where I found the information on Charlie Vertes's possible family members. I do a quick search on a phone number directory site, matching the area code with the address information I discovered, and jot down the result. I pick up my phone and dial the number, raising it to my ear. I listen as it rings over and over again, but after about a minute, I hang up and set the phone on the couch.

I start to get up when the ringer goes off, and I pick it up again. The caller ID shows the number I just called.

"Hello?" I ask after answering.

"Someone there just called this number," a young woman says.

"Yes. I'm sorry for bothering you."

"Are you selling something?"

"No. Not at all."

There's a brief pause. "Who are you trying to get a hold of?"

"Honestly, I'm not really sure."

Again, there's another length of silence on the other end. "Who is this?" the woman asks.

"My name is Ally Tanner. I live down in Duxbridge, and I was hoping to ask you...or someone, some questions."

"What kind of questions?"

"I'm researching a book, and—"

"That doesn't really answer *my* question."

"No, I guess it doesn't, sorry. I'm trying to find out more about a Charlie Vertes."

"Charlie Vertes," she says as if it's a name she hadn't heard in years...or maybe even longer.

"Yes. He was a crew member of merchant ship back in the 1800s," I say.

There's another long pause.

"Am I talking to the right person? Are you related to the Charlie Vertes I'm talking about?" I ask.

"Yes," she finally answers.

"I know this is a long shot, and I completely understand if you have no idea what I'm talking about and you want to hang up on me, but please...give me a moment."

"What is this really about?" she asks.

"I'm trying to solve a mystery," I say, holding my breath and waiting for her response.

She doesn't say anything for close to thirty seconds, but she also doesn't hang up. "You say you're in Duxbridge?" she asks.

"Yes."

"Can you come see me?" she asks.

I sit up a little straighter on the couch. "Sure. Of course. Um...we could do this over the phone if that would be easier."

"No. I'd rather meet in person if that's okay with you."

"That's fine with me."

"Okay. Are you free tomorrow?" she asks.

"Absolutely. Can you give me your address?"

She gives me the information, and I type it into my notepad app. "What time works for you?" she asks.

"Any time."

"Let's say around lunchtime?"

"That's perfect."

"All right. I'll see you then."

"Oh…sorry. I didn't get your name."

"It's Anastasia," she says.

"Perfect. I'll see you tomorrow."

"Okay. Bye."

"Bye."

I hang up and stand there for a moment, stunned that I may have found the person I was searching for. A few seconds later, the door opens, and Emily walks in carrying a pair of plastic shopping bags weighted down by their contents.

"Dinner's ready," she says with a smile and then frowns when she sees my expression, "What's the matter?"

"Nothing," I reply, shaking my head. "You up for a road trip tomorrow?"

"Absolutely! We talkin' Thelma and Louise?"

"I hope not."

"Aw…you're no fun."

~26~

"Are you guys doing okay?" Jerry asks via video.

"We're fine," I reply, smiling at him as I'm lounging on Emily's loveseat.

"No more...sightings?"

I shake my head. "No. It's been quiet."

"Good. Um...I was planning on coming back tomorrow, but things here are not going as planned. I probably won't be able to get out of here until early Sunday morning."

"That's okay. What's wrong?"

He shakes his head and grumbles. "Just 'one of those' clients."

"A real peach?"

"You can say that again."

"I want blue cabinets, but not that blue or that blue.

What do you think about green?" he says, imitating her and probably doing a terrible job.

"Lovely."

"Emily treating you well?" he asks.

"Of course, I am," she shouts from the other side of the room before I have a chance to reply. "You're going to miss the orgy, though."

"What did she say?" he asks, frowning at me.

"Nothing," I reply, shaking my head. "Anyway. It's okay that you can't get back. Emily and I are going to head up to Smithton tomorrow."

"For what?"

"I found someone related to Charlie Vertes, one of the crew members of *The Dominator*."

"Seriously?"

"Yeah, it was surprisingly easy."

"Lucky might be a better word."

"Yeah, I suppose so."

I look over at Emily. She's at her desk, studying the journal and speaking into her phone. I'm too far away to make out any of the words.

"Hey, did you know Emily's loaded?" I ask Jerry, glancing at her over the top of my phone.

"Is she?"

"I am not loaded," Emily calls from her desk.

"Really?" I ask, getting up and walking around her place while showing Jerry the interior of her massive loft apartment.

"Wow! My house could fit in there twice," Jerry says.

"You guys are so funny."

"And you are so loaded."

"Whatever. Haven't we been over this already?" she asks, looking up from the diary.

"Yeah, but it's so much fun," I reply with a grin, and she just shakes her head. I turn my attention back to Jerry and walk slowly toward my bedroom door.

"No sexting back there," Emily shouts. "I just had the sheets cleaned!"

"Oh my God," I say, rolling my eyes, before closing the door. I sit down on the bed and smile at Jerry. "I miss you," I say, surprised that I even said it...but now it's too late to take it back.

"Me too," he replies with a warm smile. "I've been thinking about you all day."

"Well," I say with a sly grin, "don't get distracted and shoot a nail through your foot."

"I won't." He pauses for a moment, and I can see his expression change.

"What's the matter?" I ask.

He looks right and then left but won't make eye contact with me, as if he wants to say something, but he's not sure how to say it.

"Jerry, what's wrong?"

"This isn't moving too fast between us, is it?" he asks, a worried expression on his face.

"What do you mean, too fast?"

He sighs and shakes his head. "I just...I don't want you to think I pressured you into anything...."

"Jerry," I say softly, "when you get to know me a little more, you'll understand that there's no way that you could pressure me into anything."

"I mean...I...I already know that, but...it's been a long

time since I've been involved with anyone, and I can't remember how fast things should be going."

"First off, do you think we're 'involved?'" I ask, grinning at him.

"Well...I mean...I..."

"It's okay, Jerry," I say, smiling now. "I'm just messing with you a little bit. I would say we're involved."

His shoulders slump, he looks at me and shakes his head. "That was messed up."

"Yeah...I guess it was. Sorry."

"It's okay. I guess I should've been prepared for what I was getting myself into."

I nod and smile at him, and then my expression changes. "Listen, after Steven passed, I didn't think I would find anyone or even want to find anyone for a very long time. But life comes at you full force. You need to be ready to open yourself up to whatever comes your way, or you'll end up sad and alone and wishing for things that could have been but never will be."

He nods and sighs. "That's...that's how I feel."

"Good. Then we're on the same page. So, as far as whether or not we're moving too fast," I say, pausing for a few seconds. "I don't think so. There may be some people who will think I didn't wait long enough or haven't grieved long enough, but I would tell those people that until they experience what I've experienced, they should just shut the hell up."

At first, Jerry doesn't respond, but then, finally, he smiles. "Good, because I don't think we are, either."

I smile, and I get that little tickle deep down in my belly. "I'm glad to hear that," I say. "I've been nervous about bringing any of this up. I didn't want to risk what we've got...what we've been building."

"You've been nervous? I've felt like throwing up ever since I started thinking about it."

He smiles, and I chuckle quietly because that's exactly how I've been feeling, but he doesn't need to know everything, right?

"So, you guys are going to take a road trip tomorrow?" he asks.

"Yeah. It's not too far. It's only Smithton."

"You riding her bike?"

"Are you kidding me? I don't mind tooling around town, but there's no way I'm riding shotgun on that thing all the way there."

He's just about to respond when there's a knock on the door.

"Are you decent?" Emily asks without opening it.

I look at Jerry and shake my head. "Yes, I'm decent."

She opens the door, peeks in, and then frowns. "That's a shame," she says, grinning at me.

"Will you stop that already? What did you need?"

"You need to hear some of this shit," she says, holding the journal up.

* * *

"WHAT DO YOU GOT?" I ask as I'm reclining on the sectional. I have my phone propped up against a pillow on the back of the sofa so that Jerry can hear everything as well.

"Okay," Emily says as she's pacing back and forth in

front of me. "I'm not done yet, because she wrote a lot of stuff...I mean, a lot of stuff."

"Yeah, I noticed that. I guess that diary was her Facebook of the 1800s."

"Yeah, probably. Anyway, let's start with the fact that Duxbridge was a real prick, I mean a massive, stinking, disgusting piece of crap."

"That's what she wrote?" I ask, grinning at her.

"No. Those are my words. I'm just paraphrasing."

"What did you find out?"

"Well, he was sort of a scumbag, and every time Oliver was off on one of his voyages, he would visit Lilly, sometimes multiple times a week, even though she had gently suggested that he stop."

"What did she say, exactly?"

She picks up her phone and starts tapping the screen. Then she holds it up for us to hear. The voice is hers, but the words are Lilly's.

"William Duxbridge came by again today. I wish he would stop visiting. He only seems to be here when Oliver is not. He seems charming on the outside, but I feel as if there is some darker purpose to his attentions."

"Then there's this one," she says before continuing.

"Oliver came back today, and I was so happy, but I also told him about Duxbridge and his visits. He was properly upset and set off at once to town to confront him."

"This is from a few days later; I'm not sure what was said between Duxbridge and Oliver, as he has been reluctant to speak of it, but I'm not sure if this has made the situation better or worse. I don't think I should press the matter."

She pauses for a moment and looks at me and then at Jerry, who is still on video.

"That doesn't sound good," I say.

"I'd agree," Jerry adds.

"Is there anything else about Oliver talking to him?"

"Not that I've come across yet."

"Okay. What else is there?"

"A lot of the entries are rather mundane, everyday things. The tone seems to change, however, for the better. She talks a lot about Oliver and how happy she was when he was home and how sad she was when he was gone, but it seemed like she was starting to get used to it. She did mention how she started walking out to the top of the cliff and sitting and watching for Oliver's ship, although I have a feeling she probably couldn't have seen it from there anyway. He sailed out of Boston from what I discovered, and that's way too far away."

"Did she mention anything about a lantern?"

"Not directly," she replies. "But she did say that she would often walk up there in the evening, so she probably did have one with her."

"That makes sense."

"There was this entry, though," she says, tapping the screen on her phone. "I went into town today and had a pleasant time of it. One of the shopkeepers asked me about my nightly walks up along the cliff's edge, and I said that it helped to soothe my worry and my mood when Oliver is away from home. He warned me that I should use care when traversing the uneven terrain in the dark. I told him I always carry a lantern with me, and he made a joke about a ship mistaking the light from my lantern for a lighthouse. I told him my little lamp would hardly be visible from any sort of distance."

"Well, that's interesting," Jerry says.

"If the townspeople knew about her taking those walks and standing or sitting on the cliff with her light," I say, pausing for a moment.

"Then when the ships started crashing on the rocks, they would have automatically assumed it was her fault," Emily says, finishing my thought.

"Maybe."

"With someone's help," Jerry adds, and Emily and I frown.

"Exactly."

"What else did you find?"

"There are some not-so-great entries a little bit after that," she replies quietly.

"About what?"

"She and Oliver were trying to have a baby, and she did get pregnant, or at least they thought she was, but after he left again for England, something happened, and she lost it. There are a lot of very dark days where she talked about feeling like a failure, how much Oliver would hate her for losing their child, and she wrote a lot about how she would sit on the edge of the cliff up there and look down at the ocean and wonder if she would feel anything if she just tumbled off into the sea."

"Jesus," Jerry says, but I don't say anything.

I just stare off into the distance, my thoughts drifting back to my own…fears and doubts not that long ago.

"Ally?" Emily asks, and I look up at her as if coming out of a dream. "You okay?"

"Yeah…yeah…um, I'm good."

"How long did this last with her?" Jerry asks.

"From what I can tell, a few months, until Oliver returned, and then her mood seems to shift dramatically again when instead of being angry with her, he's caring and sympathetic and even cried with her, even though she made a note that no one should ever know about that."

"Anything else?" I ask.

"Just some more entries like this one. 'Mr. Duxbridge continues to make unwelcome visits to the house. I know Oliver talked with him, but it does not seem to have deterred him. Yesterday he encountered me in town and attempted to start a conversation around the possibility of selling the cottage. I insisted that we had no intention of doing any such thing. He did not seem to take my word to heart and was, in fact, quite cross with me. I excused myself and made my way into one of the closest shops, even though I was not interested in purchasing any of their wares. I just wanted to be rid of him and be amongst other people, hoping that would deter any additional conversation.'"

"Damn. He really was an asshole," I say, shaking my head and frowning.

"I think we already knew that," Jerry says.

"I know, but hearing it in her words, makes it that much more real."

"Anything else beyond that?" Jerry asks.

Emily shakes her head. "That's as far as I've gotten, and I'm starting to get a headache, so I think I'm done for the day," she replies.

"Yeah, I think we all are," I say, picking up my phone and looking into Jerry's face. "You look tired, too."

"I am. You two need to get some rest since you've got that drive ahead of you tomorrow."

I nod and sigh quietly, and Emily catches my eye and smiles before closing up the journal and putting it in the desk drawer.

"All right. I'll see you on Sunday, right?" I ask.

"That's the plan."

"Okay. Night, Jerry."

"Night, Ally."

I reluctantly hit the "End Call" button, shutting off the video. Emily walks over and sits down on the couch, facing me.

"What about a nightcap?" she asks.

"That sounds like a good idea."

~27~

"*A*re you ready to go yet?" I shout up the stairs.

"Almost!" she replies.

I sigh and shake my head, walking back to my car and slipping in behind the wheel. I leave the door open to allow the cool early morning air to fill the cabin. I lean my head back and close my eyes for a moment.

"Are you sleeping?" Emily asks as she climbs into the passenger seat.

"I'm just waiting for you."

"Well, I'm here now. Can we go?"

"That's rude," I say, putting the car into gear and backing slowly out of the space.

"That's just the way it is," she says, grinning at me.

I start down Main Street, in the direction of my house.

"What about breakfast?" Emily asks as we're approaching the diner.

"Well, we'd have time if someone had been ready when they said they'd be ready," I reply.

"I called ahead. Just pull over."

I stop in front of the café and put the car into park. Emily climbs out and then leans in through the window.

"Do you want anything special?" she asks.

"I thought you ordered already."

"I did, but I can add on anything you want."

"Just a danish."

"Fruit or cinnamon?"

"Hmmm?" I say, thinking about it for a moment. "Let's do cinnamon."

"Got it. Be right back."

I give her a quick smile, and she darts off to the diner, slipping inside as soon as two other customers make their way out the doors. I look down the street and watch a few pedestrians window shopping in some of the little stores. Suddenly, I feel a chill invade the car, and a parade of goose bumps march up and down my arms. I look around, but I don't see anything—no sign of Lilly, the sailor...or Duxbridge, but something tells me that we need to get moving as soon as possible.

I look toward the diner, and I see Emily inside, leaning against the counter while a couple of customers talk with her. I hit the horn. She looks out the window, and I wave her back toward me. She snatches two white paper sacks off the counter, along with two large coffees, and pushes her way out the door. As soon as she's back in the car, I frown at her.

"What's the matter?" she asks.

"Something's here," I say, and her eyes go wide before she hops into the car, pulling the door shut behind her.

She shivers and then frowns. "I feel it."

I back out of the space, then shift the car into drive, and race away from the diner, even though I'm not really sure exactly what we're running from. I keep glancing in the rearview and side mirrors as I drive, searching for any sign of pursuers, but there's nothing there. As we're approaching the cottage, a second chill passes over my skin, and suddenly, Emily grabs my arm and points past me and out the window.

"Over there!" she says.

When I look across the field on the left side of the road, I spot a black shadow racing toward us, skimming across the surface of the grass. It almost looks like a mass of tiny, black flies, but it's moving way too fast, and it's coming directly for us.

"It's him, isn't it?" Emily asks.

"It looks like it."

I press the accelerator, and we speed up, the landscape zipping by the windows. I look in the rearview mirror and watch as the dark cloud passes through a wooden fence and onto the road behind us. Emily is sitting and staring out the back window.

"Might want to go faster," she says.

I glance at the speedometer. "I'm already going over sixty!"

"Well, that thing is doing over seventy or more!"

We rocket past the museum, but the road changes from straight and flat to winding and sloping. The tires screech as we go around a curve, and I have to struggle to maintain control.

"It's almost on us!" Emily shouts.

I look over at the side mirror, and the dark shadow is all I can see. "I don't know what to do!" I shout.

Emily shrugs and shakes her head. "You're asking me?" she replies, and then suddenly, the shadow is in the car, moving across the back seat toward us.

Emily grabs her throat, her eyes wide, as the temperature in the car seems to drop thirty degrees in a matter of seconds. Emily stares at me as she tries to draw in a breath. I feel the cold chill of the shadow flow across me. I glimpse the sign that bids visitors farewell from Duxbridge, and instantly, the shadow is gone, and Emily sucks in mouthful after mouthful of air. I instantly pull over onto the shoulder, skidding to a stop and slamming the car into park.

"Are you okay?" I ask, my heart racing and my eyes wide.

She nods and looks back toward town. "What the hell happened?" she asks while sitting back in her seat.

"I don't know," I reply, and then I remember the sign. "Wait. We just passed the edge of town. I wonder if he can't go beyond the borders."

"Maybe, but if that's true, it doesn't make me feel great about coming back later today."

"Yeah. Me either."

We sit for a few minutes on the side of the road, and then Emily looks at me.

"You still want your breakfast?" she asks.

"That's what you're thinking about?"

"Hey," she says, grinning at me, "we gotta eat, right?"

I shake my head and then smile at her. "I guess we do. Give me that danish."

* * *

"ARE WE THERE YET?" Emily asks.

I look over at her and shake my head. "Don't make me pull this car over."

"Sorry, Dad," she says with a chuckle. "But seriously, how much farther?"

"You can read the GPS, right?"

"I don't feel like it," she says, whining and frowning at me as she's leaning back against the door.

I sigh and glance at the screen. "It's like you're a child," I say, shaking my head. "We should be there in about ten minutes."

"That's not too bad."

"I'm starting to wonder why I brought you along."

"Because I'm so much fun."

"When does that begin?" I ask before coming to a stop at a four-way intersection. "I thought you were working on the diary."

"I can't read anymore while we're driving. It's making my stomach sick."

I pull across and down the slowly curving, narrow, two-lane highway. A few moments later, we pass the first small house and then a few more just seconds later. The little town comes into view in the distance, situated on top of a small rise, surrounded by rolling hills, farmland, and large stretches of pines and other trees. The road winds gently through the woods for a mile or so, and then the trees recede, and we drive into the tiny hamlet.

There are only four or five buildings, a few of which are unoccupied with sun-faded "For Rent" signs in their windows. One tiny restaurant with a couple of cars parked outside on the street is the only business that seems to be still in operation.

"Wow. I thought Duxbridge was small," Emily says, sitting up and looking out the windshield.

"It doesn't look like this place will be here much longer," I say with a sad tone.

"Yeah. Unfortunately. So, where does this lady live?"

"She said it was just past the town, in a little blue and white cottage."

We roll through the rest of the sad little village, and then for the next mile or so, we don't see any other buildings or signs of habitation, but then Emily leans forward and peers through the windshield.

"Is that it?" she asks, pointing at a small house on the left side of the road.

"It must be," I reply while slowing down and coming to a stop after pulling over onto the grassy shoulder.

The house is small but looks well cared for.

"Shit. This place is old," Emily says as we're climbing out of the car.

"Late 1700s?"

"Looks like it."

I come around the side of the car, and Emily and I walk up the short path to the front door, passing the mailbox on the road with the name "Vertes" painted in bold, white block letters. I knock quietly, and we wait. A few seconds later, it opens, and a young woman with long blond hair and bright-green eyes looks at us through the screen door.

"Ally?" she asks.

"Anastasia, right?"

"Yeah. That's me."

"Great…um…this is Emily. I hope it's okay that I brought her along."

"Of course," she replies as she's pushing open the door.

We walk into a small living room with a large fireplace off to the left. The room is furnished with an impressive collection of antiques, all of them in impeccable condition. We follow her down the central hallway, past the main staircase, and into the kitchen at the back of the house. There's a small table set against the wall, with three wooden chairs. Even though the appliances have been updated to 2020 standards, the kitchen retains the feeling of an older time, much like my own.

"You can take a seat," Anastasia says, gesturing toward the table. "Do you want something to drink?"

"Sure," I reply. "Thanks."

"You can call me Stasia if you want," she says as she's opening the refrigerator door.

"Okay. Anastasia is such a pretty name, though."

"Yeah," she says, walking over to the table with three bottled beers in her hands. "But it seems so formal."

"I guess so," I say, taking one of the chilled beers.

She sits down, twists off the top, and casually tosses it onto the table. Emily looks at the bottle for a moment and then smiles before taking a drink.

"You have good taste," she says to Stasia. "This is some fine beer."

"Thanks," she replies before taking a swig from her bottle. "So, you said you're doing some research for a book?"

I look over at Emily for a moment and then back at Stasia. "Honestly. Not really."

She frowns at me. "Then why are you asking about this?"

Now it's my turn to pause.

"Because we've got a fuckin' ghost that's trying to kill us," Emily says.

Stasia doesn't seem particularly phased by this response. "Is it the black shadow?" she asks, and I nearly choke on my beer.

"What?" I ask, looking at Emily for a moment.

"It's Duxbridge's ghost," she says without batting an eye.

"How do you know that?"

"Because it's been haunting my family for the last two hundred years."

I sit back in my chair, and I just stare at her for a few seconds.

"Did you buy the Blackwater cottage?" she asks.

"Yeah."

"That explains a lot," she says, taking another drink from her bottle.

"So then, you are related to Charlie Vertes?" I ask.

"Yes. He was my great-great-great-great-grandfather... or something like that."

"And he was the Charlie Vertes who sailed on *The Dominator* out of Boston."

"He was."

"I thought the ship sank in 1820."

She pauses for a moment and sighs. "That's what everyone was supposed to think."

"What does that mean?"

"Maybe I should start from the beginning."

28

~28~

"Charlie had been sailing with Blackwater for close to ten years. He was one of his most trusted crew members and worked his way up to boatswain. They had been all around the world together more than once when they began working on *The Dominator*," Stasia says.

There are six empty bottles in the center of the table, and we each have another in our hands. There's also a large wooden box with low sides and a curved wooden lid, reinforced with metal straps, sitting amongst the bottles.

"So, he's your what…great, great, great grandfather?" Emily asks.

"One more great on top of that."

"I'm assuming he knew Larsen and Duxbridge," I say.

"Yes," she says, opening the lid of the chest and

clinking into a couple of the bottles. She pulls an old, leather-bound book out, opens it, and begins reading from some of the passages:

"May 5,1820. Randolph Larsen met with Oliver and me today. He seemed agitated about something, but he would not tell us what it was about. He told us that we were to leave for England within two weeks, which seems like a rather short time to properly provision the ship. I told Oliver I was concerned about Larsen's behavior, but he dismissed my worries and told me to set about preparing the ship."

"May 9,1820. I spotted Larsen meeting with Duxbridge in a small tavern in town today. They were being very secretive and speaking in hushed tones in a darkened corner of the otherwise busy inn. I know Oliver has had some dealings with Duxbridge in the past concerning his cottage and Lilly. I don't know if I should tell him about this or not."

"May 12, 1820. I have come to the decision to tell Oliver about Larsen and Duxbridge."

"May 14,1820. Oliver was very upset when I told him about the meeting I witnessed, and he went off at once to confront Duxbridge."

"May 19,1820. I have not heard from Oliver since the 14th, and I am very concerned about his whereabouts. I was considering traveling down to Duxbridge to see Lilly, but there is not enough time, as I am in the middle of preparing the ship to depart in two days. I have also not heard from Larsen, but we have a schedule to maintain."

I'm sitting across from her, shaking my head, trying to absorb everything she's telling us.

"It gets worse," she says as if she read my thoughts.

"May 23, 1820. We set out from port today without Oliver. Another man came on board, one I had never seen before, and announced that he was the new captain. We asked what had become of Oliver, but he could not—or would not—answer our questions."

"July 15, 1820. I am writing this in secret. Approximately a week from our destination of Liverpool, we were instructed to dump one of the lifeboats overboard and to change the name of the ship to *The Black Lilly*. There have been some grumbles amongst the crew as we carry out these odd requests, but no action has been taken against them...including by me."

"Jesus," Emily mutters quietly.

"I can't believe this," I say.

"It's all true," Stasia says.

"Oh...I know it's all true. That's not what I meant. I just can't believe we may actually solve this mystery."

"Do you want to hear more?" she asks.

"Of course."

"July 27, 1820. We docked to today in Portsmouth instead of Liverpool. Once we made landfall, we were each given a purse of gold pieces and told that we could not return to the United States."

"Couldn't return?" Emily asks, sitting up straighter in her chair.

Stasia nods. "Yes."

"I'm assuming he did," I say.

She smiles and nods. "Yes. Later on, he talks about how he and a few others decided to change their names and return on the next ship they could either book passage or sign on as crew members. From what I could discover—and from our family history—when Charlie returned, he had taken the name Lillard. Instead of Boston, he sailed into New York and then made his way back to Smithton."

"What did he say had happened?" I ask.

"He never did. When he came back, he had the money he had been given, which apparently must have been a fairly impressive amount, and he used it to build this house and purchase the farmland around it."

"What about the name? How did he explain that to his wife?"

She frowns and sighs. "I really don't know what he did about that, but back in that time, if the man said something had to be done, I think she would have just gone along with it, without any questions."

"Maybe," I reply. "Is there anything else?"

"Charlie was racked with guilt for the rest of his life for not coming forward about any of this, especially after learning about Lilly Blackwater's death. I think he regretted taking the money, even though it allowed him to build a life. He never went to sea again. He told his son that the joy of it had gone out after *The Dominator*."

"Did he ever try to go see Lilly or talk to her before she died?"

"He thought about it," she says, flipping through some of the pages of the old diary before stopping and starting to read aloud again. "I am ashamed about my part in the tragedy that befell Oliver. I am not sure what has happened to him, but I feel certain that William Duxbridge is to blame and that Oliver is dead. I wish I had the courage to find and speak with Lilly about the true fate of her husband, but I fear Duxbridge's wrath and the discovery that I have returned to the States. I am such a small man."

"That's sad," Emily says. "None of it was his fault."

"No," she says, "but it haunted him until the day he died."

I shake my head and sigh quietly. "Well, at least this proves *The Dominator* never sank, and Oliver didn't die at sea."

"And Duxbridge had something to do with it," Emily adds.

"Yeah, but I'm still not sure it helps us discover what the ghosts want," I say, and then I look over at Stasia.

"You have more than one ghost?"

"Yeah. We have at least three in total."

"Who are they?"

"Lilly and one of the sailors who died on the rock below the cliff near her cottage."

"Damn."

"Wait a minute. How did you know about Duxbridge's ghost?" I ask.

"Because I've seen it."

"You have? Where?"

"At that museum. The one they opened inside his old mansion," she replies. "I was looking for some more information on *The Dominator* and this Larsen person. It attacked me there."

"Yeah. Us too," Emily says.

I sit back in my chair, take a breath, and hold it for a moment before releasing it again. "You changed your name back, from Lillard to Vertes," I say, recalling the mailbox out front.

"Yeah. That was Charlie's last request. He left it in his will. After the death of his son, my great, great, great grandfather, we should retake the name Vertes and try to live down some of the shame that he had brought upon it," she says, sounding much older than she appears.

"I don't think he had much choice in the matter," I say. "Duxbridge and Larsen are to blame."

"I know," she replies. "I just wish he had felt that way."

"Well, maybe he'll be able to rest a little easier if we can solve this mystery once and for all."

"So, what do we do now?" Emily asks, looking over at me.

"I think we need to head back to Duxbridge, and you need to translate the rest of Lilly's diary. I think the final clue may be in there."

* * *

"WE'VE FOUND out some stuff, but I'm not sure how it helps us figure out what the ghosts want or need," Emily says as we're driving back.

"Neither do I, actually."

"I'm not too keen about running into Duxbridge again when we get back."

"Yeah. I know, but we don't really have a choice."

"The biggest problem is that we don't have any way of fighting him off, other than running away...apparently."

"Exactly," I respond with a frown.

She shakes her head and pulls the diary out of her bag.

She opens it to where she has a small bookmark peeking out of the top of the pages. I drive while she reads out loud, sometimes stopping in the middle of a passage and starting a new one if there doesn't seem to be any pertinent information.

"I thought reading in the car made you sick."

"I'm powering through," she replies before continuing. "I just came back from the cliff tonight, and I saw another lantern, although a much more powerful one, not far from where I am accustomed to sitting. I cannot tell who is there, but I am happy to have the company when I am feeling low."

I frown and shake my head. "If she only knew."

"Oh, God. Listen to this one. Mr. Duxbridge came by again this evening, just before sunset, to offer his condolences on the loss of our child, and although I accepted them as politely as I could manage, I cannot help feeling that he was disappointed that I was not as broken in spirit as he had expected."

"What a slimeball."

"You can say that again."

We drive for a while, while Emily mutters words every now and then as she searches the journal for more clues.

"This one is from early 1820," she says.

"When?"

"Um...May 22nd."

"That's one day before *The Dominator* left Boston."

"Oliver left today for England, but he said he had a meeting with Mr. Larsen near Pilson before they departed. It's a little hamlet about halfway between Duxbridge and Boston. I asked him what the meeting was about. He stated he didn't know, but he was sure it must have something to do with his latest voyage."

"So, he met with Larsen and then never showed up in Boston."

"Apparently. Have we been able to find out anything about him?"

"Nothing. I can't find any records online, and Kitty didn't have anything, either."

"Not that it probably matters, anyway," she says, shaking her head. "Trying to solve a two-hundred-year-old murder is not as easy as you think."

"You got that right," I reply with a quiet chuckle.

She goes back to reading, and I return my focus to the road, although my mind is constantly mulling over the details of the "case" and trying to figure out what we should do next.

"Listen to this one. There are rumblings in the town about a ship that crashed on the rocks not far from my cottage. I can't imagine the horror of being battered to death against the boulders or drowning in the churning waves. My heart goes out to those men and their families. I hope that something like that never befalls my sweet Oliver."

She skips forward over many pages, and then she suddenly stops and just stares at the diary.

"What's the matter?" I ask, glancing over at her.

She starts reading from Lilly's entry. "Oliver's ship is overdue today. I spoke with a few people in town, and they encouraged me not to be too worried. Ships are often late, and it's only been three days, but I have a bad feeling about this."

My heart sinks. I know it's been hundreds of years since this tragedy, but I feel like I know Lilly at this point, and her pain seems that much more real to me.

"Then there's this," Emily says. "It's been three weeks now. The ship has yet to appear, and I am beginning to lose hope. Dispatches have been sent to England, but they will not arrive there for at least two months, maybe longer. I don't know what to do, other than to try to maintain the house and property as best I can lest my Oliver return."

"Damn," I mutter quietly.

"I'm sure the not knowing was worse than anything else," Emily says.

"Yeah, and back then, it was just a waiting game."

She passes a few pages without saying anything and then stops again. "Duxbridge came to the house again today. His very presence makes my skin crawl and my stomach sick. He asked if there was anything he could do for me, but I know his offer was not genuine. There is always a smile hidden under his disingenuous frown of concern. I told him no and bade him to not return unless requested. He agreed to my request, but he did not seem happy about it."

We pass the welcome sign for Duxbridge, and I immediately feel tense and nervous, my eyes darting around, searching for any sign of the ghostly shadow.

"Where do you want to go?" I ask.

"I think my place is still safer than yours, at least for the time being."

I nod in agreement. A few moments later, we pass the museum, and both of us watch out the windows, nervously waiting for Duxbridge's ghost to appear, but he doesn't. I continue past the entrance for my cottage and to the downtown area. When we reach her loft, I pull the car around back, parking it in a narrow alley between her building and the neighboring one. I feel a little silly doing it, but I notice that we both climb out and immediately head directly inside through the rear entrance.

We race up the stairs, and as soon as we're inside, Emily double locks the doors.

"Yeah. That'll keep him out," I say, grinning at her, and she shakes her head.

"I don't know what else to do," she replies, setting her stuff on the little table and carrying the journal over to her desk.

"Me either."

"Do you think he knows about this place?" she asks.

I shake my head and sigh. "I don't know for sure, but hopefully, not."

"Beer?" Emily asks as she's walking toward the kitchen.

"Sure," I reply, moving to the sectional and flopping down after setting my bag off to the side.

I close my eyes and let out a long, slow breath until it feels like every last bit of oxygen has been expelled from my lungs. After a few moments, my brow furrows when Emily has yet to return with the bottle.

"Ally," Emily says.

"What? What do you need?" I ask, still not opening my eyes.

A moment later, a chill passes over my skin, and I sit straight up.

"I think someone is here to see you," she says from over by the kitchen.

I jump up off the couch and freeze in place. Lilly is standing a few feet from Emily, staring straight at her. Emily has the refrigerator partially open as she stands there with her hand still on the top of the door.

"Lilly," I say, calling to her.

She turns her head and looks at me, her mouth partially open and her long, dark hair flowing slowly around her, as it always does. I swallow hard and take a step forward.

"We're close," I say. "We're close to being able to help you."

She turns her head and looks at Emily again.

"She's helping me help you," I say, and she turns her gaze back to me again after studying Emily for a few seconds.

She moves toward me as if she's gliding through the air just a few inches above the floor. She stops just in front of me and pauses. I look over at Emily, and she stares at me, wide-eyed and unmoving, the door to the refrigerator still open.

Lilly raises her hand and holds it out to me. I look over at Emily, and she shakes her head, but I reach out and take Lilly's hand.

~29~

'm standing in my cottage, except it's not my cottage. It's Lilly Blackwater's cottage. Lilly is standing in the tiny kitchen. There's a fire burning in the living room fireplace, but not in the kitchen. There's a small lantern on the table near where Lilly is standing. She picks it up and walks over to the fire. There she lights a long piece of straw before transferring the flame to the little candle inside the lamp.

I watch as she moves to the kitchen fireplace, kneeling in front of the opening, and pulls the handle for the damper. She picks up a leather-wrapped bundle off the small table beside the fireplace and carefully pushes it inside the chimney, and then closes the damper again. Walking over to the living room fireplace, she reaches under the edge of the mantle and removes a small piece of wood. She pulls a tiny key out of the pocket of her dress and inserts it into a slot in the piece of wood and reinserts it into the mantle.

She looks at a small portrait of a handsome man hanging above the fireplace and reaches out and touches it. "I hope someone finds these someday," she says to herself. "And maybe they will discover your true fate. I am weary of writing, as none of my days are filled with anything but sadness and loss. I love you, Oliver. I always will."

I study her face for a moment. She's much more beautiful in "real-life" than I thought. Her features are delicate, and she radiates an aura of kindness. She carries the lamp to the door and sets it on the floor before pulling on a long, black cloak and hood that was hanging on a hook on the wall. Just as on the ship, she doesn't seem to notice me, as if this is a recording, and I'm just watching it. She opens the door and walks outside, carrying the lamp at her side.

The sun has set far off to the west, and the air is chilly. She begins walking up toward the cliff when the sounds of people behind us alert her. Lilly turns and looks down the hill toward town. A crowd of about a dozen people carrying torches and lanterns is marching in our direction. Lilly stops and starts to walk back down the hill to meet them when someone within the crowd yells out.

"There she is, and she has the lantern! She's the one who caused the ships to crash!"

Several other members of the crowd begin shouting, and they begin charging up the hill. Lilly turns immediately and flees, racing up the slope toward the cliff's edge.

Within a few moments, they have her trapped. As they move forward, she moves back until she's standing on the very precipice of the rocky outcropping.

"What do you want?" she screams at them, holding the lantern in front of herself.

"You caused the ships to crash into the rocks. You killed all those sailors!" someone shouts.

"I did not!"

"You guided them with your lamp!"

"We have to stop her!" the same voice from earlier shouts, and it seems to inflame the mob.

Someone throws a rock, which strikes her in the side. She stumbles back, and the ground beneath her foot gives way. She tumbles off the edge of the cliff, screaming as she falls. Some in the group scream as well, while others run to the edge and look over, but the majority simply stand and watch. They soon move away, heading back down the hill, their torches and lamps growing smaller and smaller in the distance, except for one figure in a dark coat and hat. It turns and looks in my direction, and I immediately know it's Duxbridge.

He smirks and then turns away, following the mob back down the hill toward town.

Instantly, I'm back in Emily's apartment. I collapse to my knees and then onto my side as I sob uncontrollably. Emily darts to my side, pulling me into a fierce embrace.

"What happened?" she asks.

"I saw it," I mumble between sobs.

"Saw what?"

"I saw him kill her."

"Duxbridge? You saw him kill Lilly?" she asks, a look of horror on her face.

I nod in response as I try to stem the flood of tears. I finally manage to gain some control, and I look around the loft.

"Where is she?" I ask, my breath coming in uneven spurts.

"Lilly? She's gone. She vanished just before you collapsed."

Emily helps me sit up, and I wipe my face with my hand.

"I saw him drive Lilly off the cliff at my house. He brought a mob of townspeople with him and goaded them on."

"Oh my God," Emily says quietly, her hand over her mouth.

She helps me to my feet, and we walk over to the couch. We sit down, facing each other. She still looks worried.

"Are you sure you're okay?" she asks.

"I'm fine," I say with a small smile.

"So, what do we do now?" she asks.

"We need to stop this son of a bitch."

"How are we going to do that?"

"I have no idea. Can we try to get the rest of the diary finished? I hope there's something in there."

"Absolutely," she says, jumping up and darting over to the desk.

I stand slowly and walk into the kitchen. I open the refrigerator and grab a bottle of water. As I'm closing the door, I look over at Emily, and she's staring back at me.

"What?" I ask. "What's wrong?"

She lifts up the journal and turns it around so that it's facing me. Written across the pages, in a large, flowing script, are the words "See what he sees."

"What does that mean?" Emily asks.

"I know what it means; I just don't know how I'm supposed to do it."

My phone suddenly rings, and both Emily and I jump. I swipe the screen, and Jerry appears on the video.

"Hi," he says, smiling at me.

"Hey, Jerry."

"How are you doing?"

"Pretty good. We just got back from our road trip."

"Oh yeah. How did that go? Did you find out anything?"

"It was good. We did find out that *The Dominator* didn't sink, and Oliver was never on it during 'its last voyage.'"

"Really? Where was he?"

I pause for a moment before answering. "I think he was dead."

"You think Duxbridge killed him?"

"I think so, and then he paid or blackmailed Larsen into faking the loss of the ship."

"Damn," he says, shaking his head. "That's a long way to go to get your hands on a little cottage and a piece of property."

"That's what I was thinking. He was a seriously fucked up individual."

"Tell him the rest," Emily calls from over in the kitchen.

Jerry frowns at me, and I shake my head.

"Lilly was here. She showed me what happened to her."

"Showed you. You mean like the sailor showed you?"

"Yeah. Exactly."

"And?"

"He killed her, too. He convinced the townspeople that she was the cause of the shipwrecks and the deaths of the sailors."

"But he was the one who did it."

"Yeah. He and a mob of people basically chased her to her death."

"Jesus. So, what does she want you to do to help her? Have you figured that out yet?"

"Not at all," I reply with a sigh.

* * *

I HANG up with Jerry after he promises to be home some-time tomorrow. Emily and I turn off most of the lights and take up positions on the couch, an open bottle of wine on the coffee table and half-filled glasses in our hands.

"You said you knew what she meant about 'see what he sees.' What does it mean?"

"She wants me to see what he did, sort of through his eyes."

"You're talking about what Lilly did to you. Touching you."

"Yeah," I reply, taking a mouthful of wine from my glass.

"That means getting close enough to touch him."

I don't answer, and she shakes her head.

"I mean, you didn't ask my opinion, but I'm going to give it anyway. That seems like a colossally terrible idea."

"I'm well aware."

"Why would she ask you to do that?"

"Because I think she thinks I might be able to discover the final clue, so we can figure out what she and the sailor need us to do to help them."

"That really seems like a longshot."

"I think this whole thing has been a longshot."

"I have to agree with you on that."

I suddenly yawn, and it seems to infect Emily a moment later. "I think we should get some sleep," I say, setting my glass on the table.

"Probably a good idea."

I start to pick up the bottle and glass, and Emily waves me off.

"Don't worry about it," she says. "We can clean up in the morning."

"Okay," I reply with a smile. "That works for me."

Emily shuts off the rest of the lights and ensures that the front door is locked before we head to our bedrooms.

"Night," she says, smiling at me from partially behind her door.

"Night. See you in the morning."

We close our doors, and I immediately strip out of my clothes and walk into the attached bathroom. I turn on the shower and climb in, letting the water flow all across me, from my head to my toes. I close my eyes and stand under the spray for a few minutes before shutting it off and pulling the towel off the bar attached to the glass wall on the outside of the stall. I look into the foggy mirror, fully expecting to find some sort of message scrawled in the mist, but there's nothing there.

After toweling off, I walk back into the bedroom, fold back the covers, climb onto the mattress, and slip under the sheets. The only light in the room is coming from a small bedside lamp. I switch it off and lie there for a few minutes with my eyes closed before letting out a sigh and reaching over and picking up my phone.

I tap the screen and pull up Jerry's number. I pause with my finger just above the call button before finally hitting it. It rings a few times, and then I'm looking into Jerry's smiling face.

"Hey," he says. "Everything all right?"

"Yeah. Everything's good."

He frowns and cocks his head slightly to the side. "Are you sure?"

"I just wanted to ask you something."

"Okay. Shoot."

"The other day when I said 'honey,' by accident," I say.

"I remember," he replies, grinning at me. "And I think I said 'honey' back to you."

"Yeah. What if I didn't say it accidentally...from now on? Would that be all right with you?"

"I think that would be all right."

"And what if I said something like...babe."

"That would be all right, too."

"Okay," I say, letting out a breath I didn't realize I'd been holding in.

"This seems like an odd thing to ask about, considering everything that's happening…you know…ghosts trying to kill you and stuff."

"I know. It's just been bothering me every time we're on the phone and say hello or goodbye…I wanted to say something, but I'm afraid."

"What are you afraid of?"

"That we're moving too fast…that…I don't know," I reply, my words trailing off.

"Listen, we talked about this already. We're not moving too fast…at least I don't think so. Do you?"

"No. Not at all."

"Well then, there's no problem…baby."

When he says that last word, I get a little thrill that races through me, like a tiny bolt of electricity that ricochets off my insides for what seems like minutes.

"Okay," I reply with a warm smile. "I just needed to be sure."

"So, what's the latest on the ghost front?"

"Lilly told me that I need to 'see what he sees,'" I reply, frowning slightly.

"Does that mean Duxbridge?"

"I'm pretty sure it does."

He shakes his head and frowns back at me. "I really don't like the sound of that."

"Me either, but if it helps end this once and for all, then I have to do it."

He falls silent for a moment, his expression thoughtful. "Like I said, I don't like it."

"That's what Emily said."

"Well, for once, I agree with her."

I sigh and then shift my pillows to lie on my back. "So, tell me about your day," I say, rolling over onto my side.

"Are you changing the subject?"

"Yeah, I am. I need to get some sleep."

"Are you saying I had a boring day?" he asks, grinning at me.

"A lot more boring than mine."

"Touché."

~30~

"*H*ow the hell are we going to do this?" Emily asks as we're driving back to my house.

"I don't know. How do you attract a ghost?"

"You got me…even though we seem pretty good at it."

I laugh and shake my head. I make the turn into my driveway, passing the two stone columns and heading up the winding gravel trail. I have a sudden feeling of dread descend upon me as the cottage comes into view. The sun is shining brightly in the sky above our heads, but it feels as if it's powerless to banish the dark pall that is hanging over the day.

"So, what's your plan if Duxbridge shows up here?" Emily asks as we're climbing out of the car.

"Who has a plan?" I ask, shaking my head and smiling grimly. "I have to grab a ghost."

"Well, stranger things have happened."

We walk past her bike and up to the front door. I look up toward the cliff, and I have an overpowering urge to burst into tears as I think about what Lilly went through those last few minutes of her life. We walk inside, and I drop my keys onto the kitchen counter.

Emily looks around and shakes her head. "Are we just going to sit and wait for him to show up?"

"I'm not sure what else to do."

"We could go to the museum."

I look at her and frown, and I'm about to call her crazy when I stop for a moment and consider her suggestion. "That's not a bad idea," I reply.

"Really? I was only kidding."

"It should be easy to draw him out. We've already encountered him there twice."

"True. But going into the lion's den to catch a lion is not the best idea."

"Yeah, that does make sense."

I start to walk back to my bedroom before stopping just before the hallway. "Shit. I left my laptop in the car," I say.

I walk past Emily, who has her head in the fridge, toward the front door. The second I touch the knob, I feel a chill, and I spin around, looking at Emily. She's staring back at me.

"I feel it," she says.

I look around, searching for any sign of Duxbridge, but we seem to be alone. When I look back at Emily, my breath catches in my throat. The dark figure is standing directly behind her.

"Emily!" I scream.

She spins around, and Duxbridge tosses her into the cabinets with a flick of his wrist. She collapses to the floor, and he charges at me, his red eyes filled with rage and hate. At first, I start to flee, but then I stop and turn back to face him, planting my feet even though all I want to do is run. He raises his arm to strike me, but I lift my hand and grab his arm. He stares at me, his face contorted in confusion and anger, and honestly, I'm as surprised as he is. He tries to pull away, but I hold fast, my fingers gripping his phantom arm.

There's a bright flash, and then I'm in a tavern, filled with smoke and the smells of food, beer, and sweat. Duxbridge is sitting at a small table tucked into a darkened corner. A man approaches, moving quickly and constantly watching the people around him.

"You're late, Larsen," Duxbridge says as the man takes a seat, his small, beady eyes constantly shifting from one place to another.

"I came as soon as I could manage," the other man replies.

"Is it set?"

"It is. The ship will leave in two days."

"Good. You found a captain?"

"Yes," he replies with a little sigh. "I don't feel good about this."

"Maybe this will help," Duxbridge says, pushing a small, leather pouch across the table.

Larsen sits for a moment and then snatches the bag and tucks it into his jacket.

"Don't ever contact me again," Duxbridge says.

"Don't worry," Larsen says before getting to his feet and rushing out of the tavern.

An instant later, I'm standing in the woods, unsure exactly where I am. Duxbridge is standing by a large tree, his eyes darting here and there as if he's waiting for someone. A second man steps out of the trees and strides over to him.

"Duxbridge!" the second man says angrily.

"Blackwater," he replies with a sneer.

"I understand you have met with Randolph Larsen," he says.

"We have business dealings. They are of no concern to you."

Blackwater eyes him suspiciously. "That may be true, so I will leave that between the two of you, but we have other matters to discuss."

"Such as?"

"I've told you to leave Lilly alone, and you have ignored my wishes more than once."

"That's why I agreed to meet you here. I wanted to apologize."

"Apologize?" Blackwater asks, looking suspiciously at him.

"Yes. Sometimes I make poor decisions, and I am sorry it has caused your wife any distress."

Blackwater nods but doesn't say anything in response. Duxbridge extends his hand, and Oliver pauses for a moment before extending in return. Duxbridge holds his hand firmly. Then suddenly, he pulls Blackwater close while quickly producing a blade from under his left sleeve and plunging the knife into Blackwater's side, twisting the weapon.

Oliver stumbles back, holding the wound as blood begins staining his shirt, and then he rushes at Duxbridge, reaching for the knife, but his opponent is too fast and lands a second blow with the knife deep into his chest. Oliver drops to one knee and then collapses onto the leaf-covered ground.

There's another flash, and I'm standing on a cliff overlooking the ocean, with darkness all around and rain pouring down in buckets. At first, I think it's the cliff by my cottage, but then I realize it's the neighboring one, and I see Duxbridge standing on the peak, holding a large black lantern high in the air. Suddenly, the screams of people can be heard rising up from the ocean below, and the sound of a ship being smashed to bits on the rocks far below fills the air.

I watch as tiny lights, almost like fireflies, drift up from the churning waters and seem to be drawn into the lantern. Duxbridge closes two small folding doors on the front of the lamp and lowers it, but it becomes snagged on something momentarily before he frees it again. He looks down at his coat and utters a curse, then trudges back down the hill.

Another flash nearly blinds me, and I'm outside the cottage, watching the crowd advancing on Lilly. Duxbridge is tucked into the mob, hidden from view, only his dark jacket visible to me. He's also carrying the lantern again. After they chase Lilly off the cliff, he continues up to the edge and looks over. While he's peering down, I spot another tiny speck of light float up and then move into the lamp.

I release Duxbridge's arm and stumble backward, trying to catch my breath. Emily is at my side. I look around, my eyes wide. She has an angry scratch on her cheek.

"Where is he?" I ask.

"He's gone...for now," she says. "Are you okay?"

"Yeah." I grab her hand and look deep into her eyes. "It's the lamp. We have to get the lamp. They're trapped in it."

* * *

A FEW MINUTES LATER, we're zipping down the driveway toward the highway. Emily is driving her bike, and I'm on the back, my arms wrapped tightly around her waist.

"You sure about this?" she shouts back to me, her voice muted by the helmet.

"As sure as I can be!"

"I guess that's as good as it gets."

We roar onto the road, skidding for a second as Emily makes the turn. She guns the engine, and we literally fly down the highway. It only takes a minute or two to reach the museum. Emily races into the parking lot and slides to a stop just in front of the doors. There are no other cars out front, and I look at the little sign hanging on the knob.

"Shit! They're closed," I say, looking at Emily.

"Do you know where the lantern is?" she asks.

"I think I saw it the other day. It's just inside the living room, hanging from the ceiling."

"All right then," she says, walking over and picking up a rock from the landscaping around the front of the building. She marches up to one of the windows to the right of the door and smashes the glass out of the frame. She reaches inside and undoes the lock, pulling the other two panes open.

"Emily!"

"What? Do you want to get the lamp and stop Duxbridge, or do you want to wait until next Tuesday?" she asks.

I shake my head and dart over and climb through the opening. Emily follows directly behind me, and we run into the living room, looking up at the dark rafters as we go.

"Is that it?" Emily asks, pointing to a large black lantern with folding doors.

"That's it!"

We push a small table over underneath the lamp, knocking a few things onto the floor in the process. I climb up while Emily steadies me. I reach up, but I can't quite get it.

"Dammit!"

A chill passes over my skin, and I look at Emily.

"He's coming!" I say, and she nods.

She grabs a chair from near the fireplace, and we lift it onto the table. I scamper onto the chair and reach upward, finally getting a grip on the bottom of the lamp. I push up and lift it off its hook.

"Come on! We gotta go!" Emily says.

I jump down, and we race for the front door, pushing them open and dashing for the bike. I turn and look and spot Duxbridge's ghost glaring at us from just inside the entryway.

"Go! Go! Go!" I shout, and Emily kicks the bike to life and twists the throttle.

We dart out of the parking lot and back onto the road. I'm holding onto her with one hand and the lantern with the other as we race down the highway again. Glancing back, I can see the dark shadow chasing us.

"Faster!" I shout, and Emily speeds up, the little engine roaring as the landscape flashes by us on both sides.

"Hold on!" she shouts as she hits the brakes and makes the turn up my driveway.

Gravel and stones fly up in the air as the back tire throws them in all directions. Looking back again, Duxbridge is only a few yards behind us.

"He's gaining on us!"

"This is all she's got!"

We go airborne for a couple of seconds when we reach the top of the slope, just in front of the house.

"Keep going!" I shout, tapping her on the shoulder and pointing to the cliff in the distance.

Suddenly, something hits us from behind, and Emily loses control of the bike. The front tire turns sideways and digs into the rough, grassy terrain, and we're both thrown off. I hit the ground hard and lose my grip on the lantern, striking my head on a large stone. Duxbridge is on me immediately, his hands wrapped around my throat, the cold of his touch burning my skin.

"Death *is* here," he says, his voice cruel and his face full of fury.

I gasp for air, but I can't get even get in a whisp. I feel myself blacking out when I hear Emily's voice.

"Hey! Dickhead!" she shouts, and Duxbridge looks toward her, his ghostly grip on my throat lessening. She's standing on the edge of the cliff, the lantern in hand. Blood is running down the side of her face from a gash on her forehead. "Fuck you!" she says and hurls the lamp far out toward the ocean with a grunt.

Duxbridge races for it, but it's too little too late. It tumbles out of sight, and then suddenly, there's an ear-piercing screech, and dozens of phantoms come streaming up from the ocean, materializing on the cliff and hemming in Duxbridge. I spot the sailor, standing amongst close to fifty of his comrades.

Emily comes running over to me and helps me to my feet. I look back toward the cottage, and Lilly is approaching the group, hovering just above the ground. She passes us by and moves to join the rest of the ghosts. For a moment, I think they're going to attack Duxbridge, but instead, one by one, the other spirits slowly begin to dissolve and fade away, expressions of incredible relief on their faces. Before he vanishes, the sailor looks over at me and nods slightly, and a moment later, he's gone.

Duxbridge seems transfixed and unable to move as Lilly approaches him. She stops a few feet from him, and he sneers at her.

"Va au diable," she says in a clear and lyrical voice.

Duxbridge begins trembling, and instead of fading away like the sailor and his companions, he suddenly bursts into phantom flames of red and black and then vanishes.

Finally, she turns and looks at us. Lilly smiles, her face as beautiful in death as it was in life. "Thank you," she whispers and then slowly dissolves and drifts upward into the sky.

"What did she say to him?" I ask Emily.

"Go to hell," she replies with a smile.

* * *

"HOLLY!" I shout as I run outside to greet her.

She's just climbing out of her car, a wide smile on her face. "Oh my God, Ally. You look great!" she says, and we embrace each other for nearly a minute.

When we finally step apart, there are tears in both our eyes.

"Thanks," I say. "It's so good to see you."

"You too, baby."

She looks at me and frowns. "What's that?" she asks, pointing to the bruise and bump on my forehead.

"Oh…it's nothing. Just a little mishap."

She nods and then looks at the cottage and smiles. "This is place is so adorable," she says.

"It is nice, isn't it?"

She looks out toward the ocean and shakes her head. "What a view."

"Yeah. It sure is."

"So, how have you been?" she asks as we're walking toward the house.

"Busy."

"Really. Doing what? Are you working again?"

"Not yet. I've just been working on a project with my new friend, Emily."

"Really?" she asks as we walk inside. "You're making friends?"

"Oh yeah. She's the best."

"I'm happy for you. Just don't forget about me," she says with a laugh.

"Never."

"So, what's this project. You have to tell me all about it."

I shrug.

"Maybe someday. It's a little boring."

"Yeah, somehow, I doubt that."

"Do you want a tour?" I ask her, trying to change the subject.

"Absolutely."

About fifteen minutes later, we're walking back into the kitchen when I hear Jerry's truck pulling up outside.

"Who's that?" she asks, looking out the front window.

"Just someone I want you to meet," I reply, smiling broadly.

The End

Made in the USA
Monee, IL
18 September 2023

42961291R00174